# HAUNTED CASTLES

TONY WALKER

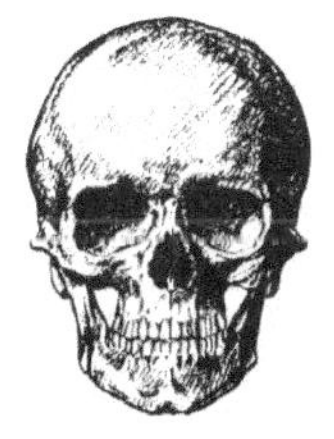

*For Sheila*

# CONTENTS

# INTRODUCTION

I read Ray Russell's Haunted Castles at the beginning of COVID lockdown and it inspired me to write The Schloss Von Hohenwald. I wanted to try something Gothic and was definitely influenced by his style. I published that story in *Horror Stories for Halloween* but over the winter of 2020-21, I decided to look over my old stories, re-work them and put them together under the theme of Haunted Castles.

It seems I have long been interested in the Gothic. Because it is so well established as a genre, there are real risks in attempting to write gothic stories. They can become very camp very quickly and the terror turn to mirth. Still, Ray Russell manages it in *Sardonicus,* as does Poppy Z. Brite in for example, *His Mouth Will Taste of Wormwood,* though I do not compare my own efforts to theirs in anything other than theme.

The second story Dalston Hall grew out of my live storytelling project and may still bear the marks of a story to be real aloud. There are patterns of repetition, especially towards the end that I draw out to enhance the tension and I think there is a free audiobook version of this floating about the internet somewhere. It is my great privilege to be pirated. Someone must have thought it worth copying!

The third story is the Tower of Ker-Zu. Well, Ker-Zu is Breton for the "Black Fortress". I had been intending at least a quartet of haunted castle stories set in the Celtic countries.

There is Dungarvan Castle set in the once Gaelic speaking Highlands of Scotland, Tullabeg Castle (not included in this volume) set in Ireland, Dalston Hall has the Cumbric speaking spectre Gospatric Map Bennog, who was a real person and who was indeed lord of Catterlen in the twelfth Century, and The Tower of Ker-Zu is my Breton story. Brittany is full of legends.

Ker-Zu is a dark fantasy, really and somewhat more erotic than most of the others. I generally avoid writing about carnal relations as it brings a blush to my cheeks, but this story turns on the sensuality of the dark lady Melusin, and was necessary.

The final story is the longest, a novella at forty thousand plus words. This was previously published but is extensively re-worked. The early versions were written when I was watching a lot of David Lynch, and what David Lynch can get away with I cannot. So, the early versions drew on unconscious imagery and felt very dreamlike. This version has a proper story, and is more folk-horror than surreal. I think it is a better story now. But what do I know?

In terms of story genres as per Blake Snyder and Save the Cat, for those who are interested. I think that Schloss Von Hohenwald is a 'Dude With A Problem", while Dalston Hall is definitely 'Monster In the House', Ker-Zu is a 'Rites of Passage' as I think is Dungarvan. In both these two, the man in the stories has to seriously rethink how he treats women. These two may even be considered romances rather than horror stories.

Ultimately, none of this is important. What is important is that you enjoy the stories themselves.

I read other peoples' stories out on *The Classic Ghost Stories Podcast*. Catch me there for free.

Tony Walker, March 2021.

∿

Steppenwolf

> *You can see my eyes are lupine,*
> *The liquid golden fires glare,*
> *My loping walk, my slinking spine,*
> *Are signs that there is something there.*
> *The way my nostrils flare for odour,*
> *The way my ears prick up for sound;*
> *My hair's electrically aware,*
> *Tells me things for miles around.*
>
> *I am a man-wolf, I am a wolf man.*
> *I have half a canine mind.*
> *I have half the mind of man.*
> *I am neither of one kind.*

Robert Calvert

# PART ONE
# DALSTON HALL

CHAPTER

# ONE

I 322, and the winter was the hardest and coldest anyone remembered. The ground lay heavy under snow long frozen and the land was locked with ice. Without expectation, the Scottish army came south. Perhaps hunger drove, or perhaps cruelty, for Cumberland had been harried and burned by the Scots year after year since the English defeat at Bannockburn.

As the short day waned, Lord Henry Dalston stood tall on the red sandstone battlements of his pele tower. The River Caldew flowed through woods and fields to the east of the high tower but it was from the cold north that the threat would most likely come.

He had heard how they crossed the frozen Esk at Longtown, reached Kirklinton and then besieged the great walled city of Carlisle. Most likely raiding parties would soon come to Dalston. The cold wind ruffled his greying hair. Lord Dalston saw no livestock in the fields as the farmers had moved them south already. Lord Dalston had sent all servants but one home to their families. Only Mary remained, a woman of middle years who had no family.

No livestock, but plenty of black crows on bare treetops. Lord Dalston scanned the horizon but his eye was caught by a dark figure in the middle distance. The figure stood tall in a black cloak and hood against the white snow. He did not move, merely stared at the tower.

Dalston thought the man better seek shelter lest he fall prey to the swift Scottish horsemen on their small grey ponies. Dalston hailed him with a yell and a wave of his arm, but the man did not respond. He shouted again, but again the man did not respond and finally with a shrug Dalston pulled up the trapdoor and took the wooden stairs back down into the security of his tower.

In his day chamber with its tapestries of hunting scenes from the Inglewood Forest, its glass windows, its wooden floors, Dalston spoke to his wife Edith. 'Do you really think they will come, Henry?' she asked.

Dalston rubbed his eyes. 'I do. They will be scouting the area for victuals to take back to the besieging army at Carlisle. Mid-winter is a foolish time to start a war.'

'And that's why they caught us by surprise.'

He stroked her hair. 'I think I'll take a glass of wine, even though it is early.'

'I'll ask Mary to prepare food sooner tonight. There are only the two of us. I hope everyone else has got safe home.'

Dalston reached inside his doublet and pulled a great black iron key on a leather thong that he kept around his neck. He smiled gravely. 'We are safe inside with the door locked. They won't bring siege equipment on their raids for food. They can take what they wish from the hall below; we can't stop them. But they'll not get into the tower. It was built secure and no raider has ever gained entry in once the door is locked.

DARKNESS FELL EARLY on that winter night and dinner was served in their bedroom where they sat quiet in the gloom lit by flickering candles. Lady Edith wore sable around her shoulder and a shawl of wool to keep her warm and she worked at her embroidery, but every now and again looked nervously up to check on her husband. He sat deep in thought, sipping his white rhenish wine.

She said, 'We have food in?'

He nodded. 'We had plenty in for the winter in any case. It'll go further if it's just we three.'

After a while, she asked, 'Are you worried?'

Dalston gave a weary smile. 'We've been through it before. They won't spare siege engines from Carlisle for such a little place as we are.'

THEY RETIRED TO BED EARLY, but Dalston slept little. His dreams were troubled with scenes of fire and pillage. In the deep of night, he awoke suddenly, thinking he heard the sound of soldiers and horses outside, but when he listened, it was only the soft sound of the north wind blowing round the pele tower. He slept again and when he awoke, it was day and Edith was already up.

They breakfasted together and then climbed to the tower roof to observe whether there were signs of trouble from the north. On the tower, a slight breeze blew but it was cold. The mountains to the south were white, the trees dark, but the ground pale and frozen.

Great palls of smoke rose from where they knew Carlisle to be under attack.

And then Edith said, 'Look, Henry, who is that?'

And there, standing in the same place he had been the day before was the black-clad stranger.

Lord Henry Dalston said. 'I saw that man yesterday, and he was stood exactly where he is now.'

'Well, he must have sought shelter overnight,' said his wife, 'for he would have frozen otherwise.'

Dalston nodded. 'I wonder who he is. I should call down and offer him shelter.'

But Edith put her hand on her husband's arm as if to stay him. He turned and regarded her, 'What, Edith? You are usually the first to offer succour to waifs and strays.'

She paused. 'He seems so strange.'

'I will go down and see him.'

'If you do, take your sword.'

He smiled. 'If it makes you feel better, I will, of course.'

'It would. I'm sure it's nothing, but he looks so odd standing there without moving.'

Lord Henry Dalston made his way down from the roof and down the spiral stone staircase inside the tower. He strapped his sword to his waist to please his wife, then went down past his room and the room below until he came to the great iron door. It was a latticework of painted iron bars and had been there for centuries. Once it had been the main entrance to the tower, when the tower stood alone, but now it gave entry to the Baronial Hall. He drew the heavy key on its thong from around his neck, and the iron was warm from where it had lain pressed against his heart. He put it in the lock and turned the key. The key turned easily in the greased lock.

Henry Dalston walked through the deserted Baronial Hall. As many of the valuables as could be moved had already been put in the pele tower for safety. His boots echoed on the stone floor. He went to the main door and pushed it open. Outside, his feet crunched on the frozen snow. He walked round the tower until he came in sight of where the dark-clad stranger stood in the middle distance. Dalston hailed him. 'Halloo! Stranger, can I help you?'

The man didn't speak. Dalston's hand went to the hilt of his sword and he went closer. He stopped twenty yards away. The man wore a long black cloak ragged at the bottom. The cloak's hood was up, throwing his face into shadow. He had on a breastplate that looked old-fashioned. He wore a sword on a belt at his side and leather trousers with knee-length boots.

Dalston shouted again, 'Hello there, stranger. I am Henry Dalston, Lord of this tower.'

For the first time the man spoke. His voice was slow and accented such as Dalston remembered folk speaking in his grandfather's time.

'Lord Dalston,' the man said. 'I greet you. I am Gospatric Map Bennog, Lord of Cadeirleng.'

Dalston recognised the old-fashioned name Gospatric and the fashion of using the patronymic 'map', to show he was son of Bennog, was as the old Cumbrians had done. Also his pronunciation of his home as Cadeirleng was not like the more familiar and modern Catterlen. The names were old Cumbrian too, in the language that no one now spoke.

Dalston said, 'I am sorry, sir. I do not know you. As far as I was aware, the lord of Catterlen is Herbert de Vaux.'

The dark clad man said, 'I know of no De Vaux, and I assure you I am lord of Cadeirleng and always was.'

'Enough of this, sir. You risk your life here, if you are English, for the Scottish army is abroad and seeking plunder, or hadn't you heard?'

'I am neither English nor Scottish, Lord Dalston.'

'Are you French then?'

'I am not. I am of this place.'

Dalston began to grow angry at the manner of this stranger who claimed honours he could not possibly have, and what did he mean that he was not English, Scottish nor French?

Dalston spoke, 'I was going to invite you into my tower for your own safety, as a matter of common courtesy. '

The stranger said, in his strangely accented voice, 'I accept your courtesy, Lord Dalston. I will be honoured to be your guest. At least for a while.'

Now Dalston remembered his wife's misgivings about the stranger; strange for Edith to be so disquieted, but the man also made a strange impression on him with his old-fashioned name and clothes.

He wished he had not made the invitation he unfortunately had just made. But what could he do? He could not leave anyone to the mercy of rampaging soldiers who would not care who they killed, whether he claimed not to be English or whatever he said.

Dalston narrowed his lips. 'Come then, Gospatric Map Bennog. I will find a room for you. We have only one servant staying with us, so please forgive my poor hospitality.'

The dark-clad man moved closer to Henry Dalston, almost seeming to glide over the snow, so lightly he walked. Dalston, for some odd reason not wanting to be close to the stranger hurried away and Gospatric Map Bennog followed him to his own front door.

Mary the maid, was found and was told to prepare the guest room on the floor above Lord and Lady Dalston's own room, just below the servant floor where Mary slept. From the way she looked at the man, who stood inside the Baronial Hall with his hood still up, Dalston thought that Mary did not care for him either.

Still, hospitality was a duty, and Dalston had made the invitation for the stranger to enter his tower.

Dalston accompanied his mysterious visitor and Mary up the spiral staircase to the floor where his chambers were.

'I'll leave you then, sir. You can go and rest until it is time to eat, for I believe you were all night in the cold.' Dalston said this pointedly, but his guest's pale face registered no emotion, nor did he reply, he simply went up after Mary who showed him to his chambers.

'He is a very strange man,' Lady Dalston said as they sat in their chambers. Dalston had just come down from the tower's roof. 'He makes me feel very ill at ease.'

Dalston shrugged. Whatever thoughts he had about Gospatric Map Bennog, he didn't share them.

Have the soldiers come, or is there any sign of them?' she asked.

'Smoke from Carlisle. New fires over towards Cardew and Cumdivock, but no sign of the soldiers themselves.'

'That's good, isn't it?' she said hesitantly. 'Perhaps they won't come.'

'Perhaps.'

'But even if they do, the tower is secure.'

Against most things, thought Dalston, but he said, 'Yes, yes of course. Try not to worry.'

They lapsed into a troubled silence and as dark was falling, Mary came to light the tapers.

'Is our noble guest settled in his chambers.'

'I think so,' said Mary, a lit spill cupped in her hand.

Lady Dalston said, 'Have you lit the tapers in his chambers?'

Mary shook her head. 'I knocked and asked to come in to do it, but there was no answer. I knocked several times,' she said, as if to reassure her lord she had done her duty.

'He must like to sit in the dark,' Lady Dalston said.

'Perhaps he went out?' Mary said.

Lord Dalston shook his head. 'The gate is locked and I have the only key.'

Lady Dalston began, 'He makes me—'

But Dalston signed for her to hold her peace in front of the servants and Lady Dalston blushed and fell silent.

'Your dinner will be ready in an hour. I have prepared some pullets,' Mary said.

Dalston nodded. 'You have done well, Mary. Knock again on our visitor's door just before food is laid out. We will eat in the old dining room.'

The old dining room was the room in the pele tower that had been used for eating before the Baronial Hall was built. There was a large fireplace, which was rarely lit these days. Dalston had had one of the male servants lay the fire of dry logs and tinder before he left to go to his family.

But when they sat in the red sandstone dining chamber, with its old-fashioned tapestries and tapers held in standing candle holders of black iron, there was no sign of Gospatric Map Bennog.

'Did you knock?' Lady Dalston said, as Mary served the meal.

'Aye, my lady, but he did not answer.'

Dalston was tired. The strain of waiting for the Scottish soldiers had eroded his patience. 'We will eat anyway. If he chooses not to eat, then that is up to him.'

Mary filled Lord Dalston's goblet with wine, then went to Lady Dalston, who refused the wine and had clear spring water instead.

The fire burned in its hearth, casting shadows across the walls. Outside night had fallen and the chill of the winter came through the walls held at bay by the warmth of the flickering flames. They talked of this and that, of happier times and summer and their daughters who were married, and further south, safe.

After they had eaten and Mary had cleared away the platters, Dalston asked if there was any sign of Lord Gospatric. Mary shook her head.

He left Edith to her embroidery and mounted the stairs to the guest chamber. Standing outside, he knocked the heavy wooden door. No response came. He knocked again, harder this time. Again nothing so he called out, 'Lord Gospatric, are you not hungry?'

The wind whistled outside but otherwise there was no sound. Lord Dalston felt the cold come from under the door. No sign of light seeped out. Perhaps their guest was so tired, that he had fallen into a deep sleep. If that was so, he would wake hungry for breakfast.

Dalston descended. His wife raised an eyebrow. 'Any sign of him?'

'No,' Dalston said. 'He must be asleep.'

'He must.'

The tapers burned low. Dalston was tired, his limbs felt heavy. He nodded in his chair and then his wife said, 'Time for sleep. Who knows what tomorrow will bring.'

'Who knows?'

'Perhaps they will lift the siege and return whence they came,' said his wife.'

'Perhaps.' He went over and kissed his wife on the forehead. He took her hand and led her bed, then called Mary to help her undress.

When Edith was in bed, he dismissed Mary with a smile. 'Thank you for staying, Mary,' he said and she curtsied with a smile. 'I couldn't leave you, my Lord.'

LADY DALSTON FELL into a deep sleep, the night was so dark and silent. Only the wind fretted and moaned outside the windows. Then a scream tore through the building. She awoke with a start, sitting bolt upright. Her husband woke beside her. 'What was what, Henry?'

'I don't know.'

'I think it was Mary. Have the soldiers got into the tower?'

Dalston's voice was troubled. 'No, that can't be. I have the key. And besides they would have to come past our door, and there would be such a noise of them breaking down the gate and mounting the stairs.'

'Then what is it then?' Lady Dalston asked, a terrible fear growing in her heart. 'It was Mary's cry. I know her voice so well.'

'I will go,' Lord Dalston said, rising in his night shirt.

'Take your sword, ' she said.

It was dark, but he had flint and iron and lit a flame in the tinder from which he kindled a taper. 'Light a candle for me,' she said. Without speaking he did so, pulled on his doublet and breeches and hurried.

It was raining heavily outside their window.

Lady Dalston watched her husband leave, sighing and trembling, waiting for him to return.

But minutes went by then quarter of an hour, and still he did not return.

Lady Dalston half expected to hear sounds of fighting or shouts and alarms, but there was only silence. After a while, she rose and went to the door. 'Henry! Henry! What keeps you?' she yelled, but there was no reply.

With her hand to her throat, she fetched a taper and trembled, peering up into the gloom of the spiral stone staircase that led up to Mary's chamber.

'Husband, are you there?' She shouted, but her only answer was the sighing of the wind.

'Henry, please tell me you are well.' She yelled, but her only answer was a flutter of the taper burning in her hand.

'Henry!' she called again. 'Please speak!' But the only answer she got was the pitter patter of soft rain.

With taper in hand, she finally summoned her courage, and stepped out onto the stairs of the tower, the stone cold under her bare feet. 'Henry?' She called, but her voice was quieter now as if she no longer expected an answer.

Lady Dalston heard someone coming down from above.

Whoever came was not in hurry, he came, almost silently, down and down, towards her, step by step by step.

Lady Dalston stood shaking. She could not run and she could not stay. She didn't know what to do.

And the footsteps came down, almost in sight now, just round the corner of the spiral stairs.

And instead of climbing, Lady Dalston descended, taper in hand.

She jumped down the steps, hurrying in her panic, and always behind her came the soft footfall descending.

And then, her heart pounding in her chest, she came to the bottom of the tower. But at the bottom was the heavy black iron lattice gate that had stood for centuries keeping intruders out. And stood now, keeping her in.

Lady Dalston pulled at the gate; she pushed at the gate; she heaved at the gate, but it was to no avail. It was heavy and iron and locked against her. Lady Dalston strained and tugged and moaned in her fear. And behind her, someone came round the turn of the stairs.

Lady Dalston held up her taper and screamed.

Lord Gospatric descended the stairs. His eyes were yellow like fever and his cheeks as pale as snow. His lips were red as blood and blood was on his chin, and blood ran over his cuffs and blood was on his fingernails. And as he came closer, Lord Gospatric smiled.

Lady Dalston saw Lord Gospatric's teeth were long and white and sharp.

And even though he had eaten, Lord Gospatric was still hungry.

Lady Dalston shook the strong iron door but she could not get out.

And, as Lord Gospatric's cold red fingers touched her, she wished her husband had never let him in.

# PART TWO
# SCHLOSS VON HOHENWALD

CHAPTER

# ONE

Ralph Waters-Wyn sat in the passenger seat beside his friend, as Gerald Anderson pulled his Rover 10 in by the Schönbrunn Palace. He left the engine idling because he said he wouldn't stop long and because the Rover was a bugger to start again. He helped Ralph retrieve his luggage from the boot while the horse-drawn carriages and other motors filed past.

"You're still going the long way round?" Ralph said, valise in hand.

Gerald nodded. "Via Styria."

"Backwoods country there. Make sure you don't break down, or we may never see you again. It's a very superstitious part of the country. I don't think they see many foreigners."

Gerald laughed. "Don't worry about me."

Ralph frowned. "Seriously. Why don't you go a more direct way – through more civilised parts?"

"You know me, old man. I like an adventure."

"That's all well and good, but don't get involved in anybody else's problems, and — I know you — don't try to fix things that are not your to fix. Remember you never know who you can trust in foreign parts."

"And you sell lots of paintings so you can buy me dinner in a nice little place by the Blue Mosque."

They said goodbye, and Ralph, who was spending time with wealthy clients in Vienna, promised to meet Gerald again in Istanbul, although that would not be for several weeks.

Ralph stood on the pavement as Gerald pulled the Rover off onto the road. He saw him wave through the window but then lost him sight of him in the traffic.


THE TWO FRIENDS PARTED, and Gerald took the road south. He planned to take the long route to Istanbul to while away the time until he met his friend, and divert south through the ruins of the Austro-Hungarian Empire, sight-seeing across Styria until he crossed the border into the new country of Yugoslavia, and from there he would thread his way south-east through the Balkans to Turkey and Thrace.

The weather was not in his favour, though Gerald should have guessed late October was not the time for pleasure-touring, but he wanted to return to England in time for Christmas, so it was October or never. He crossed the regional boundary into Styria and found the mountainous, heavily-forested land strange and forbidding. The leaves in the lower deciduous woodlands had turned iron, gold and bronze. The drizzle pattered on his windscreen, and the wind smelled of winter.

It was a beautiful country, but a mysterious country, and a country where each vista through the woods and each glimpse of a rustic village suggested secrets long kept. Since the War, the area received few visitors, most inns were boarded, and such rural folk as Gerald spotted from his speeding Rover 10 looked poverty-ridden and downtrodden.

Gerald drove through village after village, seeking somewhere to stop, but settlements were few among the mountains and forests, and villages with inns fewer still. Nowhere did he see anything like welcoming accommodation, and so he pressed on hoping the next town, or then the next, would offer something appropriate, but by the tenth hour of driving, he would have happily stayed anywhere with a roof.

Gerald arrived at Geistthall as darkness fell, and with the darkness came vicious, squalling rain. The gloomy pines all around the village thrashed in the wind, and as he scanned the narrow main street, he despaired of finding somewhere comfortable to stay. To be sure, there was a small inn there, called *Zum Schwarzen Wolf*, but when Gerald stopped to enquire, collar up against the shower, a middle-aged woman with dark hair answered his knocking. He had trouble making her understand his German at first, but then she seemed to get it and shook her head with a smile. She told him the inn sold beer and wine but had no rooms. "Sorry, Mein Herr, better luck somewhere else." She was mid-sentence when a mutton-chopped man with a sour face came up beside her.

He glared at the woman who winced as if expecting a blow, then he said in English, "No rooms! No rooms!"

Gerald bit his tongue. It looked as though the woman were afraid of this man whom he guessed to be her husband, who snarled at his wife to get in.

"Hang on a second..." Gerald said.

The landlord stuck his index finger up in warning. "You mind your own business, or you will have more trouble than you imagine."

Gerald fixed him with a stare. "Treat your wife decently, or you'll have me to answer to."

The man's face dropped, and he stepped back. It seemed he was a coward, as most bullies are.

But Gerald decided to mark his card. "I will be back, and I will ask, and if you have laid a finger on her, I'll lay more than a finger on you."

The man hurriedly pushed the door closed. With a final scowl, Gerald turned. The wind blew the rain in his face. His Rover was parked about fifty yards away, and as he approached, he saw a man in a raincoat and hat admiring it. It looked like he was stroking the bonnet, and he stepped back guiltily as Gerald approached.

"Rover 10?" The man said in German, then he said, "English?"

Gerald nodded. The man wore a clerical collar: a priest. "She runs well, yes. Just doing a bit of touring."

"Bad weather for touring."

"You're telling me. Do you know of anywhere to stay hereabouts?"

The priest shook his head. Bizarrely, he had white powder on his coat sleeve; it looked like he'd caught it in the sugar bowl. He said, "No, sorry. The *Schwarzen Wolf* doesn't have rooms."

Gerald gave a bitter laugh. "So, I understand. Anyway, off I go. Perhaps I'll find somewhere further on."

"Perhaps you'll find somewhere," the man said.

"I'm just passing through, anyway."

The man nodded. "Styria is old and full of secrets. Best pass through."

Gerald laughed. "I'm all the more determined to keep going then."

"Good luck!"

Gerald got in the Rover as the priest walked away. It struck him that this was the second time he'd been wished luck in a short space of time. He hoped he wouldn't need it.

And so, Gerald was forced to drive on. The road from Geistthall was narrow and steep with huge boulders at the margins that had clearly tumbled from the mountain to block the way but were since cleared to allow passage. The Rover's engine laboured as it took the slope, the road twisting like a corkscrew on a steep climb through wildly moving pine trees. The car began to misfire long before he reached the top.

"Damn, just what I need," Gerald muttered. He had a set of spanners to do minor running repairs, but he was no mechanic and did not relish trying to fix anything in this weather. As he leant forward over the steering wheel, urging the car on yard after yard, the engine sputtered and coughed and lost power, once, twice, three times, just to surge on before coughing and sputtering once more.

The road went on and on, and up and up, and round and round, spiralling into the mist, and on each twist, Gerald hoped he was nearing the summit of the pass. If the engine failed after he reached the top, he could simply coast downhill and thus escape being marooned on this damned mountain.

What a ridiculous time of year to drive through these Styrian Alps. Why hadn't he taken the usual route to Istanbul? Why hadn't he waited for Ralph in Vienna? But restlessness and a need for novelty had always been Gerald's downfall. He couldn't resist pushing everything a little further than anyone else.

Well before the top, the engine backfired mightily, like something had blown and quickly lost power, the engine noise suddenly dying away. Gerald cursed and prayed. "Just get me through this, Lord, and I promise I'll go to church every Sunday for the next month." How frequently how men find faith in times of crisis.

As if the Lord heard him, the engine caught and resumed feeble traction, and the Rover climbed on. However, Gerald was still far short of the crest of the pass when the car spluttered and died, standing motionless on the side of the wild Austrian road, the only sounds a faint ticking from the engine and a slow hiss of steam. Gerald gazed through the fogged-up windows, but no sign of human habitation met his eye; even the road looked rarely used.

The heavy rain had formed rivulets that flooded downhill over the pitted tarmac. Slumping on the wheel, he remembered he had seen no traffic since long before Geistthall, so he hardly expected rescue now.

Just then, to his horror, the asphalt road surface shifted under the car. Gerald shoved the driver door open and leapt out. The road underfoot was moving as the rain undermined the surface, and as he stared, the vehicle began to slide. It shifted a few feet sideways but didn't tip off the road. Gerald feared that if he stayed the night in his car, he would wake to find himself tumbling down the mountainside.

But if he didn't stay in the car, where would he find shelter? He looked around, getting steadily drenched standing there. For a few moments only, he considered going under the trees, but he would be soaked within minutes and never sleep. In great trepidation, as if it were a dog that might bite him, he approached the car, snatched open the rear door and grabbed his mackintosh from the back seat.

Gerald was already wet-through under the coat, but the mackintosh absorbed some of the downpour as he trudged up the dismal road, making sure to keep away from the edge. Grey fog hung in tatters across the highway and drifted through the trees. The only thing that raised his spirits, and that not by much, was his hope that there were sometimes inns at the top of passes in these countries.

# TWO

In the end, it was not an inn he found, but a castle: a Styrian Schloss buried behind serried ranks of trees. The old fortress was ruinous in parts, but lights gleamed through the mist: two of them, one on the ground floor but one through a smaller window high up in the left-hand tower.

A castle! It was like something out of a penny-dreadful story, and the Gothic grandeur of it set him back and made him even fearful, but what choice did he have? He would have to knock on the great oak door.

Cautiously, Gerald approached the dark building. Its battlements loomed above, and its windows watched, all of them dark except the two showing lamps, and those two he imagined concealing peering eyes of persons keen on keeping their secrets, and keen on knowing his.

A foreboding came over him as he crossed the drawbridge. He guessed at one time, the bridge would be drawn up for defence but looked now as if centuries had gone by since it last lifted.

Finally, Gerald stood before the huge oak and iron door. In this massive door was cut a smaller entrance, sized for a man. This was a door cut for convenience of human buildings, so no matter how monstrous the place appeared, some human lived here, and surely no human could turn him or anyone else away on such a night as this?

As if to emphasise the sharpness of his predicament, lightning cracked the sky behind him, flashing white on the ivy-draped walls in front.

His mouth was dry and his hand trembled. Why was he so nervous? But then, of course, the car breaking down, his aloneness in a strange land, the weather, the cold, his shivering, these were surely enough to explain his anxiety. The sight of this place and the dread it had caused him were due to his overwrought nerves, not to any real threat.

Overcoming the seeping unease, Gerald reached and gripped the heavy iron knocker in the shape of a wolf's head. He lifted it and rammed it down three times, and the heavy blows echoed deep within the building, but no one came.

He reasoned: there were lights here, so there were people. Why did they not come? Perhaps they hadn't heard his forlorn knocking, so Gerald lifted the iron wolf's head again and beat it a further three times. Nine times now, he hammered down the wolf's-head knocker, and nine times the echoes went forth, summoning whoever was within while nine times the lightning cracked behind him, sparkling and dancing against an ominous background of clouds.

Still no one emerged from the fortress, and Gerald was about to retreat into the night and go who knows where, when he heard a sound. Bolts drew back, and chains were unshackled, and the door groaned open to reveal a hollow-faced man in servant's attire, standing with a golden candelabra in which flared seven candles. The flames fluttered, the wild wind threatening to extinguish them, as the servant glared coldly.

Gerald spoke in German, "Excuse me, my car broke down. I have nowhere to stay, and the weather..."

The man looked at him a long time as if digesting the words.

Gerald wondered whether he had made himself plain and cleared his throat to say more, but before he could speak, the servant said, "My master does not receive guests."

Gerald stood bewildered, one arm gesturing to the storm. More lightning split the sky to support his entreaty. "But the weather....?"

The grave-faced man repeated himself. "My master does not receive guests."   At the door, in despair, Gerald begged the servant, and the man finally sighed and went to his master. It transpired that his master was kinder, or more curious, than the servant and Gerald was allowed in out of the rain.

GERALD STOOD DRIPPING in the vast entrance hall of the castle, and the door closed behind him to keep out the storm. He stood, head back, amazed. It was as if he had been transported back to the Middle Ages. Faded tapestries hung on the walls and substantial black-iron candelabras dangled from the ceiling, their crowns of candles unlit but dripping with stalactites of frozen wax to show that once, perhaps long ago, they had burned with life.  But what life was here now? Staring around, all seemed gloom.

The only illumination in the hall came from the triple candelabra the servant retrieved from the top of a scarred oak bookcase. He'd placed it there so the gusting wind did not extinguish the light when he closed the door.

The servant led Gerald through stone passages past open doors that showed shadowed rooms but did not permit enough light to enter to unmask their secrets. As they walked, Gerald imagined centuries worth of heirlooms— priceless antiques mixed with worthless junk, unsorted and left long alone. He followed the servant who strode down passages and stalked along hallways, Gerald walked behind and the servant didn't speak while Gerald hoped for a fire, and possibly food.

Finally, they came to a great hall. The hearth was ten feet wide and eight feet tall and blazed with massive logs, culled, Gerald supposed, from the trees that encircled the schloss like a besieging army awaiting their chance to throw all of this down and restore the land to wild nature. He craned his neck. The ceiling of the Great Hall rose to the height of two rooms, but the enormous fire was enough to heat it, and even from here, the flames scorched Gerald's cold cheeks.

Turkish carpets lay one upon the other on the stone floor in vibrant patterns of red and green and black and yellow. They too looked ancient as if they dated from the time, centuries ago, when the Turks harried the borders of Austria. The stone walls were dressed in tapestry, all faded, all showing hunting parties, all except one strange scene that appeared to depict a wedding between a man and a wolf standing on her hind legs.

Baroque suits of armour huddled in corners, too rococo surely ever to have been worn in a fight, and above them, racks and rows of broadswords and halberds. Ancient muskets and fusils decorated the other walls and everywhere stood tables and tall cabinets over-stuffed with china and porcelain. Items from the orient: China, India and Japan filled gaps around the hall's edge, and then there were heaps of books, old books, shelves of books, hundreds of books, leather books, cloth books, paperback books, but none looking as if they had been read in years.

The flickering light in the Great Hall came from the wide iron crowns of candles hung on black chains from the ceiling. Unlike the dead candelabras in the entrance, these danced with rippling flames, shifting in currents of unquiet air. A long table ran along the centre of the room for almost its full length.

But the chief wonder of the room was the host. He sat in a tall chair, dressed in black, silently observing Gerald's entry, and Gerald could not tell his age, fifty at least, maybe older. This noble-looking man sat, thin, and high-cheek-boned, with black hair pulled from his forehead in a severe widow's peak. He watched Gerald with eyes as blue as glacier ice compressed for ten thousand years and his face was unnaturally pale as if sunlight never fell upon it.

"Allow me to introduce myself," Gerald said, as soon as his astonishment at the room and its contents subsided. He had been in castles in England of course, but none so grand or ancient-looking as this.

His host nodded to acknowledge Gerald speaking but did not get up from his wing-backed chair.

"I'm Gerald Anderson, from Sussex, England. I live some of the year in London." Gerald jerked a hand in the direction he supposed his lonely car to lie abandoned in the howling storm. "My car broke down, you see."

Gerald spoke German. The man answered in English. "I see, Mr Anderson. Thank you for your introduction. I do not normally receive guests, but the hour is late and the weather most inhospitable. Because of this, I have made an exception for you. We have ancient laws of hospitality in this country. I'm sure you can have your car repaired tomorrow and be on your way. Vincent in the village is an excellent mechanic."

"I thank you, sir, but you have the advantage over me..."

He nodded. "I am the Graf von Hohenwald. My family have lived here for many centuries. My brother was Graf before me, our father before him, and so on, *et cetera, et cetera, in saecula saeculorum.*"

Gerald was dripping and inched closer to the fire, and soon steam rose from his clothes.

"You are cold and wet," the Graf said. "Do you have dry clothes?"

Gerald had dry clothes in his suitcase, but that was locked in the boot of his car, and he didn't relish going out to fetch it. Gerald's hesitation caused the Graf to mutter to his servant and order him to set out some dry clothes. The Graf then turned to Gerald, and his glacier eyes pierced the Englishman like a moth on a pin. "Change, then I will ask Tobias to provide food. At this time of night, it will be cold meat, cheese and bread only, and wine, if you drink alcohol?"

Gerald smiled. "I do. That is most kind of you."

"Go now."

. . .

THUS DISMISSED, Gerald followed Tobias from the Great Hall, dripping still. Gerald's room was in the tower. It was clean, but felt cold and damp as if no one had lived in it for a long time. There was a window shuttered in dark, varnished wood, and the wind screamed outside, so he did not open it, though he thought there might be a beautiful view from this room in the morning as it was so high.

But he had no plans to stay. This old place felt strange. Whatever mysteries it held were of no concern to travelling Englishmen: let the Styrians keep their secrets. As soon as his car got fixed he would be gone.

The clothes set out were plain and old, but in good order, no holes or wear. There were even soft leather shoes that looked Victorian in style but were a reasonable fit.

Someone had laid out towels, and someone, possibly the same someone had put a warming-pan in the bed to air it. The linen smelled fresh. There was another bookshelf, but Gerald had no time to peruse the volumes after drying and changing before a soft knocking came on the door. It was the hollow-faced servant, Tobias.

"Your dinner awaits you, sir." He said.

Gerald wasn't sure whether it was his imagination, but Tobias seemed slightly warmer in demeanour as if he'd seen his master be courteous towards Gerald and decided to follow his lead.

GERALD TROTTED after Tobias and arrived again in the Great Hall with its blazing fire. Now, the long wooden table was set for dinner with only one place. Silver candelabras brightly polished with new white candles stood lit on the table, the flames gleaming in the varnish. The Graf sat in the same chair by the fire and told Gerald he had already eaten.

Gerald didn't speak while he ate, and the Graf's silent gaze, as he stuffed his mouth, made him uneasy, but he quelled the anxiety with the Graf's excellent red wine, sipping from a fine crystal glass. From the quality of the cutlery and the excellence of the wine, Gerald didn't doubt that someone living here had once had a lot of money, maybe not now, but certainly then.

When Gerald finished, he sat back and dabbed his mouth with the crisp linen napkin, his wine-stained lips left traces of red on the white. Still the Graf sat silent.

To make conversation, Gerald said, "I thank you for your hospitality. I must admit I feared I would die of cold out in the storm."

"The weather here in October is terrible. We are high, you see," the Graf said.

Silence. After several minutes of awkwardness, Gerald said, "You say there is a mechanic in the village?"

The Graf nodded. "Vincent. Yes. He has a workshop next to the inn. I will ask Tobias to take you in the morning."

"Good. Well, I am very obliged you let me stay." Gerald felt a little impertinent as he added, "Especially given that you do not normally receive visitors."

The Graf studied him. Finally, he said, "I must admit I was curious."

Gerald was taken aback. "Curious? About what? Me?"

"Yes. You."

"Me? Why on earth would you be curious about me? If my car hadn't broken down, I wouldn't be here at all."

The Graf smiled a slow smile. "A strange coincidence, don't you think? That you should break down almost outside my door, when there is no other house for miles. It was as if by magic."

Gerald frowned. "Whatever can you mean by that?"

The Graf kept staring. "Just that we have been expecting a visitor. Someone who might not be honest about who he really was."

Gerald's frown deepened. "What?"

The Graf considered his long fingers. "We are not wholly certain in what guise our expected visitor will come."

Gerald shook his head. "You are expecting someone, but you don't know who they are?"

"Exactly."

'That's quite strange."

"We have known about them for years, but the visit becomes imminent. I wondered perhaps if our long-expected visitor was you."

"Me? But I had no intention at all of stopping here."

"But he would say that."

"We English are plain-speaking folk. So forgive me if I ask you plainly, why do you expect this visitor now? And more especially why do you think it might be me, given that I assure you my arriving here is pure fluke?"

"The answers to these questions are all my business, not yours."

How rude the man was. Gerald forced a smile and thought it best change the subject. He cleared his throat. "It's a big place. It must be odd living in a castle."

"Must it?"

"It's so large and old for one person."

The Graf nodded. "It is large and old."

"You live alone here, I presume?"

"You presume?"

"Ah. So you have a family. But I see no sign of anyone else."

The Graf pursed his lips. After five minutes more of silence, Gerald decided he would go to bed. The sooner he was away from the Schloss Hohenwald, the better.

CHAPTER

# THREE

The next morning, after getting out of bed, Gerald drew back the wooden shutters of the circular tower room, revealing ancient and irregular glass panes, and through them, as he had guessed, a most beautiful vista over the Styrian Alps. The forest stretched miles and away in all directions, cladding the hills and valleys and giving the impression there was no other world than that blanketing overcoat of swaying green. Again, he had a feeling of unease, but still, Gerald felt better for his rest. There was even blue sky; the dawn had washed away the rain, leaving a pleasant Autumn freshness. The forests hereabout were pine and spruce, and Gerald guessed the hills kept this aspect of foreboding green, so dark as to be almost black, from season to season, and season to season after that. What mysteries must be concealed in these forests? What had they seen over the centuries and what tales and folklore had they given rise to? But he was letting his imagination run away with him, a thing most unlike him. He was usually a practical man.

Startling him from his reverie, crows rose cawing from the closest trees across from the window, and Gerald felt his stomach rumble—time for breakfast.

He wandered down the stone spiral stairs from the tower room and encountered no one. His footsteps echoed on old stone, and he paused to admire the ancient suits of armour dotted on landings and in halls and wondered whether they had belonged to the Graf's martial ancestors.

Eventually, Gerald saw the door to the Great Hall and strolled in there. His watch told him it was after 10 am. He had slept late.

The fire was burning. The smell of woodsmoke met his nose but also the aroma of food. Someone was cooking bacon. He saw the long wooden table had been laid for breakfast, but just one place. Gerald shrugged. It must be for him, so he went and sat down. There was a napkin, antique-looking silver knives and forks that weighed more than any modern ones. He waited, and within minutes, Tobias emerged, as expressionless as always.

"The Graf asked me to give you breakfast. He said you would enjoy this." In his hand, held with a serving cloth, was a large white china plate and on the plate, a heap of bacon and eggs and black bread with butter. There was also a silver pot of coffee and a smaller, china pot of milk decorated with blue flowers.

"Please, thank your master. Is he around? I feel I left abruptly last night, but I was exhausted."

"The Graf is indisposed this morning, but I have, on his instructions, telephoned the mechanic, Vincent, and asked him to collect your car for repair."

Gerald raised his eyebrows. "You have a telephone?" He found the idea surprising in that vast, ancient fortress; it seemed out of place, somehow too modern in a place that reeked of time.

Tobias nodded. "Yes, sir."

"Well, that's very kind of you. And did the mechanic collect the car?"

Tobias nodded. "I should imagine. I rang him much earlier."

"And did Vincent have any idea when the car would be fixed?"

"He did not, sir. He had not examined it at the time of our conversation."

"But I could phone him, I suppose."

"As you wish, sir."

"Will you show me the telephone? After my breakfast, of course. It smells delicious."

"After your breakfast." And Tobias departed.

Tobias left Gerald alone in the large room with the blazing log fire. The fire gave off pleasant warmth on that cold morning, and the wood smoke smelled sweet as if the logs were hewn of cherry or apple. Gazing around, Gerald took in again the tapestries and banners and oriental ornaments and antique bookcases filled with leather-bound, gilt-embossed books, and then the halberds and pikes and shields. For the first time, he noticed their heraldic designs. He guessed they bore the heraldic arms of the Graf's family and their allies in marriage. The Von Hohenwald family emblem seemed to be the snarling head of a black wolf on a yellow background.

That the Graf was not there, did not concern him. The Graf didn't seem much of a man for company, and perhaps he preferred to avoid dealings with Gerald. Still, that strange story of the long-awaited visitor, a visitor whose actual identity was still unknown was intriguing. If odd. Gerald chuckled. It was all very rich, a peculiar adventure indeed, and a story to dine out on when Gerald returned to England, but the sooner he was in his trusty Rover and away on the next leg of his travels, the better. He planned to get to Ljubljana as quickly as possible and then spend a day or so doing nothing much.

Gerald finished his breakfast. Tobias hadn't come back to clear up or show him the telephone. In any case, there was little likelihood of the mechanic having fixed the car yet, so Gerald decided to explore the castle. He wandered to the suits of armour and ran his finger over the old metal: no dust, so someone cleaned them scrupulously. He idly perused the bookcases filled with tomes about history as well as German classics. Then he sauntered out of the Great Hall and went to see what of interest he could find to fill the time until his Rover was repaired.

He wondered whether he might even run across the telephone or Tobias in his travels. As he wandered, he found a wide oak staircase of polished wood with faded stair carpets held by brass runners. Gerald scratched his head. The place was enormous. He knew his room was off one of the towers, and he did not remember using this staircase. There were two towers, and one was in ruins, at least at the top. It was unlikely this broad stairway led to either of them, so it seemed most likely it led to the main body of the Schloss. Having nothing better to do and enjoying the excitement of exploration, he mounted the stairs. If he bumped into the Graf or Tobias he would merely tell them he was looking for the telephone, after all, there was no one around to show him and if he was not allowed in these areas he could easily claim to have got lost.

Gerald was struck by the dearth of servants. There was Tobias, but surely such a huge and draughty pile as this needed maids and gardeners and whatever? Still, there was no one around, and as he explored the first floor, Gerald's excitement changed to a less pleasant emotion. There was an atmosphere to the place, haunted almost—and he didn't mean by ghosts—though by rights there should have been plenty of these, but by a certain air of despondency as if something unresolved hung over the place.

Gerald grew tired of wandering the passages that led endlessly on to other rooms, mostly featureless. Most were locked, some were not, but those that were not had shuttered windows, dust-sheets draped over furniture and beds stripped of linen, just bare mattresses. No one came here, he saw that now, and it seemed the Graf lived all alone, despite his hint of family, but whether his solitariness was by choice, or because no one sought out his company, it was hard to say, but not so hard to guess.

And as Gerald wandered, the weather, as he observed it from the windows of those rooms that were not shuttered, or from the panes along the passages that ran parallel with the outside of the building, or even from the odd ornate skylight, changed and grew altogether darker; the blue sky was gone, replaced by smothering cloud. Gerald sighed. He had taken against the place; it was too old, too dark, too haunted by alien memories that hung heavy in the air, impure, implicit and impenetrable. He now wanted to find the telephone, ring the mechanic and leave.

But it was not easy finding his way back. By accident, he came across a part of the schloss that seemed almost set apart. There was something in the furnishings and decoration that suggested it had been used by someone else. Gerald couldn't exactly say why it was different, but it *was* different. There was a plain wooden door, and there had been many of those of course, and this one was closed, as were most of the others, but there was something that set this door apart, an aura, unseen, but noticeable. It almost had a taste—acrid, and animal, unusual and unpleasant.

Curiosity aroused, Gerald tried the handle, but it was locked, again nothing novel in this, but as he was about to turn and leave, he heard something or someone move inside. Halting and pressing his ear to the door, he listened. There was definitely someone inside. He considered whether this might be the Graf's private apartment, but if anything, this part of the castle seemed too feminine for that austere gentleman.

Finally, "Hallo?" he called out.

"Hallo," came the reply: a woman's voice.

"I'm sorry to disturb you," Gerald said, in place of any other sensible response.

The anonymous female voice whispered, "Please, don't leave."

Gerald cleared his throat. "I'm Gerald Anderson, an Englishman. I stayed here last night as a guest of the Graf."

"A guest of the Graf?" Her voice grew suddenly anxious. "Are you then a friend of his?"

"No, I came upon the place in last night's storm. My car broke down. He was kind enough to let me stay."

"So, not his friend?"

Gerald shrugged. "I owe him a debt, but, no, I wouldn't consider myself his friend, nor, I guess, would he consider me a friend either. We hardly know each other."

"You must help me," she said abruptly.

Gerald stood back. Help her? What with for Heaven's sake? But he paused. Last night it had been he who needed the help and now some resident of this castle was requesting his aid.

The woman blurted, "I am Amaris. The Graf keeps me prisoner here."

"Prisoner?" How bizarre, but the girl went on.

"The Graf is my uncle. He keeps me locked up."

Locked up? What kind of a tangle was he getting himself into by coming here? Gerald said simply, "Why on earth would he do that?"

"The Graf is a wicked man. He fears my birthday."

"He fears your birthday? Why in Heaven would he fear your birthday?" This grew odder by the minute.

Amaris said, "Because when I am twenty-one, I come into my estate, and this castle will be mine. It is not his, never his. It was my father's, and Alexander is only Graf here while I am a minor, and soon I will have my birthday, and he will be deposed, so that is why he fears me, and keeps me locked way, but you—you can set me free."

It occurred to Gerald that the Graf might have locked this girl Amaris away because she was insane. Such things happened, even recently, even in England. He hesitated, unsure of how to respond.

"There is a key," she said. She was driving the situation faster than he could think.

"A key?" He hesitated. He should speak of this to the Graf, or, easier still, walk away and never mention it to anyone. Equally, her story might even be true and she might indeed be the victim of a great wrong. How was he to truly know?

Gerald Anderson was not a dishonourable man. He had fought bravely in the war, and would never let down a friend or a comrade, but this peculiar situation was far beyond his experience, and it left him uncomfortable. He sighed deeply. Where did his loyalty lie—to the Graf whom he hardly knew, but who had showed him hospitality, or to this strange girl, whom he did not know at all and who might easily be mad and locked away for her safety and the safety of others?

Amaris continued. "Yes, behind you, is a rosewood cabinet. In the top drawer, is a key to the outer door here. Unlock it, and we can speak more freely."

"It only unlocks the outer door?"

"Yes, sadly. But still, even with one door opened, we can talk better."

At least he could give her the benefit of an honest hearing. His sense of fair play wouldn't let him leave a woman locked up without hearing her out.

Gerald turned and saw the cabinet—it was a chest of drawers more properly and seemed designed for the keeping of linen. He approached it and again feeling he was been driven by the girl's demands and not knowing how reasonably to refuse her, he dragged open the topmost drawer. In it was indeed a key. Slowly, as if it might bite, he took it. He rubbed his chin and looked at the key in his right hand. Ah, well.

Gerald unlocked the door. His heart beat a little faster as he opened the door. He didn't know whether he expected her to rush at him, but he needn't have worried. This outer door now opened onto a suite of rooms. There had been a door at the end of the short corridor, but that had been removed, and now there was an iron grille. Behind the latticed iron stood a young, black-haired woman. She looked around twenty and was, to all appearances, in good health. It seemed the Graf did not starve her at least, and her clothes, though plain, were clean. She was also extraordinarily beautiful.

She said, "I am Amaris Von Hohenwald, the rightful heir of this castle. Thank you, Mr Anderson, for opening the door."

Gerald could see from where he stood that there was a lock on the grille. It seemed another key was needed to free her completely.

Yes, she was rather striking. The sort of woman you could look at all day and not grow tired.

Amaris smiled. "I sense my freedom is at hand." She paused. "I had expected another to come and rescue me. He long ago promised he would come on my twenty-first birthday, but perhaps he has been killed. I cannot think he would abandon me if he still lived."

He gestured. "The iron lattice here is locked as well."

"Yes, Mr Anderson, that is the next step." Amaris Von Hohenwald had the face of an angel and a voice was as sweet as Alpine honey made from the brightest and freshest wildflowers in the highest, cleanest meadows.

"Will you help me?"

The least he could do was to wait while she told him her tale of woe.

# FOUR

Gerald stood, one step away from the iron grating that imprisoned Amaris. Not that he suspected anyone so slender and lovely could do him harm, or even reach her hand through the grille. As he stood, she told him her story.

"My father, Joachim Von Hohenwald, was the rightful Graf and owner of this castle. He was the elder of the two brothers. The current Graf that you have met is Alexander, the younger. The family disapproved of my father's marriage. My mother was a commoner, in trade, and a Hungarian. Her father was a watchmaker and far below the Von Hohenwalds in social standing. This was just before the end of the last war when the old empire was dying and the country was in turmoil. Alexander saw a way of gaining an advantage over my father, and he poisoned my grandparent's minds against my mother. I believe Alexander killed my mother, and my father took his own life because of grief."

"The Graf murdered your mother?"

"With poison, yes. There is no proof. Still, I believe it."

"But your grandparents?"

"Are now dead, but they agreed that Alexander would be my

guardian. He was kind enough to me while they lived, I remember him being sweet, but once they were dead and he was Graf, he put me in this suite of rooms, installed the cage, locked the door, and I have been here since."

Gerald paused. "But why didn't he kill you? If he was wicked enough to poison your mother, why did he simply not do away with you, once your grandparents were gone? I'm sorry to be so blunt, but perhaps you are mistaken, and your mother died of natural causes."

Her eyes blazed. "So, you are on his side?"

Gerald gestured helplessly. "No, I didn't say that."

"If he was innocent, why has he locked me up here?"

It struck Gerald that he didn't actually know that the Graf had locked her up here, or for how long, or indeed whether she was really his niece. But she was locked in, that was for sure. It certainly seemed like devilry. He said, "I don't know."

She implored him. "Please, Mr Anderson, you must help me escape!" Her eyes were blue as spring crocuses with a yellow star flare around the iris, unusual and fascinating

"But how do I do that?"

"My uncle has a key," she said.

"If your story is true—"

"—it is true, I swear."

"Then surely, he won't just give it to me."

She shook her pretty head. "Of course not. But he keeps it in his room."

"I don't know where his room is."

"It's up the broken tower."

Gerald frowned. "You can't expect me to go into his room and steal it."

Tears flowed from her eyes and ran down her cheeks. "Of course, you are right. For a second, I had hope. But clearly, it is too much to ask you to do for me. I am a stranger to you after all."

Then a thought occurred to him. "What if I try to reason with him? Find the facts and point out other courses of action."

"My uncle Alexander will not see reason on this matter. He is my gaoler. Please do not expect him to listen to you." Her voice went quiet as if she was afraid. "Please, do not even mention my name. If he knows you have found me, and that you have given me hope, I fear for my life."

This was all too strange. Gerald knew he should turn his back on this. Who knew the truth of anything here? But some Chivalric impulse pulled at him. "So, you want me to go and get the key?"

"And then take me away, to Vienna, to anywhere."

"I thought you wanted to claim your inheritance?"

"In time, but first, I need to be safe from his murderous rage. Once he realises I have escaped, he will seek to destroy me, and you for helping me. So we must get safe, then speak to a lawyer."

A lawyer! At last, the real world intruded. Gerald would undoubtedly trust the mundane workings of the Law. He said, "So, you say it's in his room?"

"Yes, but please, be quick. Then we can leave."

Gerald noticed the emphasis on 'we' as if she had twined his fate with hers. All of a sudden he imagined them together, years from now, remembered their daring escape from her wicked uncle. Then he shook his head. What was coming over him? He needed some space to think. "His room's in the ruined tower?"

She put her hand up to the bars of her cage. "Yes, please hurry back with the key."

GERALD LEFT Amaris in her prison. He had no idea what to do. Or rather he clearly knew he should leave all of this well alone. But that would mean leaving her to his fate, and he struggled to do that—a poor young woman like that must be innocent. She seemed too pure and, indeed too beautiful for it all to be a lie. He would speak to the Graf, hear his side of the story. Surely something could be worked out.

He retraced his steps to the Great Hall with a heavy heart. The fire had been banked up, and the plates cleared away, but of Tobias or his master Graf Alexander, there was no sign. This was a very strange place.

As he looked around the hall with its ancient weapons and its even more ancient traditions, there was no sign of anyone. Gerald thought on what Amaris said: that the Graf would fly into a mad rage and kill them both. A nobleman such as the Graf could probably do whatever he wanted out here, and get away with it.

He wasn't frightened of that, but there was no point walking straight into a fight.

He sat on a chair. Gerald considered going to the village and finding the local policeman. But then, of course, any police officers in this isolated neck of the woods would be deferential to the local lord, so he could expect little from them. He held his head in his hands. Maybe, he actually would have to rescue her himself.

Gerald decided to go looking for the Graf's room. He hadn't actually made his mind up to ransack the room looking for the key, that would be such a gross trespass on the Graf's hospitality to him. First he would find the Graf's chamber, and decide what to do then.


GERALD SPENT over an hour wandering over the vast, many-roomed schloss, getting lost, retracing his steps, finding himself and losing himself multiple times until he had the glimmer of a clue of his way around the castle and where the broken tower could be found. The broken tower was the twin of the tower where his room was, and the schloss was broadly symmetrical, though there were particular idiosyncrasies and he guessed each Graf had added a little bit to the place, some more than others.

But finally, he had it. He knew where the Graf's room was. He didn't know where the Graf was though, and it was very possible he was in his chamber.

Gerald stood, like a novice burglar with stage fright outside the door on the long, empty corridor. No one came. He stood there five or six minutes. Gerald put his hand on the crystal doorknob. Shaking his head, he turned it.

If the key were in the Graf's room then Amaris's story rang true and the Graf must be complicit in her imprisonment. Then he would go back and unlock Amaris. He wasn't a cad and he wasn't a coward. He would find out the truth and then act accordingly.

The knob turned, and the door clicked open. Gerald thought anyone within twenty yards would hear the hammering of his heart, but there was no sound from within the Graf's room. He pushed the door gently and coughed. Again, if the Graf was inside, he would say outright that he'd found Amaris and do him the courtesy of asking him for his side of the story.

No alarm was raised at the opening of the door and thereby emboldened, Gerald pushed it open the length of his arm, expecting some cry or shout, but still, no words were yelled or even whispered. The Graf wasn't there. More confidently, Gerald opened the door and peered around.

The room was panelled in walnut. There was a four-poster bed with silk hangings in yellow with a stylised wolf's head emblazoned on them. The sheets were undisturbed. Either the bed had just been made, or the Graf hadn't been sleeping here. Perhaps he'd got the wrong room? But in any case, where the hell did the man spend his days?

Gerald scanned the chamber. A window looked out onto the rain-swept forest, and grey light percolated in through undrawn curtains. It was a dull day, and would soon be dark again. The room had more bookshelves, armoires and chests, more porcelain and brass oil lamps with frosted glass globes, but no Graf.

He went to the first chest of drawers. All the while, he looked around the room, on the nightstand and the top of the bookcase to see if there was any sign of this key. Nothing was visible, so he dragged open the top drawer and found old clothes that stunk of camphor. He yanked the next drawer, and saw yet more ancient clothing that looked like it had not been worn for decades.

This was like looking for a needle in a haystack, but, as he hovered, ready to search another drawer, some sixth sense prickled the hairs on the back of his neck: someone was coming.

As quietly, but as quickly as he could, he pushed the drawer closed. Gerald hadn't shut the chamber door properly behind him, and it sat about six inches open. He slipped behind the door so he would be hidden behind it should anyone enter. Of course, if they came fully into the room, he would be exposed, and the Graf was sure to come into his own room.

Gerald heard steps along the passage outside. The stone was carpeted, but the tread was heavy enough for him to know it belonged to a man and that he was coming this way.

Gerald stopped breathing. As he waited, eyes closed, to be revealed.

Then, whoever it was stopped. Gerald heard him pause and put his hand to the door, and the door moved slightly open. Then, he pulled the door shut from outside. Closed, but thankfully not locked. And he left.

It must have been Tobias walking past, thinking the Graf hadn't shut his bedroom door properly. But what if he wondered why and came back to check the Graf was well? Gerald needed to get out of the room right away, key or no key. All this skulking wasn't his style. He didn't know what had come over him to be so shifty.

He gave it five minutes then opened the door, listened and heard nothing.

It was impossible to find a hidden key among all the items in that overstuffed bedchamber. He would have to try something else. Gerald left the room, making sure to close it tightly behind him.

GERALD HURRIED DOWN THE CORRIDOR. He found his way back to the Great Hall. This time Tobias was there.

"Ah, sir, I came looking for you, but you weren't in your room."

"I went to the library. I presume it's a library, there are lots of books!" He had seen a library on his travels, but not entered. He might not be a cad or a coward, but here and now he was a liar. What was this place doing to him?

Tobias studied him as if he knew he was lying, then said, "The mechanic telephoned. He told me he ordered a part from Graz this morning and is expecting it this afternoon. He fully anticipates having your car fixed ready for you to leave this evening."

Tobias clearly didn't want him to stay another night. He had to find a way of releasing Amaris before then.

Will you require food before you leave?" Tobias asked.

Gerald said, "Is the Graf around?"

"No sir, he is currently indisposed."

Gerald put his hand to his mouth the said, "Tobias, does anyone else live here in the castle?"

Tobias cocked his head. "Have you found anyone in your wanderings?"

He wasn't going to give his master's game away. Gerald felt foolish for even trying to wheedle the information out of him. Whatever he was, Tobias was not disloyal.

Gerald thought he would get his car and bring it back and then figure out another way or releasing Amaris or at least get better directions to where the key might be kept. There might even be a locksmith in the village. He couldn't expect the locksmith to help, but he might be able to get a loan of his tools and hope he could figure out how to use them in lieu of a key. Gerald said, "I suppose I can get food in the inn?"

"Of sorts."

"I'll do that then. I'll get the car and fetch it back up. Is there someone who can take me down?"

"I can, sir. We have a horse and trap. But I have some jobs to do first. If you would be happy to wait half an hour?"

"That'll be fine."

CHAPTER

# FIVE

It was getting dark as Gerald sat in a borrowed fur coat next to Tobias on the Graf's carriage pulled by two black horses. They clip-clopped down the pass at an amiable speed. From a distance, Gerald heard a deep baying howl, and started in his seat.

Tobias chuckled. "The English herr is frightened at the sound of a wolf."

"A wolf?"

"More than one. There are still wolf packs in Styria."

"My goodness." Gerald glanced all around. "Will they bother the horses?"

"They are usually timid." Then he smiled. "Unless they are hungry."

They kept on going down the pass, the way was steep, and Gerald nervously glanced at the tree-line on either side of the road just in case wolves emerged. They didn't, but as they trotted along, the wind blew the clouds away, and a large moon rose. The orb seemed bigger than usual and tinged with red.

"Full moon," he said.

"The Hunter's Moon, they call it," Tobias said. "It makes the wolves brave."

He knew Tobias was teasing him. How these people liked to manipulate his emotions. Gerald heard the wolves again, but they were calling a long way off. Still, he had no idea how fast they ran. In his Rover, he would have felt safe; there was a metal door between him and them, but here he was sitting on an open trap. He willed the horses to trot more swiftly, but they just kept the same steady pace.

They were about halfway to the village when Gerald finally worked up his courage. "Does the Graf have any family, Tobias?"

Tobias nodded. "He has only one niece. She is his only living relative."

"His sister's or his brother's child?"

"Brother's, but Graf Joachim died, and Graf Alexander has looked after her since."

"What do they call her?"

"That would be Lady Amaris."

So Amaris had told the truth, she was the Graf's niece. But why would he lock her up, unless she was telling the truth about the inheritance?

"Tobias, where does Amaris live, if the Graf looks after her?"

"Why she lives in the castle with us," Tobias said. "I believe you may have met her. Amaris's mind wanders. I wouldn't give credence to what she says. She likes to play with our guests."

They had arrived on the village street. Gerald's mind whirled. Who actually was telling the truth here?

Tobias dropped him off by the inn: *Zum Schwarzen Wolf.*

Gerald desperately wanted to know more. "Will you come in for a beer, Tobias?" Gerald said. "I'll treat you for bringing me all the way down."

With the same expressionless face, Tobias declined. "No, I must hurry back to the castle. The Graf will be waking soon and I must attend to him."

"Waking? But it's evening!"

"The Graf is an aristocrat. His ways are not our ways." Tobias flicked the switch over the horses' backs and they turned to head back up the pass, the way they'd come, and Gerald's chance of finding out more was gone.

Gerald looked around. So, they knew he'd met Amaris. But who'd told them? Perhaps Amaris herself, perhaps she and they were part of some strange conspiracy. But why? And then the Graf getting up at this time of the day? Even if ancient aristocratic families always felt above bourgeois conventions, getting up at this time wasn't natural. And where had he slept all day? It certainly wasn't his chamber.

Gerald yanked open the rough door of the inn and stepped into the aroma of tobacco, goulash and beer. A gipsy-looking man fiddled wild airs on the violin and villagers played backgammon and laughed uproariously. All that stopped as Gerald entered. He was clearly foreign, but after the obligatory gawp, the locals had the manners to continue with their revelry. Gerald was hungry, but first he needed to get his car. He asked the mutton-chop whiskered man, the landlord, who was cleaning pewter tankards with a clean linen cloth where he could find the mechanic, Vincent. The man clearly remembered Gerald too and was overly deferential.

With a fawning smile, the landlord told him the mechanic's workshop was three houses down; he couldn't fail to see the petrol pump outside it, he said. Gerald hurried back to the door, and with his hand on the doorknob, he hesitated. Inside, it was warm and convivial; the food smelled good, and the dark beer that foamed from tankards on the long wooden tables or held in the hands of the chattering men had great appeal. Outside, it was cold where the clear skies and sanguineous moon had sucked away any warmth that lingered under the clouds. But there would be time for a beer once he had the car fixed. Gerald turned up the collar of his borrowed coat.

As he pulled tight his coat, he remembered it wasn't his. Damn, he was not rid of the Graf just yet.

Once he retrieved his car, he would stop at the castle again. He would find a way to free Amaris. As he walked from the inn to the mechanic's shop, strange imaginings filled his mind. Gerald certainly wasn't given to wild fantasies, yet with each step he pictured himself confronting the Graf, appealing to his humanity, or threatening him with the law, and taking the beautiful Amaris with him. He imagined them in Ljubljana or Istanbul, she so young and beautiful and so very grateful.

He shook his head to try and clear it. He even wondered whether they had bewitched him, the Graf and Amaris together.

GERALD FOUND the mechanic's workshop. The door of the garage was open, and electric lamps lit up his work. The bonnet of his Rover was open, and the blonde head of the man he presumed to be Vincent was studying the engine. He hailed him, and the mechanic looked up, surprised.

"Gerald Anderson," Gerald said. "This is my car you're working on."

"Ah, Herr Anderson." Vincent grimaced. "I'm sorry, it's not ready yet."

That was a blow. "Oh? I thought you ordered the necessary part."

Vincent took off his gloves a finger at a time and pushed back the blond forelock that fell over his creased forehead. "I did, I did..."

"So, didn't it arrive?"

He sighed. "It needed new filters. One arrived, but it was not quite the right one. English parts are hard to get here. I thought it would do as it was the closest in size, but the thread is the wrong way."

"Damnation. So, when do you think it'll be ready."

"I am afraid, Herr Anderson, that it will not be tonight. I will send for the replacement first thing tomorrow. It could arrive tomorrow night, but more likely the day after tomorrow."

Gerald felt like he'd been punched. "The day after tomorrow? Oh, no! Can't you do it sooner?"

Vincent seemed a decent man. "I will try, I promise you, but it's better to be realistic."

"By the way, do you have any bolt cutters?"

"Bolt cutters? No, why?"

Gerald frowned. "Or is there a locksmith in the village? Someone who would lend me his tools?"

Vincent stared at him a second then said, "No, no locksmith in Geistthall. Is there anything I can help you with?"

"I just need something that can cut metal."

Vincent scratched his head. "I have some shears. I use them for slicing through the bodywork of wrecked cars."

He went and fetched some heavy black metal shears about three feet long with leather handles. The blades were big and sharp. They looked like they might do the job.

"Can I borrow them?"

Vincent said, "I don't use them all the time. I'd need them back. But yes, I suppose. What do you need them for?"

Gerald sucked his teeth. "I really can't say. Please honour my confidence. I'll bring you them back when I'd done with them."

"Do you want them now?"

"No. Can you put them in the back seat of my car? I don't need them until my car's fixed."

Vincent looked genuinely bewildered but promised to do as Gerald asked.

They talked briefly, but there was no point in lingering. It was cold and Gerald's belly growled. At the door of the mechanic's workshop, Gerald turned. "You said the car needed a new filter. I had all the filters changed before I left England."

Vincent shrugged. "I think there was something wrong with your fuel. It was sticky and congealed, blocking the filter."

. . .

GERALD WALKED DESPONDENTLY BACK to the inn. He needed some beer. Back in the busy tavern, he smiled at the innkeeper's wife. She didn't greet him but he got the impression she remembered him. Probably they had so few tourists that he stuck out like a sore thumb. Gerald found a table by the fire and ordered a *stein* of dark beer, a plate of beef goulash and bread and butter. He was despondent at the thought of returning to the castle, and because he'd dismissed Tobias and his ponies, it looked like he'd be walking. He certainly didn't relish that long walk up the pass in this cold with those wolves howling all around. Then halfway through his beer, Gerald remembered that the castle had a telephone. He would ring and ask Tobias to come and fetch him!

Goulash finished, the innkeeper's wife came and collected his pewter dish, and Gerald ordered another dark beer, and gave her a tip of a few groschen.

"I hope you found accommodation," she said.

He nodded. "Yes, at the castle."

"The castle?" She seemed alarmed, but she took away his dish without further comment and went to fetch the beer. When she returned with it, she whispered, "Is the kind *herr* staying still at the Schloss Hohenwald?"

He nodded sadly. "For longer than I anticipated."

She shook her head, and continued in a low voice as if she didn't wish to be overheard. "It is a bad place, the Schloss Hohenwald."

He had formed the same opinion himself but he imagined the local peasants were in awe of the Graf, so he smiled indulgently, "And why do you say that?"

She shook her head. "It is cursed. The Von Hohenwald family are all cursed."

Gerald sat back. He could at least fish for information about Amaris. "I heard there was a tragedy in the family. The late Graf died."

"Graf Joachim. Yes, a good man. He killed himself, yes. He could not bear what he had allowed."

"Allowed?"

"His daughter."

"And her name was?"

"The Lady Amaris. It was not her fault. It was in her blood."

"The Graf's blood?"

"No, from the other side—her cursed mother!"

Gerald decided to risk asking a potentially explosive question. "I heard Graf Alexander killed Amaris's mother, is that true?"

The woman seemed taken aback. "No! That is a lie! For all his faults, Alexander did not kill her. Her father Joachim killed her himself. For the child was not his."

"Not his?"

"Amaris was conceived in fornication, out of wedlock, in adultery."

"And Graf Joachim killed his wife for that?"

"Aye, and for other sins. And then he took his own life in grief."

The mutton-chopped husband was calling her back. The fire burned and the chatter ebbed and flowed in the tavern. The woman hesitated then took the crucifix from her neck. "Please, will the kind *herr* take this cross? It is for protection."

He frowned. "From what?"

"From the evil that lurks there."

"It's very kind of you," Gerald said, "But it's yours." He thought her superstitious gesture wouldn't help him much, as well-intentioned as it undoubtedly was. He pushed it back. "Thank you but I can't take your crucifix."

She looked at him with what appeared to be a genuine concern as she backed away and then turned to go to her tasks.

The tavern owner was increasingly impatient. He yelled over. She had been wasting time talking to Gerald when there was work to be done. Then he recognised Gerald. A look of fear came over his face and he stepped back into the kitchen.

CHAPTER

# SIX

As the innkeeper's wife walked away, the door opened, letting the cold in and a slender man entered wearing clerical garb. It was the priest who had admired his Rover—a priest coming for his pint of ale, well why not?

Gerald watched him scan the bar. When he saw Gerald, he gave a smile and came over. Gerald sat back. What did this portend?

The priest spoke in English, "Hello, you are Mr Anderson?"

Taken aback, Gerald said, "I am. Nice to meet you, Father, but how do you know me?"

"We met briefly."

"I remember, but you know my name."

The priest said. "Foreign visitors are not common. Word gets around, even to the ears of the parish priest."

The priest shook his hand limply. He was very pale and his hair dark. Gerald saw that though the man had clearly shaved, he had a shadow of stubble on his chin. His hair was so dark he probably had to shave twice a day to get rid of that shadow.

The priest pointed to the table. "May I join you?"

Gerald shrugged. Why not? He would phone Tobias when he'd finished his beer.

The priest sat. "I am Father László János."

Gerald said, "You sound Hungarian from your name."

"Very observant. I am. I am a stranger in Styria. I've only been here a month."

"A month? And how do you find the locals? I hope they've welcomed you."

The priest smiled, and Gerald took it they hadn't. When when the the innkeeper's wife came back, János ordered a beer. Father János sipped it when it was brought. "It's fine. I didn't expect them to wholly see eye to eye with me. I think they find some of my ideas too modern. I'm from Budapest, so I have an urban mentality, perhaps." He shrugged.

"So the story of my car breaking down is common knowledge?"

"It's not a big community. That and the story of your stay at the castle soon got around, and I was curious. Not many people stay at the castle. Few indeed of the villagers have been inside it."

Gerald smiled. "A strange place, the castle."

János said. "I've never been invited."

"No, the Graf doesn't strike me as particularly pious. You know he disappears during the day?"

"Perhaps he's a vampire?" Father János said with a smile.

Gerald said, "Well, I haven't yet discounted the idea."

János said, "I've never met him, or even seen him. He doesn't come to the village. I hear he goes to Vienna, or even Venice but never Geistthall."

Gerald was guarded. "The Graf has been hospitable enough. I wouldn't want to speak ill of him."

"Many do," Father János said.

Gerald raised an eyebrow. More fishing. "Really? Pray, tell."

János said, "Have you met his niece?"

He tried not to let his surprise show. "His niece? He has one?"

"Apparently. His brother's daughter. She's called Amaris Von Hohenwald."

"Ah," Gerald said.

"So, you've met her?"

He couldn't lie to a man of the cloth. He was always uncomfortable lying anyway. "Yes, I met her."

"They say she's quite beautiful."

Gerald wondered what interest a priest had in beautiful young women, but shrugged. "I suppose she is." He decided to keep quiet about her being locked up for now.

"You've heard the story?" János said.

Gerald shook his head. "What story?"

János sat back. "Ah, well. The locals say his brother Joachim's wife was afflicted with a strange disease. It was in her bloodline. The wife fell pregnant, and Amaris was born. Apparently, Joachim realised his wife would die slowly and in pain from this mysterious illness. It was said her mother suffered from it too, and so would Amaris. Joachim strangled his wife."

"He strangled her?" The story of Amaris's birth and her mother's death seemed to change with whoever was telling it.

János said, "Out of mercy."

"A strange kind of mercy."

"Joachim's wife asked him to, so it's said, but his heart was broken. They say that this illness comes out in adulthood and there was every chance that Amaris would carry it too, and Joachim knew he should destroy his infant daughter, but he couldn't bring himself to do it. He left Amaris outside one cold winter's night, expecting her to die quietly of cold, and then Joachim took his own life."

"And Alexander found her?"

"Made her his ward."

"So what was this disease?"

"Some congenital defect of the blood that curses certain families."

"But if that's the case then Amaris is heir to the castle."

"I imagine so. I'm sure she is of age now, or soon will be to inherit. Would you like another beer, Mr Anderson?"

Gerald sighed. "I have to get back to the castle eventually and I have no transport. I will need to phone the Graf's servant for a lift, or walk."

János said, "I can drive you."

Gerald raised his eyebrows. "You have a car?"

"I do."

Hearing that, Gerald agreed to another beer. The thought of a lift cheered him, even if the anticipation of another night in the castle didn't. Into his third pint, Gerald said. "He locks her up, you know."

János looked shocked. "He locks her up?"

So the priest hadn't heard that. Gerald nodded. "Behind an iron grille."

"How strange. And is there a key?"

"Apparently."

"Do you know where it is?"

Gerald shook his head.

János peered at him. "But why does the Graf lock her up?"

"She says that he keeps her prisoner because he doesn't want her to inherit the castle and turn him out."

Father János shrugged. "Perhaps it's true. But maybe he keeps her prisoner because he is afraid of this illness she is supposed to carry."

Gerald frowned. "Surely, he should seek treatment for her."

János said, "You're right, but he doesn't sound like a forward-thinking man. Maybe he doesn't think there's a cure."

Gerald said, "How would he know? He's no doctor." He took a gulp of beer. He had an idea. Gerald said, "We should persuade him to let us take her to a hospital."

"Should we?"

"Well, if she is sick, then she needs medical help."

János nodded thoughtfully. "I understand what you're saying."

Gerald rubbed his eyes; the smoke from the fire made them sting, and the beer was made him woozy, but he still knew the difference between right and wrong. "I was planning to have a word with the Graf."

"Really? Good luck."

"But, I suppose a man like that can do what he wants and get away with it."

"Especially if he's a vampire."

Gerald blinked. "Of course he's not really. Vampires don't exist." Gerald thought quickly. János could be a good ally, if he could persuade him to help. It made sense to use the power of the Church — confront the Graf and shame him into freeing Amaris. He wouldn't dare kill a clergyman.

Gerald nodded. "What if we two go and have a word with the Graf and if he doesn't release her, we will threaten to call the police."

"I would imaging the police here would be deferential to the Graf. They would take his side rather than that of a foreign tourist."

"But what about you? You're a man of the Church."

"And a foreigner too."

"But still, the parish priest. You must have some standing."

"Less than you'd think."

Gerald said, "But we can't leave her. It's immoral."

"I agree."

"Then will you help me?"

János gave a strange smile. "I'm not sure the Bishop would be too happy about me calling the police on the Graf."

"But you're a Christian, you must do what's right."

János grinned. "I must."

"Then will you help me?"

"To try and talk sense into the Graf?"

"Yes, just that. We won't come to blows. I can't imagine you're much of a fighter—no offence."

The priest shrugged. "Well, I'm happy to come. It's a very humane idea of yours. I approve."

And if talking didn't work, Gerald had the shears in his car.

. . .

THEY DECIDED NOT to have another drink. Gerald waited inside the inn door while Father János fetched his car. As he stood there, the innkeeper's wife who had served him beer came up. She had something in her hand, and, thinking it was the crucifix, he turned to refuse it, but it was a small glass bottle.

She held it up. "If you will not take the holy cross, take this herb."

"A herb?" Gerald peered at it. In his warm drunken fuddle, he took the bottle from her to see it better.

The woman said, "It is aconite. It is poison," and with that, the woman gave him a sad look, turned and went back into the smoky inn. The glass bottle remained in Gerald's hand as he wondered what he was meant to do with it. Poison? But whom to poison?

Father János pulled the tavern door open, revealing the dark night without. "Ready?"

Gerald was going to ask him about aconite, but János seemed in a hurry, so Gerald stuffed the glass bottle with aconite in it into his inside pocket, planning to ask the priest what he thought about it later.

"Do you mind if we go by the mechanic's shop? There is something I need to fetch from my car."

János shrugged. "That is not a problem."


VINCENT HAD GONE to bed when Gerald called. He came downstairs, in his vest and opened the door a crack. "Ah, it's you."

"Yes, sorry. But you know those shears?"

"Yes."

"I need them now."

"Now? But it's late."

"Honestly, I need them. Can I get them?"

Vincent shrugged. "I guess. The garage is open. But bring them back tomorrow."

"I will. I'll fetch them back when I get my car."

The garage was indeed open—such a trusting village.

GERALD BUNDLED the shears in his coat and placed them on the back seat. In the dark it would just like the coat was just a coat.

The trip up the pass in Father János's Hungarian Magomix was quicker than the trip down in the pony and trap. Gerald hadn't expected a Catholic priest to have a car, but it seemed Fr János was extremely interested in motors, and they chatted about Rover and Vauxhall and Rolls-Royce. Halfway up, Gerald peered out of the window. "At least the weather's improved." There was no rain, and the red moon sat halfway across the sky like an enormous Chinese lantern above the dark Styrian forest. Once again, the wolves howled. János saw his alarm and laughed. "Don't be frightened of the wolves, Mr Anderson. They call all night to their friends."

They pulled up outside the Schloss Hohenwald. Gerald hesitated; his idea of trying to make the Graf see sense and let his niece go now seemed rather doomed to failure, even with the priest on board. These aristocrats were too used to getting their own way, probably even a priest would make him hesitate.

"Listen, father," Gerald said.

"László, please. I think we are friends, no?"

Gerald nodded. He still felt drunk. "Yes, of course. But listen. I am guessing you've never come to blows with anyone."

"Oh, I don't know. I was a boy once and like all boys had a few scraps."

"But you've never been in combat."

János sat in the car, his leather-gloved hands gripping the steering wheel.

"You see, if the Graf is the tyrant we think he is—"

"—and we do."

"It seems that way. You know, it's possible he may not give Amaris up without a fight."

"Ah."

"So, I think: don't fight. If he cuts up rough. We back off."

"Back off?"

"Yes, retreat. Pretend he's won."

"I see. And then what? If he 'cuts up rough' as you say, then surely that proves he is indeed a tyrant and Amaris will suddenly be in greater danger once he knows the game is up."

"I've thought of that." Gerald reached over and pulled up his coat. He took out the shears. The moonlight illuminated them.

"Goodness," János said.

Gerald smiled grimly. "We retreat and use these to snip the lock off. Then we get her out."

"It seems like you've have it all planned out."

Gerald shrugged. "Desperate times. We can't leave her to that monster."

"No, indeed."

"And now the castle."

They were parked just outside. "I've never been inside," János said. He smiled. "But now's the time."

"It's pretty much what you'd expect, I suppose," Gerald said.

János patted Gerald on the shoulder. "You're a good man, Mr Anderson, very honourable."

"I hope so,"

János seemed keen. "Let us begin."

Gerald nodded. Tight lipped, he walked over the drawbridge to the castle door, and János followed as the old walls stared down at them. János grinned standing at the door; there was something about him, not like a priest at all. Gerald frowned; and it was odd the priest was so keen to go in, but Gerald pounded the door with the wolf's head knocker as János stood beside him, almost expectantly.

After he knocked, Gerald stood back, holding his coat that concealed the shears.

Eventually, Tobias answered. He registered no surprise to see Father János in his clerical garb beside Gerald.

Gerald muttered, "The car wasn't fixed."

"I'm sorry to hear that, sir."

"It leaves me at a disadvantage. I would have taken a room at the inn—"

"—But there aren't any," Father János said.

Tobias regarded the priest for the first time. "Indeed."

"So," Gerald said."I'm afraid I need to put upon your hospitality again."

Tobias nodded gravely. "I will ask the Graf, sir."

They waited there, the light of the baleful mood washing the forecourt of the schloss in blood orange.

"Very decent of you to come with me," Gerald said to János.

"Not a problem. Glad to be able to help." The priest smirked. Inexplicably, he seemed to find the situation amusing. Gerald felt suddenly dizzy. He rubbed his eyes.

"Are you quite well?" János asked.

"Probably just the beer."

"It's strong."

"Yes."

They waited.

Eventually, Tobias returned. He nodded and said, "Please come this way."

Once inside the Entrance Hall, Tobias stopped and chained the doors behind him. He shot the bolt and turned the heavy key. "Let us go," he said.

Gerald hung back. He put the shears behind one of the chairs that flanked the hall. They weren't hidden, but there was no one about to find them anyway.

CHAPTER

# SEVEN

Gerald and Father János followed Tobias to the Great Hall, where the fire blazed. The Graf sat inscrutably in his wing-backed chair with his black hair and his piercing blue eyes. "Mr Anderson, I thought we had lost you."

"My car didn't get fixed."

"That's a pity."

"It leaves me without anywhere to stay."

The Graf nodded. "I see. And I expect you will need breakfast also."

"If you don't mind."

The Graf studied the two of them silently. He did not greet the priest until Father János said, "I am László János, the new priest in the village."

Without looking at him directly, the Graf said, "I have heard of you. You have modern ideas, not suited to Styria. We are an old-fashioned people here who like old-fashioned things."

János said, "With due respect, Graf, I believe that if we are to rejuvenate the area, we need to be bold."

"And you are Hungarian."

"I am."

The Graf said, "I do not like Hungarians."

"That is unfortunate."

Gerald thought he'd better get it over with, so he said, "Before we retire, Graf, I would like to speak of Amaris."

The Graf said, "Of Amaris?"

"Your niece, whom you have locked up in a room of the schloss."

"Sequestered. Yes."

"Whatever you call it, it's not right."

"You know nothing about it. Best keep your nose out of this, Englishman."

"You can't just lock someone away."

"Apparently I have."

"Such things must be against the law, even here."

"What would you do with her? You seem to know it all, so please enlighten me as to what other possible course of action there could be? Should I have killed her?"

"Of course not. She's your own niece."

"I'm not sure about that."

Gerald thought he was referring to the tale of the adultery the innkeeper's wife repeated. Gerald said, "Please can we stop playing word games?"

The Graf stared at him with his ice-blue eyes. "Perhaps you'd like a drink? I have some good Zweigelt, so fruity, fresh and soft. It is quite the success story in Austrian winemaking. Did you know the grape was produced first in 1922 at Klosterneuburg?"

Gerald ignored the diversion. "What is your reason for locking this poor girl up?"

"Why not have some wine?"

"I'd rather sort this out first. Explain yourself, please."

"I'll have some wine," Father János said, sitting down in one of the leather chairs.

Gerald glanced at the priest, once again János appeared enormously amused. But Gerald was uneasy, though he knew János was an ally. He said, "Very well, I'll have a glass, but then tell your tale, and we can get the poor girl free. Even if she is ill, she shouldn't be locked up. I'll take her to a hospital, even if you won't."

The Graf laughed. "You'd take her with you in your little car?"

"If necessary."

"You amuse me."

Gerald saw János laughing too. What the hell was going on?

Tobias came and brought a decanter of red wine. When he poured it, he withdrew, leaving the three around the blazing fire.

"I was always suspicious of you, Mr Anderson,' The Graf said, lifting his heavy crystal goblet to his full lips. The wine stained them crimson as blood, and he wiped his mouth with the back of his pale hand.

"And me of you, Graf," Gerald said.

"Of me? Why?"

"You're a strange man. You are completely absent during the hours of the day for one thing." A chill ran up Gerald's spine as the Graf studied him.

"I sleep during the day. I am awake all night, but when the first rays of dawn break in the east, I retreat to my bed."

Gerald said, "But I entered your bedroom earlier today, and you were not there."

"Because, Mr Anderson, I do not sleep in my bedroom. I sleep elsewhere."

"Elsewhere? Why do you not sleep in your chamber?"

"Because where I sleep, it is quieter, and I get better rest."

All this while, Father János sat quietly. At a pause in the conversation, János said, "You don't like Hungarians. As a Hungarian can I ask you why? Please explain how my countrymen have offended you."

"My brother's wife was Hungarian."

János folded his arms. "I believe you were not well disposed towards her."

The Graf studied his two visitors. "Are you two in league? It makes no difference, I merely ask from curiosity."

Gerald shook his head. "I hardly know Father János. He gave me a lift. We only just met in the tavern." Then he remembered, "Ah, yes and once before, just before my car broke down."

The Graf kept his silence, but János continued, "And so your niece is half Hungarian."

A shadow crossed the Graf's brow. "Half something. Maybe more than half."

Gerald blurted, "She will take the castle from you, that's why you lock her up. You want to keep what you got from your brother."

The Graf gestured around him. "This? I care not for this. I only stay from duty."

János said, "Why don't you leave? Leave it to her. Go to Vienna or wherever you want to be. Right the ancient wrong you have perpetrated, seeking to block the natural order."

The Graf snorted. "Do you know who the Von Hohenwald family are, Hungarian? We have been in these mountains and valleys for always, all down the centuries, always carrying out our ancient duty to the Emperor and the Church. I, Alexander Von Hohenwald, will not be the one who lays down his sword and lets evil in."

Gerald pleaded, "But Graf, you can't keep a young woman locked up against her will."

The Graf shook his head. "What do you know, Englishman? Your country knows nothing of the ancient evil that plagues this land."

"I know the difference between right and wrong. You must let Amaris go."

The Graf said, "I see you have fallen under her spell. Tell me, does she look hungry or dirty?"

"No, but that still doesn't justify false imprisonment. As a gentleman, as a nobleman, I appeal to you to see sense."

This wasn't working. Gerald's suspicions of the Graf's evil intent now seemed well-founded.

The Graf sighed deeply and drained his goblet. "I cannot, and I will not let her go."

"But surely, whatever your reason for this—"

But at that moment, Father János stood and put his hand on Gerald's shoulder. "Come, Gerald. We shall free Amaris."

And then realisation dawned in the Graf's eyes. "I know who you are now."

Father János seemed amused. "Do you?" But he had little interest in the Graf now and turned to Gerald. "Show me the way to Amaris."

Gerald stood from his chair.

The Graf stood too. He rubbed his forehead. "I have been foolish. I have allowed the enemy in through my front door. Mr Anderson, do you know what you are doing?"

Gerald shrugged. "I just know it's not right to keep someone locked up behind an iron grille."

"Isn't it?" The Graf stared coldly at Gerald.

János said, "Come, Gerald, we must be quick."

As they hurried out of the Great Hall, Gerald heard the Graf calling for Tobias.


GERALD SHOWED Father János the way. The priest seemed unnaturally eager now to free Amaris. Gerald put it down to some natural sense of justice and mercy that we guess must be in all churchmen. Hurrying along the ancient echoing halls, Gerald got lost once, then he found the way.

They were in the entrance hall. Gerald saw the shears and darted across to get them.

János grinned. "Ah, your shears."

"Yes, we'll need them for the lock."

János reached out a hand. "Can I borrow them?"

Gerald frowned but handed him them anyway.

János went over and nipped through the chain that held the castle doors closed. He gave Gerald the shears back and then for good measure turned the huge black key and drew back the huge black bolt. The outer door was now unlocked.

"Come," János said.

Gerald followed the priest up the stairs. They had not got far when suddenly the electric lights were extinguished.

János laughed. "He may think that will stop us, but he's wrong."

In the dark, János's eyes gleamed strangely. "Are we near?" Then he said, "No matter, I smell her."

Gerald frowned. "Smell her?"

János said, "Perhaps you would like to leave now? Our kind is not lacking in mercy, whatever tales they tell of us."

"What? Your kind? I'm sorry, I don't understand."

Red-tinged moonlight flooded in at one of the windows that opened onto the exterior of the Schloss. It was enough to show Gerald that János's eyes glittering like rubies. Gerald put his hand to his throat. Who exactly was János? What exactly was going on?

János said, "And I am grateful to you, Gerald. Without your help, gaining entry to the castle would have been harder, and the Graf would have been alerted if I had simply come on my own."

Gerald said, "Should I come with you? Do you need me to take Amaris away in my car?" He was still holding the shears.

János shook his head. "That won't be necessary. Just take me to her prison, then, if you know what's good for you, leave."

They turned and strode down the passage to where Amaris's prison was. János had a strange loping gait, and as the moonlight struck him, his appearance rippled, like the moon on water on a winter's night. There was something very strange here. It all seemed planned and Gerald began to suspect he had been duped.

János arrived at the iron-grille that kept Amaris prisoner.

Gerald yelled, "You'll need these!" He thrust out the shears to János, but János did not need them. With enormous strength, he rent the latticed iron from its frame, and heard Amaris yell in triumph, "Father, you have finally come!"

As Gerald looked, he saw man and girl transform in the moonlight. Their forms altered until they were human no more; they were wolves — huge werewolves.

Gerald turned and fled.

Running, and almost out of breath, arriving outside the Great Hall, Gerald found two armoured figures. They wore two suits of armour that had recently lined the halls. The visors of both helmets were up, and he saw the Graf, with the Wolf Head shield of the Von Hohenwalds and beside him his squire, Tobias.

"Are they coming?" The Graf said.

Gerald nodded, unable yet to speak.

The Graf drew a longsword that glinted in the yellow flames of the fire. It gleamed, not as steel would, but with a softer glimmer, as from more noble metal: it seemed the Graf's sword was of silver. "You are far from safety, Englishman."

"They turned into wolves!" Gerald stammered. "Monstrous wolves." As he spoke the words, he still couldn't quite believe them.

"You should leave. This isn't your fight."

Gerald said, "I can't abandon you. They played me for a fool, and in my foolishness, I helped bring this upon you."

The Graf nodded. "Yes, you have been very foolish. But so have I. You have been their Trojan horse, but I let you in. And I was so stupid in letting that Hungarian into the castle. I thought that because he worse a priest's garb he could not be one of them."

Tobias said, "The power of the Church is not now what it was. They mock it now where once they cowered in fear of it."

The Graf's mouth tightened. "You still have time to go, Mr Anderson. Not much, maybe minutes."

Gerald shook his head. "I can't go. I will fight."

The Graf said, "That might also be an act of foolishness."

"I was foolish to trust Amaris."

The Graf gave a wry smile. "But she is fair while I am grim. That is why you were deceived."

Suddenly Tobias spoke up, "Evil comes in like a serpent, often wearing a mask of beauty."

The Graf said, "Tobias speaks truly. For beauty is not always truthful and the truth is rarely beautiful. Men down the ages have made the same mistake as you and trusted poisoned words spoken by a fair mouth, rather than listen to truth that wore a less appealing face."

"I will make up for my gullibility. I will stay and fight," Gerald repeated.

"Very well. I accept your offer of service. Take a weapon and stand ready. You will be tested—perhaps unto death."

Gerald selected a halberd from the rack and returned to the two steel-clad warriors. He took his place beside them.

The Graf said, "The Von Hohenwalds have protected these lands from the werewolves for centuries. It was our sacred duty handed to us by the Emperor and the Pope—to cleanse these mountains from the ancient plague of lycanthropy. And we nearly succeeded, but then, as a cruel jest, or perhaps by wicked design, my brother fell in love with a Hungarian woman who was one of them. She seduced him, and they had a child, but the girl was not his, it was fathered by the male wolf.

"Joachim was cuckolded and tricked. I tried to talk to him, but he wouldn't believe the girl wasn't his. He was so convinced, he even half convinced me. I knew she was half-wolf, but until tonight, I persuaded myself that my brother's blood ran in her veins and so she was kin to me and deserving my protection, even while I protected others from her. I should never have been so merciful."

Gerald watched the Graf's handsome, anguished face in the flickering firelight.

The Graf went on. "Before she died, my brother's Hungarian wife taunted me and said the wolves would come to rescue Amaris. And that is why I awaited the stranger." He gave a soft laugh. "For a while, I thought you might be he— an Englishman! How foolish I was, of course, it had to be a Hungarian."

Then a great howling came from outside the schloss. A great howling and pounding on the massive castle door.

The Graf said, "Our minutes are gone."

"I'm ready," Gerald said.

"Their pack is outside the main door," the Graf said.

"Do not worry, my lord," Tobias said. "I made sure I locked the door and bolted it and chained it with a heavy chain of iron. Nothing evil can enter that way."

The growling grew closer. A sad smile played on the Graf's face and he snapped down his visor. "Then at least we only have to face the two werewolves. Though that is enough. Remember your honour, gentlemen. To the fight."

With a sickness in the pit of his stomach, Gerald remembered János unlocking the door and snipping through the chain as if it were butter, snipping through the chain with the shears that Gerald had gone to such pains to bring here and leave handy for János to breach the castle door.

He was about to apologise once more for his misplaced trust when a noise of quick paws clattered down the stairway. Amaris and her true father were descending, muzzles snarling, dripping teeth, eyes blazing. Unholy fire filled their gaze, red as if the bloody moon had sunk deep within the amber orbs and now shone with fierce glee.

"There they are, lord," Tobias yelled.

"At least the pack is kept outside," the Graf muttered.

Then the castle door smashed open and the pack of cur-wolves poured in.


"To arms, and our sacred duty!" The Graf called and drew his silver sword.

"I don't understand!" Tobias cried. "How could they get in through the front door? Forgive me, lord. I bolted it."

"It doesn't matter, Tobias," The Graf said. "Stand firm." He glanced at Gerald as if to steady his nerve. Gerald was about to tell them about the door when the Graf snapped, "Stand firm, Mr

Englishman. Whatever mistakes you have made do not matter now."

Gerald turned to see the wolves come in at the door; they poured in like the froth of the sea on a wave of moonlight. The Graf and Tobias formed an arrow point, facing out on two sides with Gerald behind, inexpertly holding his weapon in front of him.

The wolves leapt, and the swords struck them down. The mortal wolves yelped as the blades cut them and their blood flowed, making the ground sticky and wet. The air filled with growls and yelps and the grunts of the fighting men. Gerald jabbed the wolves with the point of his halberd to keep them at bay. He felt, useless, superfluous. More than that, he felt duped. His gullibility was the cause of this disaster.

Amaris and János advanced and the wolf pack cleared a path for them and stood back snarling while their masters prepared to attack.

Tobias ran forward, but the Graf called him back. "You only have a steel sword, Tobias. Remember that only silver will cut these abominations!"

But rage filled Tobias, overpowering his reason, sweeping away his rationality, and he lunged at the Amaris wolf looming above him, standing seven feet tall. Lazily, she swiped him with her claws and knocked him to the floor. Tobias rolled on the stone flags, clutched his blade and didn't let it drop, and his armour prevented the worst hurt, but his steel sword couldn't hurt her.

She advanced for the kill.

Instinctively, the Graf went to protect his servant and took his eyes off his adversary, the wolf János. János roared and leapt, knocking the Graf off balance and sending him reeling. János followed up and smashed the wolf's head shield from the Graf's grasp.

Now the Graf gripped his silver sword in a double-fisted hold and faced off János while Gerald stood, helpless, the halberd keeping the natural wolves at bay, but little more.

Tobias struggled to his feet, desperate to help his lord, but as he fought to rise, the Amaris wolf seized him with her arms and with inhuman strength bit into his neck, Tobias's head lolled back to reveal an enormous gash at his throat from which arterial blood pumped in rhythm with his slowing heart.

"No!" the Graf yelled. János attacked. The Graf recovered composure enough to parry the darting claw, but he was off-balance and the János wolf knocked the silver sword from the Graf's hands sending it spinning into a corner. The wolf pack covered the dropped blade and to go among them to retrieve it would mean certain death.

Tobias lay dying in a slumped heap. There was no hope for him.

"Come!" The Graf yelled, and Gerald followed him as they retreated.

The wolves, natural and otherwise, could not overcome their bestial hunger. First the werewolves ate, and they sated themselves on the corpse of Tobias, ripping off his armour and burying their muzzles in his bloody flesh, snapping and bickering between themselves as to which of them took the tastiest organs.

After they had eaten, the wolf János and Amaris allowed the pack to take their food. János seemed so confident of his final victory that he allowed the Graf and Gerald to flee the scene of their defeat.

# EIGHT

Gerald and the Graf ran down the corridor, and then up the stairs. They ran fast.

"Let me catch my breath," Gerald said, gasping.

"Hurry. We have little time." The Graf, though older and wearing armour, paused for Gerald to recover.

"What have I just seen?" Gerald said, leaning on the wall.

"The truth! What has always been! People pretend such things do not exist and believe by turning their eyes from stranger truths, the stranger truths vanish. But they do not. There are creatures foul and dark in these woods.

Gerald heard the howling beasts not far off. Without another word, he and the Graf ran on.

The Graf said, "In my chamber is a silver dagger. It is the only other silver weapon. But I must be honest with you, our chances are slim."

As they ran, they came in sight of the Graf's room. "In there, I'll get the dagger, we can barricade the door. If we can make a stand until dawn, we may survive."

Gerald nodded, and they ran, but as they were within yards of the door and the silver dagger that lay within, the Amaris wolf appeared from the other direction, and she blocked their way.

Gerald spun round. Behind, he saw János with the full wolf pack.

Gerald knew they could not reach the Graf's door before the wolves were upon them.

What a strange and unexpected way to end his days. He had been warned not to interfere, he hadn't heeded that warning, and now it seemed he would pay the ultimate price.

The Graf hissed. "Quickly, the broken tower. We can perhaps escape over the roof."

To their left lay the dark stone steps that led up to the ruined tower. This tower struck by lightning in years gone by was open to the skies. Only a flimsy door sealed it off from the rest of the schloss.

They leapt up the stairs two at a time, but the wolves snapped at their heels. Rubble covered the ancient stone steps, and Gerald seized a stone and hurled it backwards at the pursuing wolf pack.

His aim was excellent, and he struck a wolf on the head. The beast cried out in pain, and its yelp caused the others to hold back. The werewolves were not in sight, but they couldn't be far behind.

"Hurry, Mr Anderson. Up."

Gerald hurled another stone but with less effect. Hurling rubble wouldn't save them.

"Where to now?" Gerald said as the Graf put his shoulder to the thin wooden door, bursting it open and letting in the cold October night. They climbed up the stairs and stood in the glimmer of the blood-red moon. Below them yawned the stone spiral up which the wolves and worse still, the werewolves would emerge.

Gerald looked out over the moon-drenched tiles. That was their way of escape. He prepared to step out and then, skulking, growling, baring their teeth, he saw wolves on the roof. There must be ten of them. If he stepped onto the roof he would be caught in the open between these in front and those that came up the tower behind him.

"No escape then," The Graf said. "At least we will make a noble end."

Gerald and the Graf stood side by side, the ruined tower above them like a broken tooth. The broken fragments of a stained glass window remained in its frame, jagged shards showing smashed pictures of lords and ladies long dead.

The Graf looked sadly at Gerald. "I die doing my duty, the duty my ancestors have always fulfilled, but unlike them, now I fail—a disgrace to my line. I spent my life in this isolated prison waiting for this he-wolf. And in the end, for all the years of vigilance, I let him in, duped by his clerical collar and black cloth coat."

He sighed. "You know, I would have rather have spent my years in Venice or Vienna or New York. I wanted to be a poet, not a warrior, but it was not to be." The Graf shook his head. "And you, Mr Anderson, this is not your rightful fate. I am sorry you have to die here."

Gerald shook his head. The wolves were seconds below them. "Surely, there must be some other way to kill them?"

The Graf said, "The werewolves? They are not natural creatures and can only be harmed by certain things—"

Gerald said, "—Silver, I saw that, but surely that's not the only thing that can hurt them."

The Graf shrugged. "Silver or wolfsbane."

"What's that?"

"Wolfsbane? A herb. They call it Monk's Hood, or Aconite. I am of the Von Hohenwalds. We disdained such womanly poisons and trusted instead to our silver blades."

"But your blade is lost to you now."

"Ah, yes. My pride has brought me low. What I would give now for aconite."

Gerald produced the glass bottle given to him by the barmaid. "Like this?"

The Graf's eyes narrowed. "You have aconite?"

Gerald shrugged. "I didn't know what it was. It was a gift."

"A great gift indeed. You have a good friend in whoever gave you that herb."

Gerald handed him the bottle. With shaking hand, while the wolves waited warily outside on the roof and below on the stairs, still not sure of their kill, still awaiting the coming of Amaris and János, the Graf broke off a shard of glass from the shattered window with his mailed gauntlet and, opening the bottle, squeezed the herb to produce its juice then smeared the wolfsbane on the sharp edge of the glass.

Seeing him do this, Gerald took off his jacket and using the doubled-up material to protect his hands, he too took a sliver of glass. It was not much of a weapon, but it was better than nothing. The Graf gave him the aconite, and he daubed it on the broken glass.

Then the wolves came.

The beasts could not speak. They did not bother themselves with taunts, but launched straight into the attack, thinking there was nothing now to stop them, thinking the Graf had lost his silver sword, thinking that Gerald never had anything that could hurt them anyway.

But with a full stretch of his arm, the Graf jabbed the aconite anointed glass into János's chest. The werewolf screamed as the herb seared it and seeped poison into its lupine heart. It fell back, amazed, baffled and stupefied, its amber eyes rolling, stumbling into the wolf-pack who recoiled, retreated, and ran back, dismayed at their leader's fall.

János died screaming as the wolfsbane destroyed his magical form. Soon he lay, a burned and leaking human corpse: wolf no more, merely now a thin man in priest's garb.

Amaris saw her father's death and raised her muzzle to the sanguine moon and howled.

And Gerald struck. There could be no mercy given to the wolves. Such as they would never give quarter to such as he. With shaking hand, he stabbed Amaris with glass smeared in aconite, and she died, like her father: seared and burned by the sacred herb, turning to a scorched bag of human bones, washed in the pale light of her mother the moon.

And with that, the wolf pack lifted their heads and howled, and having howled, fled.


Ralph Waters-Wynn sipped his Turkish coffee under the awning of a street cafe by the Blue Mosque in Istanbul. The day was already hot although it was just morning. The street was full of the hubbub of Turkish chatter and the sweet smell of tobacco from the hookah pipes of the customers around him.

He saw Gerald Anderson's Rover 10 appear down the road behind a donkey cart, two motorcycles and a car. Gerald was grinning through the window.

He pulled the car up and hopped out. Ralph thought his friend looked well, but he had that excited grin that Ralph knew meant he had stories to tell.

"Lovely to see you, old boy," Ralph said.

"You too, Ralphie. Anyway, did you have a nice time in Vienna?"

"Capital. Did your travels in Styria provide you with any adventures? I know how you like adventures."

"You warned me against them, Ralph!"

"Ah, yes but did you listen?"

"Not exactly, no."

# PART THREE
# THE TOWER OF KER-ZU

CHAPTER

# ONE

May time was here, and the Forest of Brec'helean was heavy with blossom as Tristan bade farewell to the fortress of Ker-Wenn. The mayflower's sweet scent haunted the avenues between the trees, and small birds flitted from shade to sunshine through the undergrowth while Tristan Mab Bennog rode his bay mare Jezebel and hummed a song of his own composing. It was a song of love and loss, for he had loved, and they had lost.

His long fingers danced over the strings of the lute cradled in his left arm. Sitting back on his head was a wide-brimmed hat with a jay's feather in its band. This hat served to keep the sun out of his eyes while he played, though the sun was yet low and screened by thick undergrowth. A bird called raucously from the bushes. It seemed that all in the world was yet well.

Early that morning, the Lady of Ker-Wenn slipped a note under his door. The message warned him that her husband suspected their dalliance and that if Tristan valued his head, he should leave before breakfast. Tristan had sighed: They made excellent breakfasts there. And he had craved one last kiss from her apple-red lips. But Tristan was fly enough to know Fate's breeze blew in his face, not at his back so long as he lingered. So, slipping to the stable below, he saddled fleet Jezebel and fled.

Tristan made a practice of moving at Lady Luck's prompting, and in this way kept her favour. From the stone bridge outside the castle, he waved a fond farewell to his latest married ladylove and left. The dawn mist lifted from the clear-running River Arzh as he rode east, choosing to take the forest track.

They said that Brec'helean Forest was haunted. Tristan himself didn't fear ghosts, but he knew others did. Even brave men, handy with a sword, avoided the haunted glades of Brec'helean, and that could be handy for a fugitive.

And Tristan was often a fugitive from love, running from husbands at least once a month, so he knew the forest well.

He rode on, playing a chord progression on the lute and guiding Jezebel with his knees. The horse seemed to need little direction to keep on the path. She was used to his inattention. Tristan's head was always full of music or fair maidens, but the mare was the only constant female in his life. Tristan was a free spirit. He was a troubadour and bard by profession, but more than his work, his true passion was women.

As he strummed a whimsical chord sequence, his memory returned to that last lady. She, whom he would forever remember fondly, though sadly never see again, and whose name grew vaguer by the mile, had one day asked him whether he loved her.

When a woman asked that particular question, Tristan pushed back his hat with its feather, grasped her white hand between both of his, and said, "How could you doubt my love for you?"

He feigned an expression to suggest infinite hurt and melt her heart. Their hearts always melted. Hers did too.

Tristan would deny that there was any bad faith in this: in his own way, he loved all the women he bedded. He loved them intensely until it was time to leave.

How could he be expected to settle with one woman? The world was filled with beautiful girls. And time and time again, he proved them ready to undo their bodices for the right song.

He knew other men were jealous of his success. He had what these louts lacked: his dark brown hair, his sea-blue eyes, his height, his lean muscled frame. Above all, he had his skill at words and music and indeed at every other art requiring delicacy of fingers or tongue.

To his mild annoyance, the last lady, one night after loving when he had intimated he had soon to move on, told him, "You should treat women better." What could she mean? When he was with them, they had his full attention and his temporary love. In any case, lady what's-her-name was the last adventure: the next lay ahead.

Jezebel plodded down the forest path where wayside flowers in yellows, blues and reds opened to the beauty of the May morning. As the mare went along, Tristran tried runs of notes that sang out sweet to his ears as his skipping fingertips strummed the catgut strings. He pushed back his hat and swept his dark hair from his brow so he could better see the frets. His finger danced, encircled by rings of silver and gold.

His placid mare strolled on. The day was warm, and the season was pleasant. For a long time, they rode along the forest road beside the brook that ran fast and clear over its bed of pebbles. Trout darted in the deep pools. Flies buzzed under the trees.

Tristan was so absorbed in his composition, that he didn't notice he was being watched. Sly faces stared from thickets, and glittering eyes watched from holes in the ground.

Then, when the day was nearly half done, his stomach told him he should soon eat. Jezebel would be glad of a chance to graze on the lush grass growing. The sun was not quite at noon, but they had started early. Tristan slung the lute on his back and leaned forward to stroke his mare's neck. "We will stop soon, Jezebel."

And then he saw a perfect place ahead. The trees widened out to his left. Here lay meadow, ankle-deep in grass, graced with yellow Tormentil and blue Speedwell. Dew starred the grass, and the meadow basked in the benediction of the morning sun.

Tristan clicked his tongue, and Jezebel neighed and slowed to a stop. Tristan slid from the saddle and took Jezebel's rein, strolling with her to the meadow. The mare grazed on the sweet grass, and he unpacked his food from the saddlebag. Here was white bread, ripe tomatoes with dried meat and dainty cakes all packed for him with love by his last lady.

He left Jezebel munching grass and sat on a flat stone by the stream. Shadowy fish darted from hiding places under rocks, and blue and crimson Kingfishers hunted them with beaks like spears, while green-gold dragonflies and iridescent damselflies darted over the rushing water. It was bliss. The words of the song that would woo his next woman came to his mind, and he sang them to the mild breeze.

VOICES RAISED in anger broke the peace, and Tristan looked round for their source. He heard two or three gruff voices and one clearer one. Someone was being set upon out of sight. Tristan sighed and put down his bread and meat. He dusted flour off his palms and stood. Was this really his fight?

Tristan looked at his boots. They were a little scuffed. He glanced at the sky and tried to concentrate on the few puffy white clouds. Then he studied the butterflies that danced around the wild iris by the stream. But it was no good. His conscience would not let him stand by while some innocent person suffered: he would have to intervene. Tristan pulled his jerkin straight and squeezed the cramp from his neck.

Jezebel had pricked up her ears and was looking in the direction from which the shouting was coming. He patted her flank. His sword was tied to his pack and still sheathed, so he reached and pulled the blade from its scabbard. As he drew it, the sun gleamed on the sword.

For a minute, he hefted the weight of the sword in his hand, trying practice feints. The shouts of the victim grew more frantic. Facing their direction, Tristan moved forward.

He pushed a weave of hazel leaves and entered another clearing. This glade was a satellite to the large meadow he had come from, smaller with one entrance. All the other sides were hedged in by thorn bushes.

Three ugly men in dirty leather armour had blades drawn a knife, a sword and an axe. A boy, with short red hair, stood at bay. Against the knife, sword and axe, the lad held only a staff.

Tristan stepped forward, swept his hair from his face and saw how the sunlight struck his sword. He took a minute to admire the decorated hilt and a further few seconds to consider how his silver and gold rings gleamed in the sun, smiling as he recalled the lovers who'd donated each one. He lifted his hand, so the gems sparkled in the sun—yes they were gorgeous, then he cleared his throat and yelled, "What's going on here? It seems a little unfair for three to be fighting one."

An ugly man turned. He had black stubble, dark bags under his eyes, a scar running down his left cheek. When he spoke, his mouth revealed only a few rotten teeth. From his air, he appeared to be their leader. "Fuck off," he said. "This ain't your fight."

"It is if I make it mine," Tristan said to the boy. "Need a hand?"

The boy nodded. "These brigands set on me as I was walking home."

Seeing the lad distracted, a brigand rushed the boy. The boy raised his staff, and the poorly aimed blow went awry. The brigand leader ran, screaming at Tristan. Tristan sidestepped. The man went past, and Tristan smacked his arse with the flat of his sword. This enraged the man who turned and swung again. But the swing was wild and undisciplined, and Tristan's same sidestep tricked him again. Another blow to the arse, but this time edge on to cut. The brigand yelped like a dog.

Tristan yawned. He could do this all day, but looking over his shoulder, he saw the boy was hard-pressed by the other two brigands. Time to finish it. When his assailant ran at him again, Tristan gutted him with the ease of a butcher filleting steak.

The man fell to his knees, a surprised look on his brutish face. He collapsed sideways, fresh blood staining his filthy jerkin.

But the boy was being beaten. Tristan narrowed his eyes, picked his target and rushed the closest brigand. The oaf turned and saw him too late, then gasped as he took the point of Tristan's sword in the eye.

They were now down to one enemy.

Tristan smiled encouragingly at the boy, and the last brigand, with a glance at each of his erstwhile comrades, turned and fled.

The boy yelled and ran after the thief waving his staff, but the man had the fear of death upon him, and the boy knew danger was past. The brigand ran for his life while the boy stopped short, panting.

WHEN THE BOY CAME BACK, Tristan was cleaning the blood off his sword on the grass.

"Thank you." The boy gasped, finally getting most of his breath back. "You saved my life."

"You're welcome," Tristan said. He winked. "Though it did interrupt my lunch."

The boy grinned. "Come back with me, and I'll make sure you get a good dinner."

Tristan sheathed his sword. "That sounds inviting. I think."

Catching sight of the rings on Tristan's hands, the boy said, "You must be rich. You should be careful in the forest."

"I'm not so rich," Tristan said. "And I can look after myself."

"I noticed." The boy extended his hand. "I'm Yann."

"A grand name," Tristan said, giving the hand a shake.

"My father had grand plans for me," said Yann. "I am named after the famous king, Yann Mab Yrien. He thought I would go to Court and win favour with the Duke."

"And you didn't?"

Yann shook his head. "Not yet."

"The Duke is overrated!" Tristan said.

"I'm surprised you dare say that."

Tristan made a show of peering around him. "I don't think his spies stretch this far."

Yann said, "You don't know who has eyes in the forest."

"The Duke?"

"Worse than the Duke."

Tristan smiled. "Come on, lead me to where I will get this dinner. And a comfortable bed, I hope?"

Yann said, "My father owns 'An Den Glas'—the Green Man—it's a famous inn in these parts." Then he paused. "The only inn in these parts."

They walked back towards where Jezebel was grazing again.

"Lovely horse," said Yann. "I look after the horses at the inn. I know a fine mare when I see one."

"She is a fine mare," Tristan said, stroking the blaze on Jezebel's brown nose. The horse snickered. Tristan felt her soft, warm breath on his palm and then stroked her nose.

"You're only light," Tristan said, looking at Yann. "I'm sure she can bear us both."

Both of them climbed on Jezebel's back, who set off without complaint to be carrying two.

The afternoon was still warm. Tristan was hungry again. "Is it far?" he said.

"Not so far."

"The forest is beautiful," Tristan said.

"She pretends to be," said the boy.

"The forest pretends to be beautiful?" Tristan said, puzzled.

"She has different moods," said the boy. "Just now she's kind and beautiful. But when the mood strikes her, she's vindictive and cruel."

"Sounds like a woman," Tristan said, smiling. The boy didn't speak. Perhaps he didn't know as much about women as Tristan did. Tristan leaned down from the saddle and plucked a long stem of grass. He chewed it thoughtfully as the horse ambled on.

"What are you doing here?" said Yann. "If I may be impertinent. I only ask because we get few visitors in these parts."

"But you run an inn!"

"Interesting visitors, I mean. We make our living selling ale to the locals and the odd bed for the night to passing merchants. Those who find the lure of profit stronger than the fear of the forest."

"Fear of the forest?" Tristan said. "Everyone talks about the haunted forest, but it's never bothered me. What's so frightening about it? Apart from brigands."

"The brigands are the least dangerous thing here." Yann paused and looked serious, sitting behind Tristan. He said, "The forest is filled with spirits."

"What kind of spirits? Brandy? Whisky? Schnapps?"

Yann frowned. "There is a tower in the middle of the forest. Though no man can find it unless the Lady of that place wishes him to."

"That sounds interesting," Tristan said. "I've never had any difficulty in making a woman want to find me."

"You're very sure of yourself."

Tristan laughed. "And who is this Lady?"

"She is a witch, but worse than that."

"Worse than a witch?"

Yann nodded. "She is a demon. If she was once human, she is not now."

"But she's still a woman, so she can be won over. Believe me." Tristan grinned.

Yann furrowed his brow. "She's no joke."

"I treat everything as a joke," Tristan said.

"Be careful," replied the young man. "One day, your pride will backfire, and someone will stop you laughing."

"You're too serious," Tristan said. He took off his jay-feather hat and twirled it around his finger. "Tell me more about this demon woman."

Yann shook his head. "She is very evil, the lady of the Dark Tower."

"And what is her name?"

"They call her the Lady Melusin."

"I will consider it a personal challenge to make her want to meet me," Tristan said.

The Green Man Inn stood by a crossroads in the middle of the forest. It took them an hour to ride there. The summer trees in their green raiment swayed in the slight breeze. There were a few dwelling houses nearby as well as an ostler, a blacksmith and a general provisions store. The cottages of the woodcutters and trappers crowded round the Green Man as if for safety. Around the hamlet's perimeter was a fence of sharpened wooden palings.

"What's the fence for?" Tristan said as he and Yann rode through the gate on the back of Jezebel.

"To keep the wolves and bears out. And the brigands," Yann said.

"But not the Lady Melusin?"

Yann whispered, "Don't joke about her. She might hear you."

CHAPTER

# TWO

They arrived at the wide wooden door of the Green Man. The building was timber-framed and stood three storeys. There was a stable around the back, and Yann yelled for the stable lad's attention. When the boy came, Tristan commended Jezebel to him and slid a few deniers into his hand, telling him to take excellent care of his horse.

"Now. I'd like you to meet my parents," Yann said.

"My honour," Tristan said as they trotted up the wooden steps to the inn's front door.

Inside, a maid fetched a middle-aged man and woman. They looked like country sorts. They nodded at Tristan but initially said nothing.

Yann put his arm around Tristan's shoulder. "This man saved my life."

Tristan bowed.

Yann's parents listened with grave faces as the boy told them about the attack and Tristan's rescue of their son from the terrifying brigands.

Yann's mother dabbed her cheeks with her linen handkerchief. "We are eternally grateful."

"We are eternally in your debt," Yann's father said. "You must stay here as our guest as long as you wish."

Tristan bowed. "I'm not much of a stayer anywhere. But I will tarry awhile in this welcoming inn, and while I'm here, I won't stay for free—I will pay you with my music."

Yann's mother raised both eyebrows." You're a minstrel?" She turned to her husband. "I do not remember us ever having a visit from a minstrel!"

Her husband clasped her hands. "It will be a great treat for the Green Man and all our customers."

Tristan bowed again. "A bard, a troubadour, a minstrel, yes. And I will sing for you tonight."

It was then that a slender blonde girl caught Tristan's eye. From habit, he beamed at her. She glanced away shyly. Tristan nudged Yann and said, "You haven't introduced me to this lovely creature."

Yann smiled but his brow furrowed. "This is my fiancée, Arc'hantael."

Tristan bowed to Arc'hantael who had stepped closer. She studied Tristan without meeting his eye.

Tristan swept his jay-feathered hat down low. "I have seen many beautiful things today, but you are the fairest by far."

The girl blushed, She didn't take her eyes off him. "It's not often we get gallant strangers here."

Tristan guessed there were plenty of rough huntsmen passing through, eager for the summer ale and a grope of her bum if she didn't move deftly out of their way and then there were the fat merchants who might try to see how far they could get if they dropped a little gold. But intelligent, lyrical, handsome artists would be few and far between in this out of the way clearing in the forest. That was his trump card.

Arc'hantael suddenly glanced at Yann, who was staring at her. He turned and clapped Tristan on the shoulder and moved him away from the girl. "Come, let me show you the rest of the inn," he said.

The guest bedrooms were on the first floor above the bar. Yann explained that the family had their quarters on the storey above that. He showed Tristan to his room. The floor was of wooden beams, planed and then varnished. It was spotless. The walls were panelled in the same wood. There was a large bed with crisp white linen sheets and heavy woollen blankets, unlikely to be needed on these summer nights. Tristan went to the window. He looked out through the trees whose leaves were fine gold as the sun shone through them. The sky was still blue, and the clouds had all but disappeared. The sunshine was turning the rich butter yellow of evening as the golden orb began to dip in the west. Butterflies and honeybees buzzed around marigolds that grew in pots set outside the window on the sill.

"What a lovely place," Tristan said. "You're very lucky to live here." He turned, "And you're fortunate to be engaged to such a beautiful young woman. She'd be a rare gem in the city, but there won't be many like her for many miles around here."

Yann frowned. "Thank you. I am fortunate, as you say."

"She's beautiful." Tristan grinned. "Have you...?"

Yann reddened. "No, it's not our way. She remains a virgin."

Tristan slapped him on the back and laughed. "Good for you."

Yann sighed. "I love her. But I worry I bore her. Her head's always full of stories, and she has ideas of travelling to Roazhon and seeing the Duke."

"You could do that," Tristan said. "Roazhon is lovely: the tall castle on the hill above the city made of gleaming white stone and the way the red-roofed houses crowd on the tongue of land between the three rivers where they come to the silver sea."

Yann said, "My future is here in this village." He sighed. "But if I were able to talk like you, Arc'hantael wouldn't find me boring."

"You have other qualities," Tristan said. "You're brave and courteous for a start."

But Yann wasn't listening. "I know it would be easy for you to take her from me. I saw her looking at you."

Tristan sighed. "It wouldn't be the act of a friend to steal another man's betrothed."

Yann said, "Thank you. I do believe you to be an honourable man. You came to save me, involving yourself in my trouble."

Tristan said, "Anyone would have done the same."

Yann shook his head. "No, most people would have walked away. I know you will always do the right thing." Yann walked to the door. As he was going out, he hesitated. "But I guess you have stolen many a man's woman."

"That was different. They weren't my friends," Tristan said. "Anyway, what time do we eat?"

After Tristan napped, he got up, washed and dressed. With the coming of evening, the forest grew cold. Through the window, the pinpricks of the stars pierced the dark blue sky. Tristan left his room, not bothering to lock it, and went down to the inn's common room.

He had his lute with him. There were long wooden trestle tables across the bar, and huge log fire burned in the hearth. Yann greeted him warmly and showed him to his table. Tristan saw that Arc'hantael was working—taking the food to the tables. Trying to be discreet, he admired her long blonde hair and her slender figure. Despite his attempt at discretion, Yann saw him looking and frowned. Not good.

Arc'hantael brought him roast pork with sweet potatoes and carrots and onions from the garden behind the inn. Then she brought him a flagon of brown ale.

She lingered as if wanting to chat. He thanked her with a smile but cut the conversation short for Yann's sake. Then he watched her walk away, and he sighed and lifted the ale to his mouth. She was stunning, and she was interested. But a promise was a promise.

Tristan glanced over to where Yann stood next to his father by the bar. Yann looked back at him with slow anger in his eyes. Tristan smiled, but the young man did not return his smile. He was doing his best not to encourage Arc'hantael. He couldn't help that she found him attractive.

Tristan smiled and mouthed, "The food was great." This time, Yann smiled back, but it was with effort, and he looked troubled.

And when he finished his meal, Yann showed him to a stool so he could play. Tristan took the lute and began to tune it, plucking at the strings and running up scales and arpeggios until he was content that the instrument sounded its best. And then, while the folk in the bar waited with quiet anticipation, he struck the first chord and sang.

Tristan's rich baritone voice rang out. He sang a song of loving and losing. His voice was rich and deep, and all the women fell in love with him with his dark hair and his clever fingers. The instrument flowed as sweet as honey and as clear as water. And then when their hearts were full of love, he sang a song of warring and winning, and their spirits grew proud with honour and camerarderie and loyalty fast unto death. All the women loved him, and all the men envied him.

Tristan sang for an hour. People bought him drinks, and he grew merrier and sang songs that made the audience laugh. Then he sang for an hour more. It was near midnight. The candles burned low and the fire went to embers and the mood changed and the shadows grew in the corners, and Tristan sang about *An Itron Gaer Zidruez,* who in French is the *La Belle Dame Sans Merci*: the beautiful woman with no kindness.

"That's a story about the Lady Melusin," a rustic chap with a leather tankard in his fist yelled. The others hissed him to be quiet. "But it is," he said, but shame-faced for speaking her name.

Another one, half-drunk said, "This singer thinks he's a charmer, but she's one woman he could never win round."

Yann's father suddenly spoke up. "Don't talk about Lady

Melusin. We don't want the Green Man to become a target of her ill-favour."

Tristan sang another song gathering nuts and kissing in the hazel bushes. Then another song, then another until the drunks were drunker than before and the lonely hearts even more misty-eyed.

And as the owls called from the trees outside, the evening's entertainment drew to a close. People applauded. They crowded round him as if they wanted to take some of him home with them—the young girls with bright eyes, the middle-aged married women with lustful ones. The men clapped him on the back and said they'd love to hear him play again sometime.

"Well, Tristan?" said Yann. "Will you stay another night?" He said it in a way that sounded as if that was the last thing he wanted.

Arc'hantael stood close by Tristan, and Yann moved to block her, but still the candles of her eyes flared when Tristan looked at her. "Please?" she said.

Tristan shrugged. "I think I'll be off tomorrow."

Yann exhaled with relief. Arc'hantael squeezed her fingers as if she was about to ask him to reconsider, but Yann turned to her, and she fell quiet. She looked at her feet then back at Tristan. Her cheeks were flushed.

Tristan thought it was time to say goodnight. He made to get up.

Arc'hantael put her hand on his arm and said, "Do you have to go to bed yet? Perhaps you could play some more?"

"It's late," Yann said.

"Aye, it's late," Tristan agreed. "I should go to bed."

"Or if you are too tired to play more, you could tell us some stories."

Arc'hantael was almost pleading.

Tristan sighed.

The bar was nearly empty now. Yann's mother was clearing up behind the bar. His father was in the kitchen. Arc'hantael sat down next to Tristan. "Tell me about Roazhon. Yann says, you know the city well. Tell me about the Duke, and especially the Duchess. Is it true that you know her?"

Yann stood behind her with eyes like thunder. "Tristan must be tired."

"Sing me a song of far off places. Somewhere you've been." Hers were misty.

"I'm tired," Tristan said, smiling.

Yann glowered at both of them for a second, and then he stalked off.

"I don't think Yann is pleased," Tristan said.

"He's jealous," said Arc'hantael, her head cocked, ignoring her fiancé and staring at Tristan as if she'd found something rare and beautiful.

Tristan said softly, "I don't want him to be jealous."

"I don't have much experience of the world," said Arc'hantael, "but I've never known anyone like you." Her voice was full of yearning. "All the boys here are farmers or woodcutters. We don't have any singers," she said with a dismissive wave of her hand. "Nobody like you."

"I was born the lowest of the low," Tristan said.

She looked at the rings on his hand, and she reached out and touched them. "To us, you seem rich."

He made a fist. "These? All gifts."

"You earned them with your talent."

He smiled thinly and said, "Yes. But not with my musical talent."

She laughed. "Then which talent?"

He thought how naïve she was and tried to shock her to scare her off. "With my talent at seduction," he said finally.

"Ah." Her speedwell-blue eyes remained on him. His comment had had the opposite effect entirely to what he'd hoped.

"I'm a virgin," she said, head down.

"And you shall stay that way, as far as I'm concerned."

Just then, Yann came to the door and barked into the room. "I thought you were going to bed, Tristan, and you have work tomorrow, Arc'hantael!"

Tristan looked up at the boy. "I am going up now," he said, his tone conciliatory.

"And you're still leaving tomorrow?" asked Arc'hantael.

"Tomorrow, I've decided I'm going to find the Lady Melusin."

Arc'hantael's eyes widened. She put her hand to her throat.

Yann shook his head scornfully. "Then you go to your death."

"I don't mind danger," Tristan said mildly.

"So how do you plan to find her?" said Arc'hantael. "They say you can't find her unless she wants you to."

"I can make her want to meet me," he said.

"You're very arrogant," Yann said.

"It suits him", Arc'hantael said. Yann watched her do it. "Be careful," she said. "Melusin likes pretty men."

"This is a very foolish thing to do." Yann said. "But it is your decision to make."

"I will head into the heart of the forest. I'm sure to find her there," Tristan said.

Yann nodded. "I disagree with you going. It's pointless throwing your life away in your silly arrogance. Melusin is wicked and cruel."

"They say no man can defeat her," said Arc'hantael.

Tristan laughed. "She'll fall as they all do—after all, she's only a woman."

IN THE MORNING, Tristan ate a leisurely breakfast sitting outside the Green Man at the back, perched on a stump of wood. Arc'hantael brought him his food and offered him beer, but he accepted only water drawn from the inn's well.

"I'm sorry you're leaving," said Arc'hantael. Her blue eyes fixed him as she stood, blonde tresses falling over her shoulders. She waited there, half-nervous, half-entranced by him. "I don't think you should go looking for trouble," she said.

He shrugged and stood. "Trouble is an adventure."

"Nobody here has much thirst for adventure."

"It's not for me to judge others," Tristan said, standing. He looked toward the stable. "Jezebel has eaten?"

"Why don't you take me with you?" She said it as if it was a joke, but he knew she was serious. "We could see all the cities and the sea and the stars over Jerusalem. Things I'd never see if I stayed here and married Yann."

Tristan smiled, trying to be kind. "Maybe I'll come back here."

Quickly, she said, "I'd like that. But you won't."

She was right. Tristan would never come back. He knew coming back would cause heartbreak, and he didn't want to hurt her or Yann. He put on his jay-feather hat and twisted the rings on his fingers, so the various runes and glittering stones faced upwards and were straight.

"Yann is bringing your horse," Arc'hantael said. "I can meet you outside the village if you wait."

"You're a bright and beautiful young woman, but your path isn't with me."

She said quietly, "Have you had a lot of women?"

He smiled but didn't answer.

"Did you ever fall in love with any of them?" she said.

He shook his head. "I've never been in love."

"So you have never lost your heart?"

"No."

"I've lost mine," she said.

She turned and reached to the rose bush behind her. The green leaves were still beaded with dew. Red roses grew on it, some in full bloom and others still buds. She plucked a bud. "Here," she said. "Remember me when you look at this."

He took the rose but said, "It will fade."

"As I will fade from your memory."

They turned to see Yann appear, leading Jezebel. Tristan stepped away from Arc'hantael. He called his horse. She looked well-rested and whinnied when she saw her master.

"Thank you," Tristan said, offering the boy a coin. Yann looked at it but did not reach out his hand. "I won't accept money from the man who saved my life."

Tristan bowed. "Thank you for your hospitality. And thank your mother and father on my behalf."

Yann bowed. "And if you ever come this way again..." Tristan knew he didn't mean it. He saw Yann glance at Arc'hantael from the corner of his eye. She stared at Tristan. No, Tristan said to himself — I won't be back.

Then Tristan mounted Jezebel. He clicked his tongue, and she moved off. Arc'hantael watched him as he disappeared into the forest, the lute on his back, a jay's feather in his broad-brimmed hat.

CHAPTER

# THREE

Tristan and Jezebel made their way into the heart of the wood, and soon they were far away from the Green Man and their only companions were the trees and the animals. The path here was much less used and more overgrown than the broad one they had taken to the inn the previous day.

With his head full of music and thoughts full of escape, Tristan forgot his quest to look for the Lady Melusin. Jezebel trotted on. Tristan was a flighty man, whose interests changed as quickly as the buzzing bees move from flowerhead to flowerhead. He now considered making his way to another castle, singing for his supper and having some fun.

Often, Tristan thought making love to a knight's bored wife was a duty. Usually, the wives were well educated, but ill-matched with a drunken boor. Always, they lapped up his news of Court, and Duke, and the city of Roazhon. Unfailingly, his music won their hearts and loosened their vows.

Tristan liked women. He liked to seduce them and make them love him. So why not Arc'hantael? He could have stayed at The Green Man a few more days.

In fact, why didn't he have his way with her and move on as usual? She had a fine body, and he knew he could please her in bed. Sadly, please her better than Yann ever would.

And as he thought this, Tristan cursed himself for a rogue — Arc'hantael was different. She was as innocent as all the other women had been worldly. He said out loud to the breeze. "Maybe I'm developing a conscience?"

He remembered his boast to make the dark lady of the forest come to him. He had spoken with bravado at the time, but in truth, when he said it, he doubted she existed — just another peasant fear of the dark.

This was no time to think of shadows and fears. It was a fine summer morning. He thought that he would head east for the town of Trec'horanteg where he would find the lovely dark-haired Klervi or her sister Solen. If he were lucky, one or both of their husbands might be away hunting.

Around lunchtime, Tristan came across a deep river. He thought this must be the River Muc'huz, named after jet because it ran almost black. An ancient bridge arched over it, of ancient appearance, built of pink granite, and below it a pool where the water ran dark from the peat in the hills from where it rose.

Tristan dismounted and opened the packet of food that Arc'hantael had prepared for him. She had put cakes and apple from Penn ar Bed as well as cuts of spicy sausage and cheese from Penn ar Menez. She had also put little violets on top of the food. He remembered that those were the flowers given by country maids to the lads they loved, and he smiled and shook his head.

Tristan sat on the bridge, dangling his legs and eating his lunch while Jezebel grazed behind him and buzzards circled on currents of air high above, the quiet broken only by their mewing cries. Bees and flies fussed around the nearby flowers, and the air hung sweet with the fragrance of purple clover and the perfume of roses and honeysuckle that came from the bushes on the other side of the bridge.

Tristan was hot. He decided to swim. He took off his jerkin and then his cambric shirt. He removed his calf-length soft leather boots and then his trousers. He then stripped of his undergarments and stood, enjoying the feel of the sun on his flesh. He was lean and long. His muscles were well defined but not bulky. His feet were strong and graced by a few sprouts of curly brown hair on their tops and on his toes. Not bad, he thought.

He dived from the bridge, and the cold of the stream shocked him. He ducked his head and swam underwater to where the river was deep, stopping at the granite margin which the water had worn away through ten thousand winter floods.

Languidly, he turned on his back and took a few backstrokes to take him where he had jumped in. He played a game, just kicking and using his hands enough to keep steady against the current as he stared at a blue sky framed by the foliage of the summer trees.

And then he heard Jezebel whinny. He raised his head, the water running from his ears and hair.

"What's the matter, my lass?" he shouted.

The horse whinnied again. It was probably nothing, but, now alert, Tristan swam to the stream's edge and pulled himself out. He stood on the pebbles, naked, water streaming down his chest and arms. He could see no one, but he sensed a presence. He walked stealthily towards Jezebel and, still naked, pulled his sword from its sheath.

At the corner of his eye, something moved. Tristan spun around, brandishing his blade before him. But nothing again. Nothing at all.

Or was there?

The undergrowth fluttered He peered into the dim forest, over-canopied by oaks and ashes. It was darker there than it should have been—as if night had visited day. Someone had been there, and it was a woman.

But now, she was gone. Tristan scanned the undergrowth on all sides, but she was nowhere to be seen. He let the warm sun dry him. Then he put his clothes back on.

• • •

Tristan mounted Jezebel and set off along the path. After a while, the track seemed to peter out.

Grass stood tall in the middle of the trail and, as he rode, all over until it was a trail no more. The ground grew rushy and damp. Low tree branches blocked it, and Tristan had to dismount. He led Jezebel by her rein, looking for any gap in the trees that might suggest better passage. He decided they had taken a wrong turn and would need to retrace their steps. But he could not find any way back to retrace nor anything that looked like a proper way.

"Hmm," he said, stroking his horse's neck. "Jezebel, I think we're lost."

They stumbled around in the wood for half an hour, then an hour, and then two hours. Tristan became more and more frustrated. He ate what was left of the food. It seemed that whatever direction he took, the woods grew thicker. And it was getting unaccountably dark.

At this time of the year in Brittany, the days were long, and the sun should not set until much later. But here, it was gloomy. He got a shiver between his shoulder blades — a feeling he was being watched.

Even Jezebel seemed wary of the shifting shadows.

"I don't like this place, my girl," Tristan said.

When the dusk was thick and the forest heavy with the stink of wild garlic, at last, they struck upon a roadway of some kind. This path was wide and well-appointed. It must come from somewhere and go to somewhere else, but still, he was suspicious. To what danger did it lead? To wander around in the darkening wood was feebleminded, but Tristan worried that taking that dim way was foolish as well. He waited a while without moving.

"What choice do we have?" he said finally to the horse.

The trail was clear enough from stray branches for him to mount now, so he swung up onto Jezebel's saddle. As they walked forward, he kept one hand on the pommel of his sword. He and Jezebel plodded their way down the track while crows cawed from their hiding places in the funereal trees that lined their road. It was too dark. Dark far sooner than it should have been.

"This is most unnatural, Jezebel," he said.

The mare whinnied and shook her mane.

The undergrowth changed. The trees were no longer the happy oaks of the wide summer forest, but instead, weed-hung things whose name Tristan did not know.

The ground either side of the path was choked in briars and bramble but here and there bloomed the bright berries of the deadly nightshade.

They walked the path for the best part of an hour, Tristan starting at shadows and drawing his sword more than once at sounds and screeches in the shadow-haunted woods.

And then, ahead of him, the battlements of a stone tower appeared. The tower rose tall above the trees, red-black and riven from volcanic rock, bloody and flat in colour, drenched in dark moods and pregnant with great melancholy. Windows ran up its length, but they lay lightless. A great door stood at the bottom, fashioned of dark wood and studded with bosses of black metal. As he grew closer, Tristan saw a heavy knocker —a twisted iron ring painted black, shaped like a serpent, and this snake's body was held in an iron devil's mouth.

"I think I've found the Dark Lady's house," he said.

TRISTAN DISMOUNTED and stepped over to the door. Behind him, Jezebel stood. She stamped her fore-hoof and shifted as he approached the massive door. Tristan hesitated then took the iron ring in his hand. It was full night, with not even a ghostly remembrance of day lingering in the western sky and there were no stars. Tristan thudded the ring against the thick wooden door. The blow echoed in the gloomy grove. Crows croaked and lifted into the air at the sound, but no human answered. He lifted the ring again and again struck the door with it. The same dull sound rang out. Disquiet possessed him as if the knocker spoke a secret name, and that name summoned something that a god-fearing man should never call. The crows flapped around the clearing, their wings fluttered in the tenebrous air above his head.

Still no one came. He turned to Jezebel. "The place must be empty."

The horse didn't answer.

"So what do I do now?" Tristan mused. He retired from the door and back to Jezebel. She was still stamping and rolling her eyes. The horse seemed keen to leave the place. Tristan looked ahead. The track they had been on led on further past the castle, going to who knows where. But who knows where might be better than here that he now knew too well. He was about to mount into the saddle when he turned to see the door to the tower open soundlessly.

"What witchcraft is this?" he said aloud. Tristan reached for his sword. He drew it from his sheath. Even in the dark, the metal shone, and that gave him comfort for he knew the sword's keen edge, and he was confident in his skill to wield it.

From nowhere, a woman's voice whispered, "Your blade will be no use to you here, minstrel."


THE VOICE that called out to Tristan from the gloom around the tower was soft as balm and sonorous. Its tone was like a song that draws deep emotions from the hearer. At first, he couldn't see the bearer of the voice, but as his eyes stared into the darkness, the shadows became a woman, and she stood, imperious and bold, beside the gate.

She was tall with sable hair, black as the raven's wing: fuliginous, lustrous, wondrous and rich. Her hair reached down her back even unto her waist, her skin was pale as January snow, and her lips were red and ripe as crimson haws.

Her teeth gleamed white and sharp, and her eyes burned so dark that they might be midnight's font and origin. This woman's black eyes followed every move Tristan made, and there was a hypnotic power in her gaze. Tristan felt a strange flood of emotions in his gut: fear, yes, but lust also, and a peculiar humility that was unfamiliar to him.

"I'm sorry, my lady. I didn't see you at first," Tristan said, but his hand still gripped the sword. He tried to unsheathe it, but his movements were dull and uncoordinated. He couldn't make his hand do what he wanted it to, and he knew she was the cause of it.

"Welcome to my home Tristan Mab Bennog," she said, "I heard you were looking for me."

"Forgive me, lady, but you are?"

She laughed. "You well know who I am. Some of your comments about me were over boastful."

He felt himself blush. How did she know that? Maybe she did have spies everywhere.

"You wanted me to come to you, so I came to find you," she said. "I enjoyed watching you swim. Your naked form pleased me."

"You know my name," Tristan said, trying to recover his composure. "But I don't know yours."

The woman laughed, mocking him gently. "I think you do. I am the Lady Melusin. I believe you said that I was *only a woman* with the implication that I would be overpowered by your beauty and wit and soon become another of your conquests."

She mocked him, and he felt a cold in his throat. Her power was almost palpable and there was something sinister and threatening about her. He as far away from any help. He tried to speak, but he was tongue-tied. He could not use his eloquence. The words that were his tools and gift stuttered, refusing to leave his mouth. A chill of fear rose in his chest, its cold reaching even to his blinking eyes, and he fought to stop it showing.

Melusin watched him with cruel amusement. "I think I will invite you into my house, where you can keep me entertained." She beckoned him with her long black-nailed finger. And Tristan walked, not of his own will, but by hers, through the heavy oak door and up the stone steps of the tower, sword still in hand, but now useless.

Despite the summer he had not long left, the tower was filled with the chill of winter. They climbed the stone spiral stairs, turn after turn until they were very high. She opened a door and led him in.

Tristan stood in a stone chamber, its walls covered by tapestries depicting murder and crucifixion. The stone floor was carpeted with rich rugs of reds and orange and brown. Wooden chairs and sofas furnished the room, draped in the furs of wolves and bears. There was a fire set in the wall. Flames of blue and white blazed around glowing coals in a deep-set stone hearth. There was only one window, a narrow slit, and by it, a perch upon which a raven sat watching him with bright eyes.

CANDLES BURNED and dripped black wax, their light flickering and throwing shadows on the stone walls.

The Lady Melusin stood watching him. She pointed to the sword in his hand and said, "You will not need that."

He looked at his sword as if just remembering it. His mind felt sluggish, thick with some intoxicant. He let the sword drop, and it hit the rug below his feet with a muffled noise.

"My horse?" he said.

The Lady Melusin smiled, her incisors were sharp, and their white enamel gleamed, her moist lips red as blood. He was close to her now. "Sit," she said.

And he sat.

In her chambers she was not disguised with shadows and he saw her clearly for the first time. She wore a cloak of raven's feathers, glittering iridescently as she moved. The pale flesh of her throat and shoulders was bare. Her gown was of a crimson samite, and sewn into it with gold thread were the images of winged demons with hawks' faces. A line of pearl buttons ran down from her pale chest.

Around her wrists were bangles of gold encrusted with gems and on her fingers rings of jade and platinum. Her nails were sharp and black. He stood befuddled while she walked towards him. Standing close, she towered over him. Her beauty filled his vision and was all he could think of.

She tilted her head and said, "And now, minstrel, will you play for me?"

"My lute is on the horse," he said.

She indicated with her eyes that his lute was beside him.

His brow furrowed. "How?"

"My servants brought it."

"I saw no servants."

She shrugged, her lustrous hair sweeping across her bare shoulders. "Servants are not to be seen."

Tristan fumbled for his lute. Though his mind felt slowed, his fingers were nimble; it seemed her magic allowed that. Quickly he ran through intricate webs of notes. He played high, and then his fingers slid to play low. He played melodies so beautiful that they brought sadness deeper than tears, a sadness that choked the listener. Though not her.

He played rapid rills of notes that resembled rain; he played quick torrents of chords to conjure flowing birdsong. Melusin watched, inscrutable, her eyes never leaving him. Sometimes she watched his fingers, and sometimes she watched his face. As he played, his mind began to clear.

He looked to see whether he pleased her, but he could not read past the faint smile on her alabaster face. He paused.

She clapped. "Bravo, you have played of life."

He bowed, smiling.

Her face grew cold, "But now," she said, "play of death."

And his fingers moved without him willing it, finding deep chords that were strange to him. The rhythm was strong and pulsing, bringing to mind the sound the oars make when we are ferried across the final river.

Tristan's skin went icy-cold as if he were dragging his fingers through the water of the river of death. The room darkened until the only thing he could see was her face — her slanted cheekbones, her full mouth and above the mouth, her awful black eyes.

He played on. Then he did not know if he was still playing, but he heard the music yet. The lute lay discarded to his side. And she was close to him, and her hands undressed him. They ran over his broad shoulders, examining them, admiring his muscles and they caressed his brown arms.

Then she undressed, dropping cloak and gown to fall around her feet. Her flesh was the white of bone against his tanned skin. Her breasts swelled like a young woman's, though she could not be young. Her nipples were red as dark grapes, and they stiffened and brushed his chest. She lent in to kiss him, and he felt the soft weight of her long hair over his face and shoulders. She settled on his thigh, and he felt her sex press against him. He felt the moist warmth of her eagerness.

The touch of her fingers was like ice; it shocked and thrilled him as her hands ran over his face. He desired her cold more than any heat he'd ever had. She was the pale moon, and for her touch, he would forsake the sun. But while her fingers and her mouth and her skin were chill, her sex was a pit of burning ice. Her fingers reached down and grasped his hardness.

How proud he was of its length and girth. How the girls had whispered of it and how they chased after him, eager to feel it inside them. The Lady Melusin guided and lowered herself onto him, sheathing it like a sword in a scabbard. All Tristan's arrogance in his skilful lovemaking was gone. First, she rode him; then she took him as a mare takes a stallion. When he was spent, she demanded more. Despite the cold of her skin, he sweated. And when he had ridden her more times than he had ridden any woman, she let him rest. He lay there, his head on her breast, and she stroked his hair like he was her pet.

"You satisfy me, Tristan."

He said nothing. He was weak from her. He was a mouse in the presence of a cat. She was the Lady Melusin, and she had taken him between her legs, but on her terms, and he knew when he failed to please her, his life would end.

Then he felt pain at his neck. He put his fingers there and drew them away covered in red. In the heat of their mating, he had not noticed, but now he looked and saw he was bleeding. The blood ran from his throat to his chest.

He stared at the red on his fingers. "What have you done?".

MELUSIN LOOKED at Tristan with an emotion in her eyes that was almost like affection, if a predator can have affection for its prey.

She ran her fingers through his brown hair. "I feed from your life, my little Tristan. With one hand, she reached and cupped his balls. "I take this," Then with the other hand, she adrew her fingers down the line of his jugular vein, "And this."

She smiled with her, and he saw the trace of his dried blood around her lips. "But in return, you get this." She stroked her mons pubis with its covering of hair black and soft as sable. "A good trade?"

He struggled to sit. He fought to wake from this dream of sex and death.

She allowed him to stand. He pulled on his trousers.

She laughed softly. "You have abused women all your life, Tristan. And now you begrudge one abusing you?"

He shook his head as he pulled on his shirt. "I abused no woman. All of them came of their own free will."

"Mostly true," she said. "But their free will was influenced by your little tricks. The way you told the ugly girls they were pretty and the way you told the pretty girls they were clever. And then your music and the honeyed promises you never meant to keep: *I love only you... You are the most beautiful... I dream of you, my love...* And to the virgin girls, you sneaked from their father's houses you'd say: *How can it be bad if we both want it?"*

"And to the married women you laid in their husband's beds, you'd whisper: *Your husband doesn't need to know... Don't you deserve some pleasure too?* Yes, Tristan, you have used your talents well. It's just a pity they were always for your own selfish ends."

Tristan pulled on his boots. He bowed, trying to muster his charm and manners. "I have enjoyed our time together, my lady." He frowned. "Indeed, I have never known lovemaking so intoxicating. But I must leave."

She was still naked. She sat, legs akimbo. The swell of her breasts, her wide hips and her sex plump and dark as a well-fed cat stiffened him again. But now his lust was sharpened by fear. He was arrogant. He had thought his charm could overcome any woman, but Melusin was different. He had no power over her.

She stood languidly and walked over to the fireplace. He watched her swaying stroll, her full buttocks, her waist, and the way her hair moved as she walked. She reached up to a crystal decanter filled with red wine.

It had not been there before: her servants again. He wondered what else they'd seen, or even if they had any interest in what their mistress did.

Melusin poured the red liquid into a crystal glass. She handed it to him, taking her his hand in hers and pressing the glass into his palm. She closed his fingers around it. "Drink."

"I must leave, my lady," he said, but took the glass anyway. He felt her influence on him again. She made him do what she wanted, not what he knew was best. He sipped. The liquid was not cold as he expected, and it was not wine. It was warm. It tasted of salt and iron. He spat it out. "Blood!"

She laughed. "I thought you needed some to replace what I took."

He wiped his mouth and put the glass on a nearby table. "This is my blood?"

She took his glass and swallowed what was left of the blood. She licked her lips, lasciviously with her pink tongue. "No, it's the blood of a virgin. Which, you cannot claim to be," she said. She found the whole thing amusing as if his revulsion was a joke.

And then the raven on its perch, which had been quiet through all their lovemaking, squawked. Tristan turned around, but the bird was looking not at him, but at the opening door.

Tristan heard steps outside the chamber, and then the door swung open. Wearing lacquered armour with a scimitar at his hip, a tall black-haired man entered. He gazed at Tristan and his lip curled with disdain. The man's eyes were red as fire, and his teeth were cruel and sharp, protruding over his swollen lips. His face was misshapen and evil radiated from him.

Tristan stepped back.

The naked Lady Melusin said, "Tristan, bid good day to my husband."

The man glowered at her nakedness then snarled at Tristan, "You are a brave man indeed to come here, or a foolish one."

"Perhaps both,' Lady Melusin said.

Tristan bowed. "I'm sorry my Lord; you have the advantage of me. I don't know your name."

The man showed rows of vicious teeth that ran down his throat like those of a shark, multiple and keen as razors. His incisors were as long as a snake's and his eyes burned with red hate for humanity.

The Lady Melusin smiled and said, "This is the Lord Iblis."

The man said disdainfully, "It seems you have just cuckolded me. You should know there is a price to pay for that."

Melusin raised a warning finger. "He's mine, and it's not the first time you've been cuckolded."

"No, you wanton. Nor the hundredth. But still, I will bleed him until his flesh is white," Lord Iblis snarled.

Melusin shook her head. "It is I who will bleed him in my own good time."

Iblis stalked fully into the room, and his armour chinked with each step. He walked with a strange grace, and Tristan felt his hair prickle as an ancient fear gripped him. He stood before humankind's predator, and terror filled him in its presence. Fighting to keep his voice steady, fixing the thing with an unblinking gaze, he muttered, "As I said, I'll be leaving."

He stooped to pick up the sword where he'd dropped it, forgotten while Melusin took her pleasure with him.

As Tristan bent, he felt Iblis's eyes burning into him, and painful fire ran down every vein of his body. Glancing up to see the cause of his pain, the monster's eyes held him, and he felt the sword fall from his numb fingers. Tristan tried to walk to the door—he forced his legs to move, but they did not obey him, it was as if they were someone else's limbs. He budged them slowly by a massive effort of will, but the distance he walked was small. His feet were heavy and unbiddable. Then his legs stopped moving altogether.

Iblis sneered, "Now, worm, you will pray to me," and Tristan felt his hands moving and forming the attitude of supplication before the thing that stood before him. Iblis laughed, showing his teeth like a cobra. Tristan struggled, but he had no power against Iblis's mocking gaze.

"Leave him," Melusin said. "He pleases me."

Her husband snapped. "Cover yourself—you disgust me."

Melusin dressed slowly, drawing out each movement to taunt him. Tristan feared that if she made him too angry, Iblis would use his will to snap him like a dry stick and upset her that way.

"There," Melusin said, buttoning up her dress and pulling the cloak of feathers onto her shoulders. "I am dressed. Now leave him."

Iblis let Tristan slump and the minstrel fell backwards onto a chair, his ringed fingers heavy and hanging; his handsome face pale, a slick of hair over his damp brow.

"If I let you keep him, what will you give me?" said Iblis to his wife.

Melusin sighed and came over to Tristan. She stood behind him and stroked his head as if he were her pet dog. "What do you want?" she said.

"I want the blonde virgin and her lover—the ones you caught today."

Melusin exhaled impatiently. "I have hardly tasted them yet."

"Give me them or I will kill your minstrel now."

With an air of terrible boredom, Melusin said, "Very well, you can have the boy. I will keep the girl."

"I want them both."

"You are greedy."

"Surely this," Iblis pointed at Tristan, "is more valuable to you than both of them together?"

Melusin considered Tristan, running her fingers over his shoulders, massaging him. "He is a fine specimen." She smiled. "My minstrel boy."

"Then the boy and the girl are both mine?" said Iblis.

She shrugged. "Very well."

Iblis smiled his evil smile. "Where are they?"

"In cells off the lower dungeon."

"I will go and visit them," Iblis said. "I hunger."

When Iblis had gone, Tristan felt relief sweep over him. He sat heavily.

Melusin said, "Do not leave this chamber while I am away. You are safe only here. Whatever he says, he will kill you, just to upset me."

But Tristan's mind was on other things. A thought occurred to him. He said, "Who are the boy and girl?"

Melusin seemed uninterested. "I don't know. They strayed near the tower today, just before you came. They are from one of the villages, though it is unusual for them to come so near. Still, it saved me the work of going looking for blood."

"Do you know their names?"

"No," Melusin said frowning. "Why would I? They are merely food. Do you ask the names of the cows that provide your beef?"

"You said the girl was blonde and a virgin."

Melusin laughed, "Indeed, she told me that as if her purity and innocence would protect her. Perhaps she thought I would feel a motherly regard for her? But I am no mother."

Tristan wanted to ask Melusin more, but she dismissed his question with a wave. "Enough of them. They'll be dead soon. Iblis doesn't draw out his kills as I do." She came and stood directly in front of Tristan. "I will sleep soon, and I want you again before I do."

Tristan said, "And what are your plans for me after that?"

Melusin took off her dress, "I will kill you eventually. But the longer you please me, the longer I will keep you alive. Think of it like Scheherezade in A Thousand and One Nights."

"But she only told stories!"

Melusin smiled and pointed. "Then tell me a story each time with that."

She laid her dress over the chair behind her. She was again naked before him. Even though he wished it would not, he felt her wicked beauty arousing him. She came close so he could smell her musk.

"So this is my fate?" he said.

"I would have thought you would have relished the challenge. The more inventive you are in bed, the longer and harder you please me, the longer you will live." She stroked his cheek, and her hand slipped to his shirt. He watched as she unbuttoned it.

"But you will still kill me in the end."

She said, absentmindedly, as she stripped him, "You are a very talented musician, you know."

He said nothing.

"Your music has great power. Perhaps instead of killing you, I could teach you magic — to enable you to use your music to conjure the dark and to bend people to your will." Melusin seemed taken with the idea. She mused "Yes, we can ride out together to the villages, and you can use the tunes I teach you to ensnare my prey."

"I would never do that," he said.

"You silly man," she said. "How late in life to develop morals."

He was naked now; his penis stiff. He hated her, but she excited him more than any woman had.

She looked down approvingly and stroked his hard length. "Stop talking and let us make love."

He stood up and pushed her down onto the furs that lay on the floor below the fire. He forced her legs apart with his knees. She laughed at his demonstration of power, and he knew that she was allowing him to take her, and if the whim struck her, she would crush him like an insect on a board.

She opened herself, her hands on his buttocks. As he pushed into her and she groaned with pleasure, he knew what he had to do: he had to rescue Arc'hantael and Yann. He was sure it was they that had come to the tower. And he guessed that somehow Arc'hantael had followed him and got herself ensnared and that Yann had followed her because he loved her.

Tristan thrust roughly in Melusin, wanting to punish her, but each time he sunk into her, she squeezed her legs around him and moaned in delight. And, he thought, I will find a way to kill you too, you evil bitch.

She made him couple with her another twice. And then she released him. "I go to sleep now," she said. He was exhausted. He lay without energy on the furs, naked and limp.

"When I sleep, the day comes; when I wake it flees," she said.

"You might prefer the day, but I counsel you to sleep at the same time as me, for when I am awake, I will need you, and I will not let you rest."

"Where do I sleep?" he said.

She pointed to a door he had not taken account of before. "Through there is a bedroom. There are heavy curtains at the window. They will keep the sunlight out."

He stood and grabbed his clothes. He walked to the door. When he got there, she was at the main door about to go out.

She turned and said, "I like you, Tristan." He hoped she did not want him to reciprocate. She looked thoughtful for a second and said, "In some ways you remind me of Iblis."

He shook his head. "What?"

"Whatever you think, like him you take whom you want and you care little for their fate, only for your own pleasure."

"That's not true. I am nothing like him."

"If you say so."

He said coldly, "I don't love you, Melusin. I never will."

"We shall see about that," she said and blew him a kiss. Then she left and closed the door.

WHEN SHE WAS GONE, Tristan went over to the heavy blue drape that was pulled over the slit in the stone wall that served as a window. He drew it back and light came spilling in. Outside, the sun was high. He could hear the small birds flitting and calling from the trees around the tower.

He walked over to the door of his bedroom and pulled it open. Inside there was a four-poster bed hung with sombre fabric. He touched the sheets; they were crisp, clean linen. On an oaken dresser, stood a ewer and jug filled with fresh cold water for him to wash. There was a fireplace stacked with logs and ready to be kindled at any time he should need it. He wondered with what. He guessed the tower's invisible servants would light the fire at his bidding, or more likely at hers.

He turned and walked out of the room. Whatever she said, he could sleep later. He walked through the chamber where he had been with Melusin. Through the door was the stairwell of the tower. He hesitated, thinking of her warning. But he reasoned, when she slept, so would Iblis. They were of the same kind. Surely it would be safe to leave his room? The thought of being a prisoner sickened him so he stepped from the chamber onto the stairs.

GREY STONE STEPS wound up and down, spiralling out of sight in both directions. As he walked down the spiral, there were other doors off the staircase, but they were locked. Then he got to the enormous front door. He pulled back the iron bolts and lifted the metal bars across it. He pulled it. Nothing happened. There should be no reason for it not to open, but it would not. He put his shoulder to it and pushed with all his strength. Still, it would not budge. He cursed the door. It was held by sorcery.

Then he looked down the stairs that descended yet further. They delved into bedrock, and he heard the drip of water. Tristan went down the steps. Torches were in sconces on the wall, flickering with unseen drafts of wind and their smoky smell tainted with the reek of the pitch they had been dipped in.

Tristan felt uneasy, and his hand strayed to the hilt of his sword, though he knew it would do no good against the lord and lady or their invisible servants. He stepped down slowly, one step at a time. The dripping water grew louder, and he saw that the steps ended and a tunnel stretched away, worse lit than above, with few torches, some burned out and others fluttering.

This was the dungeon. This was where Melusin and Iblis locked their prey.

Tristan prowled forward, his sword half drawn now. Ahead of him on the left were a series of doors. The tunnel here was cold, and the rain that had soaked through the bedrock created a damp sheen on the walls and the floor.

He came to the first door. It was wooden with a barred window. He peered through and saw it was a prison cell. A skeleton, brown-boned, long-dead, picked clean by rats or worse, lay on the floor in irons. He felt a chill of fear of that place, but he told himself not to give in to such feelings.

He looked through the next cell window and saw Yann sat on a stone shelf and laid out with her head on his knee, Arc'hantael. She looked pale and ill and was sleeping. At first, the boy did not notice him, but when he saw a face at the door, he shouted, "What? Are you here to torture us again so soon?"

"Yann," said the minstrel. "It is I—Tristan."

"Tristan?" the boy's voice sounded suddenly full of hope. "I thought it was him again," he muttered. "The Lord Iblis, who has nearly killed my Arc'hantael."

"How did you get here?" Tristan said.

Yann's voice was full of subdued anger. "It was your fault. You cast your spell on Arc'hantael. After you left, you were all she could talk about. She said she was going to follow you and that you would love her and you would live together happily in some city." Yann spat. "But her foolishness has brought us both death."

"But you got here quicker than me," Tristan said.

The boy shrugged. "The path led us straight here. We did not mean to stop at the tower, but the Lady Melusin appeared and offered us refreshment. In her passion and hurry to find you, Arc'hantael had not thought about bringing food, and we were hungry and thirsty."

"And you accepted Melusin's offer?"

"Arc'hantael did. I said I was afraid of the lady, and she told me to be a man. She said you would not have feared Melusin. I was stung. I couldn't let her go into the tower alone."

"I'm very sorry. But this is not my fault."

The boy laughed bitterly. "Perhaps you didn't tell her to come, but you knew she was fascinated with you. You made her love you as a game to entertain yourself. It is your fault."

"That's not true," Tristan said.

"Then why else do you seduce women? You don't want them. You only want them to want you, and when they do, and your ego is satisfied, you leave."

"You make me sound as much of a monster as the Lord and Lady of this place," Tristan said.

"I think you are." Yann hung his head, and his tears fell on Arc'hantael's sleeping face. "It doesn't matter," Yann said finally. "We will all be dead soon. You are here in the Tower, so you are their prisoner too, never mind that you are not in a cage. I take it the Lady Melusin captured you? After your boast that you would win her over, the joke is now on you."

Tristan felt shame rise through him. What the boy said was true. He said, "I will rescue you."

"And how will you do that?" said Yann dryly.

Tristan said, "I don't know how I will rescue us all yet. But I will think of a way."

"Then it had better come soon, for my Arc'hantael has lost much blood. The vampire drank deep from her neck."

"I will return soon."

"I don't believe you. Perhaps you even think you will, but when your life is at stake, I think you will leave to save yourself, for you are the only person you ever truly loved."

Tristan turned away. He would be back, whatever the boy said. And he somehow would deliver them from this evil.

TRISTAN FOUND the Tower's entrance hall. This huge door led to the outside. He tried to turn the heavy iron ring, but the door was locked against him. He heaved and shoved and hammered. He looked all around for a key, but there was none. He was indeed trapped in here.

Head hanging, trailing his fingers along the cold stone as he walked, he returned to his room. The birds still sang outside, and the sun still shone. Tristan looked from the window in his bedroom across the broad forest of Brec'helean. The sun stood high and free in the blue sky, but for all that Tristan could see this beautiful world outside the tower; he could not reach it.

He went back to his bed and lay on the comfortable mattress of goose down. He stretched over for his lute and began to play, singing along in a low voice. But he could not settle — even with his music, a thing that usually gave him such pleasure.

He sighed and stood up. Visions of the Lady Melusin kept coming to his mind. He thrust them away, but her image would return, and with the thoughts, his heart beat faster. He hated himself for it, but he wanted to see her again. A kind of infatuation had stolen over him.

Tristan sang to distract himself, but all the love songs were about Melusin. His rational mind knew this was some kind of sorcery, but still, the longing for her tugged at him. He threw the lute on the bed in disgust. What was the matter with him? What spell was she weaving to draw his thoughts always to her?

Or was it really love? An emotion unfamiliar to him—something he'd never felt in his life: love for a woman. Maybe love was what infected his mind. He went to the window again, but the vision of the vast forest only tantalised him. And then he walked into the hall where the raven still sat on its perch.

"You're as much a prisoner as I am," he said to the bird, but the bright-eyed creature did not reply.

He turned again. Restlessly he paced from the window around the room to the door onto the stairwell. He looked up the stone steps. She would be up there sleeping. He thought he would go and look on her resting face. Maybe he'd even wake her so she would come back to him sooner. He felt disgust, but longing too.

As he mounted the steps, he was filled with terrible jealousy towards her husband, the Lord Iblis. He ran through fantasies of how he would destroy Iblis and have Melusin to himself. And then he realised, the further he got up the stairs and the closer to her he was, the stronger his infatuation for her grew. He was near the top of the tower now. Just above him was a door where the staircase stopped. Her presence felt very strong here, but strong too was the burning fear that emanated from Lord Iblis.

Tristan stepped up to the door. He pushed at it, and it swung open on oiled hinges. The room revealed was small and square. On the wooden floor were two sarcophagi. Between them burned a single torch, its restless light lending a strange liveliness to the sculpted representations of lord and lady that decorated the coffins' tops. The coffins were carved from smooth alabaster.

Tristan walked over to them and stroked the stone face of Lady Melusin. It was exact — a perfect representation of her beauty in stone. But it was not enough to touch a carving of her. He longed to see her again. He put his weight against the sarcophagus lid and shoved. It moved far more easily than he had suspected. The stone shifted slowly with a grating sound and the inside of the casket became visible. He could see the edge of a rosewood coffin, lined with cream silk.

Tristan pushed the lid further and revealed another inch; now he saw her dark hair, but instead of the lustre it held when she was with him, it was dry and lifeless. He pushed the lid a further inch and saw half her face and gave out a cry he could not control.

Melusin's face was dry and desiccated, skin like old parchment stretched too tight on decrepit bone, sunken eyes like thumb-squeezed apples, yellow teeth on receded gums. She was dead.

His heart was beating. He didn't even know how to name the emotion—was this grief? Bereavement? Disgust? He had made love to this dead thing. He began to retch, but he had eaten nothing, and there was nothing for him to throw up. With shaking hands, he dragged the sarcophagus lid shut. Revulsion filled him, and he fled from the room.

CHAPTER

# FIVE

By the time Tristan got to his room, his shaking had steadied. He found a meal set for him on a table placed in his room by unseen hands. There was chicken and rice with peppers and a fresh tomato sauce. It was hot and set out on a crystal, with a knife and fork of antique silver, handles chased in heavy gold, on either side of the plate. By the plate, too was a golden goblet filled with crisp white wine.

Despite the gnawing of hunger in his belly, he could not face the food, but he drank the wine. He gulped it too quickly, guzzling it to quieten his nerves. Feelings hatched in his heart that she had laid like a cuckoo's egg inside him. He loved her, the Lady Melusin, but that love was not a natural growth. Like a hybrid, hothouse orchid, she had forced it. These were not his feelings, though they felt more real than any emotion he had ever known.

He placed the goblet on the table and watched amazed as it filled itself again with wine. And he thought of where he was and how he had come to this end. When he examined himself, what emotions had he ever felt other than pride at his own cleverness? How he enjoyed his beauty and talent and the fact that everyone he charmed fawned around him, congratulating him and wanting to be his friend?

Tears formed in his eyes and fell down his cheeks, but even these were tears for himself. He left the food to go cold and stepped again to his window.

He cursed his false feelings for Melusin, and he thought of Yann and Arc'hantael chained to a wall in the prison cell, and then he felt the flowering of another strange emotion — pity, and he knelt by his bed, and he prayed to a God he had long forgotten. All he said was simply, "Father, let me do good for once."

He noticed the light from the window suddenly fade as if the sun was eclipsed. A strange wind grew in the treetops outside, and the birds fell silent. The unnatural night had returned, and Tristan knew that Melusin would soon come back to him.

MELUSIN CAME LIKE A DARK WIND. The curtains over the window flapped as her presence sucked away the daylight. Tristan looked up from where he was to see the book of music she had provided for him flutter as she entered the room.

And there she was—no longer the dried dead thing he had seen in the coffin, but vibrant and living in her funereal majesty. Her dress now was dark blue edged with gold, sparkling diamonds sewn into it like glittering seeds. Her flesh was pale as a mountain snowfall, her eyes terrible as a storm. She smiled.

Against his will, his heart thrilled, and he stood to greet her. He found he was smiling back at her, and then he corrected the smile to a frown.

She was amused. "You almost looked pleased to see me, Tristan," she said. She picked up the golden goblet of wine, which was all he had taken from the meal. She said, "Good that you drank my wine. But you ate nothing, and my servants will be upset. They will take it as a personal slight."

"I wasn't hungry," he muttered.

"Love steals the appetite," she said.

"I don't love you," he said and then regretted rising to her bait.

She laughed. "Not yet, my darling. But soon."

He shook his head. He would never admit the feelings she had seeded in him. He felt like a petulant child because she was beautiful, and she was intelligent. She was magnanimous too; she forgave his petty moods. She forgave him the scoundrel he had been. Why should he not love her? He put his hands to his head as if to take the thoughts out. He knew it was the drug of her presence that made him feel like this. And the drug of her absence too, when she hadn't been there. She was the intoxicant, a dark liquor made of blood and longing.

She had gone to the raven and was stroking it. It allowed itself to be petted by her, apparently enjoying the touch. "Has Bran kept you company while I slept?" she said.

"The raven? No. He said nothing."

She smiled again, showing the tips of her teeth. "But he sees everything."

"I had supposed you had your spies," he said.

"Everywhere," she smiled. She came close to him and ran her nails across his face; lightly in a way that did not break the skin but reminded him that she was in her power. "How did you amuse yourself while I was gone?" she said.

"I explored."

"I told you not to wander."

"I found the door, but I can't get out."

"No, that is true and is my intent."

"I found the dungeons. The young couple in there."

She looked at him evenly.

"The girl will die soon," he said. "Could you not release them?"

"Why?" She seemed genuinely puzzled.

"For me. If you care about me as you say, you could release them for me."

She gazed at him. "It's true I do care for you. But those creatures are our food."

"They are people, not food!" he spat.

She explained to him slowly, as if speaking to a stupid child of whom she was fond. He had the impression that she was being particularly indulgent. She said simply, "People are my nourishment."

"That's disgusting," he said.

She spoke in the same even tone. "Do you pity the hens and the pigs you eat?"

"It's not the same."

"If you weren't so sentimental, you would see this more clearly." She stroked his arm. "But I like your sentimentality."

"So you will drink their blood until they are drained, and then they die."

She nodded. "Let's talk of something else. I don't want to fall out. Did you look at the music book?"

He shook his head and continued. "I beg you, Lady, let them go free. Find other victims."

"Ah," she said, in sudden realisation. "You knew them before, I think. They mean something to you."

"I hardly know them. I met them briefly."

"The girl is beautiful. Did you...?"

He shook his head, angrily. "No, of course not."

"Of course not?" She laughed.

His furrowed brow showed his anger.

Melusin continued. "But somehow you feel responsibility..." Then she fixed him with her piercing gaze. "I see. They came here because of you. The girl loves you!" She laughed out loud. "That is delicious. Are you sure you didn't seduce her behind her lover's back?"

Tristan shook his head vehemently. "I told you, no."

"Ah, you've changed then?" She was still mocking him.

He was serious. "I have changed," he said.

Her hand was still on his arm. He didn't pull it away.

"And what has caused this tremendous change in you?"

He bowed his head. "She changed me. Her innocence."

"The girl?" Melusin's voice was suddenly icy. "I like her less now. I won't have a rival, especially a silly human girl."

"And you've changed me too," he said.

She raised an eyebrow. "Really? How?"

"I learned what it was to be someone's plaything. To be treated not as a person but as an object."

"That is hardly fair, Tristan. I treat you well. You are my favourite pet."

Tristan stepped away from her. He went to the fire that blazed with an unnatural blue light. Still, it gave off warmth, and he stood in front of it, trying to rid himself of the chill Melusin's presence always caused. "I looked at the music," he said eventually.

She appeared pleased. "Will you play me something from it?"

He nodded. He went to his room and fetched his lute. Then he sat near her and tuned it. She observed, admiring the way his deft hands plucked the strings and made the chords. Almost shyly, he began to play one of the tunes.

She listened as he played with great emotion. When the last notes died away, she applauded. "That was my father's favourite tune."

"Your father?"

She said quietly. "Yes, I had a father. Did you think I was always thus?" She gestured to herself. She stood. "No, I was human like you before Iblis found me."

Tristan frowned. "I didn't realise."

"Our kind is made, not born. Iblis told me I was beautiful, and I believed him. I was very innocent."

"You are beautiful," Tristan said.

"Thank you," she said. "But he said he would make me more beautiful. And terrible. And I would live forever. I was seduced." She shrugged.

"Do you regret it?"

"I am past regrets, Tristan. I am what I am. I listened to him. I believed he loved me. He offered me the blood kiss, and I took it." She lowered her gaze. "That was a long time ago."

Tristan watched her as she walked over to the raven. It cocked its head and let her stroke it. She seemed deeply sad. She smiled at him, and he thought he had never seen a more beautiful woman. To see her vulnerability was too much. He could not resist her in her regret, and perhaps that was what this was all about— another trick to win him? And then he saw the tears on her cheeks were real.

"Melusin," he said, rising.

She put up her hand to stop him. "You make me feel strange things, Tristan. I have not cried for centuries. Not since I became this."

He offered her his linen handkerchief. It was a trick of his to listen to his lady loves and provide them with a handkerchief and make them believe in his great sensitivity. But this time his empathy was real.

Melusin took the handkerchief "What are we doing, Tristan? Two monsters like us. Are we becoming human?"

"I don't know."

"I joke," she said. "It is too late for me to become human. But you, you have the gift of humanity, but you have squandered it with your selfishness."

"I will change. I have changed," he said.

"But you don't have much time," she said, "Because I will kill you. No matter how much I come to care for you, I will kill you. It is my nature."

Melusin took Tristan with her out of the Tower. It was night. She mounted on a black stallion and he on his faithful Jezebel. The horse had been well fed but was pleased to see him. As they rode from the tower into the night-clad forest, Tristan said, "Where's Iblis?"

"Lord Iblis is hunting," she replied. "But we are not going to find him."

"I don't think he likes me," Tristan said. His mood was lighter now. He began to play his lute to amuse them as they rode.

Melusin laughed. "Do you blame him? He is very possessive of me and jealous of you. Normally I find a man and take him and kill him within the first hour. But it's different with you, and he doesn't like it."

"But you will kill me. You said you would."

"Don't let's talk of that," she said. "Not now."

The horses trotted down the forest road. All around the trees slept a drugged sleep as if the coming of the Lady Melusin overwhelmed even them. Even the stream flowing beside the road ran sluggish and slowly, iced over with a coverlet of snow-crystals until it too was locked up by Melusin's magic.

"Where are we going?" asked Tristan.

"To the hamlet. It's just a few houses, a place called called Tregerec."

"I don't know it."

"No."

They rode on, and then Tristan saw a cluster of rude huts — roughly made dwellings of wattle and daub with thatch roofs. When they came up to the nearest house, Melusin dismounted.

"Leave your horse here," she said.

Tristan tethered Jezebel to the rail on the house's balcony.

"Come," Melusin said.

Tristan followed her. She looked at the first house and gave a curious movement of her head as if she were sniffing. "Not this one," she said.

She walked on. They came to the second, then the third house, and still she didn't find what she wanted. Then she said, "This one."

She went to the door and tried it. "Locked," she said. "They must have been afraid I would come." There was a cross on the door.

"Good Christians," Tristan said.

"I do not fear the cross," Melusin said. "Wait while I open the door." She stood as if preparing a charm, and then she said, "No. I have a better idea."

She smiled at him. "I told you I would teach you how to weave magic into your music. Play this." She hummed a series of notes. They were simple enough, but Tristan heard strange sounds behind the ordinary music. There were notes of opening and revealing. They hung in the air like the thrumming of tuning forks.

Tristan went back to Jezebel and fetched his lute. He played the music she had sung, copying it note for note, but it was deeper and stranger than any music he had played before. It was as if the door listened to the music, and when he was finished, the door swung open. Tristan stood open-mouthed.

Melusin said, "I could have opened it with a charm, but I want to teach you the power you could have. When I have taught you, you will be able to achieve anything with the sounds of your art."

"But why make me powerful?"

"I will answer that later. Soon we will go into the house, but first I want to teach you a tune of sleeping."

And she taught him the tune. He was talented and learned it as quickly as the tune of opening. Once he had mastered it, she said, "Come."

Tristan followed Melusin into the rough peasant house and felt the inhabitants' eyes watching them with a silent terror. He heard the sudden animal sobbing of the daughter. Then he saw the woman of the house holding her infant daughter in her arms. Her face was twisted in pleading. Tears ran down her cheeks. Her husband stood, shaking and silent but brave, holding a pitchfork as if that could ward them off.

"Melusin..." Tristan said.

"Play!" she commanded.

He played his lute, and the eyes of the peasants grew heavily and finally closed. Soon they fell asleep, chins lolling on chests, snores erupting comically and incongruously, given what was about to happen.

"It's kinder for them to sleep," Melusin said. "I bear them no ill will."

"Kinder? Like stunning animals in an abattoir before the slaughter?" he said icily.

"I know you are being sarcastic," Melusin said, "but yes. Exactly. I will take only the father. The children need their mother."

"The children need their father too."

She shrugged. "I need to feed, or I will die. Will you watch?"

"No," he said. He was powerless to stop her, and he knew it. But worse than that, he understood why she did what she did. She was like any predator. Melusin didn't hate her prey; she drank their blood so that she did not die herself.

Tristan went outside. His head was whirling. And then his stomach heaved, but he had hardly eaten, and all he managed to throw up was bile.

Melusin came out around fifteen minutes later. There was blood around her mouth and her eyes were cold as she watched him. "I did not think you were so weak."

"For being sick? What did you expect? Why did you bring me here, anyhow?"

"I wanted to test you."

"To test me? For what?"

She was lost in thought for a second as if debating whether to say what was on her mind.

He said sharply. "What?"

It seemed she thought better of speaking. "Come on," she said, "back to the horses."

They walked, and he said again, "What?"

She looked at him as they walked. "I have considered offering you the blood kiss. I have never made another vampire. Iblis did not allow it."

"And why would he allow you to give it to me?"

"He wouldn't."

"Well, then."

"Help me mount," she said.

He made a cradle for her foot with his hands. Melusin could mount the horse without his aid, but it was another test of his servitude, or perhaps his devotion to her.

"Tristan, you are not a stupid man." She was hinting at something, and he was missing it.

He was baffled. "Speak plain."

She stared at him. "I want you to kill Iblis and become my mate."

THEY DID NOT SPEAK of it again until they returned to the Tower. Invisible servants took the horses. Tristan noted carefully where the horses went, to the right of the tower. He thought that he would find the stable that way. Then Tristan and Melusin went to the room where they had first met. There was food for him—ripe red apples and grapes. Tristan took a quick bite from a crisp apple, and where the blood-red skin broke, he saw the white flesh underneath.

If Iblis was in the Tower, there was no sign of him. Tristan went to the door, opened it and looked down the stone stairs. He could only imagine the state of Arc'hantael and Yann in the dungeons below. Iblis might be with them now. He hoped they still survived, but he knew Melusin would not allow him to check and any demonstration of his care for them would be used by her against them.

Melusin decided she wanted to play chess. Tristan saw for the first time there was a chessboard in the room. The squares were made of ebony and ivory, and the pieces were of gold.

Melusin played well. He didn't. He was close to losing and frustrated at his inability to concentrate on the game.

She said, "It's a pity you are squeamish about blood."

He snorted. "Why a pity?"

She reached out and stroked his hand. "Because I will live forever and you will die, unless I make you like me."

"Unless I accept your blood kiss?"

She took his hand almost tenderly. Her black eyes were filled with love. It seemed as if she had charmed him, but he had won her dark heart in return.

Then he said, "How do I kill him?"

"Not so loud!" she hissed. "The walls have ears; so does the raven."

Behind her, the bird shifted on its perch. "Though he loves me best," she added, turning to look at it. She lowered her voice. "This is what you must do. Go into the forest, cut a branch of rowan wood. Sharpen it. Then come to him while he sleeps."

"I can't get out of the Tower when you sleep."

"I think you can."

He realised she meant the musical charm of opening she had taught him.

"I could kill you too," Tristan said. "While you sleep."

"You could."

"Do you trust me with your life?" he asked.

She let go of his hand. She seemed surprised at herself. "I must do."

"Then you are very foolish," he said.

She chuckled. "Or cleverer than you think."

For the first time, she made him laugh spontaneously.

"I'm pleased I can make you laugh," she said. "But it won't stop me beating you." She moved her queen and checkmated his king. "And now, days comes and I sleep. There are rowan trees along the path to the north. About two hundred yards."

CHAPTER

# SIX

And when she left, the night left with her. Sunshine streamed in through the narrow window, casting an oblong glow on the floor and across the wall. Tristan was very tired. He hadn't slept for hours. He looked at the bed and longed for it, but he had to go out into the forest. He took his lute with him. When he got to the gate of the Tower, it was still locked. This time, instead of pushing with his shoulder, he plucked the strings of his lute, and he wove the magic sound that Melusin had taught him. The Song of Opening echoed in the stone entrance hall, and as its notes died away, the door clicked and slowly, of its own volition, swung open.

Outside the summer sun reigned. There were rabbits on the grass outside which fled as Tristan stepped out. Though he meant them no harm, they did not know that.

Swallows and swifts twittered and shrieked around the tower as they dived and jinked, hunting midges. First, Tristan went around the back of the Tower. Jezebel neighed before he saw her and he went into the stall and fetched her, leading her out and then walking her to the start of the trail that led away from the Dark Tower.

Tristan mounted Jezebel and rode a short distance before he

recognised the rowan's serrated leaves and glowing-red berries. He knew it was a wood thought to have magical properties, said to be powerful against witchery and supernatural evil.

Tristan cut a stem as thick as a spear and used his knife to sharpen it and then, carrying it as a weapon, rode Jezebel back to the tower. He tied the mare to a tree in the clearing in front. "Wait here, my lass," he said, stroking her noble head.

He left his sword but took his lute in his left hand, and in his right hand, carried the sharpened rowan stake.

From the tower's entrance hall, he descended the stone steps to the dungeon. He went anxiously, fearful of what he might find. Before he came to the door, he called. "Arc'hantael? Yann?"

Yann answered. "She is dead." The boy's voice was heavy with sorrow.

"I'm so sorry," Tristan said. He stopped at the first door, not wanting to go further so that he did not have to see the girl's lifeless body. But he took a breath and stepped forward. Through the barred window. he saw there Yann cradling the limp form of his love, and Arc'hantael's blonde hair draped over his knees and fallen to the floor. Yann was staring at her as if he thought she might move again.

"He said that he would kill me next," said Yann. "But I don't care. There is no life for me now Arc'hantael is is dead."

"I have come to take you home," Tristan said quietly.

The boy laughed, but it was a hollow and dry sound. "I'm locked in, or haven't you noticed?"

Tristan took his lute and, once again, he played the Song of Opening. As the music played, its melody entered the door's lock, and twisted it open.

Yann's jaw dropped. "How did you do that?"

"It doesn't matter. Now let us leave. Quickly. I do not know how long we have before Iblis and Melusin awake, or whether they can wake when it is still daylight."

"I can't leave her."

"No," Tristan said. "We will take her back to her family." He went and helped Yann carry the dead Arc'hantael. She was light and, slowly and with reverence, they carried her out of the Tower. They laid her on the grass. Tristan said, "There is a black stallion in the stables around the back of the Tower. Go and fetch it and you can ride it home with me."

Yann didn't move. He was staring at Arc'hantael as she lay among the grass and woodland flowers. "She loved you," said Yann. "But you didn't care for her."

"That's not true," Tristan said.

"She's dead because she followed you here; I'll never forgive you for that."

Tristan couldn't meet the boy's eyes. "And I will never forgive myself." He said finally. He turned and walked to the door of the Tower. As he was about to enter, he called back. "Get ready to leave. I won't be long."

Tristan mounted the steps up to the top of the tower. He had the sharpened stake in his hand.

TRISTAN OPENED the door to the chamber where Melusin and Iblis slept. He pushed the door cautiously as if afraid they might wake and kill him.

But there was no sound, not even the sound of breathing. And the two were not slumbering in bed, they were dead in their coffins.

In the room were the twin sarcophagi, the reliefs on them cast in flickering shadows by the single torch. Tristan went to Melusin's tomb. He placed the rowan stake on the floor and pushed the lid.

Even though he had seen it before, revulsion at her dry, dead face, seized him. He stepped back but, forcing himself to do a task that disgusted and frightened him, pushed the lid further open. The sound of the stone grating open resonated in the room. Melusin's hands were folded over her chest.

Above them, he saw her robe where it covered her heart. That was where he would strike. He picked up the stake then. He had it ready to push into her dry body. Then he hesitated. Sweat beaded on his face, running into his eyes. He wiped them with the back of his shirtsleeve.

"The other first," he said to the quiet room.

He turned to Lord Iblis's tomb. Pushing pushed aside the lid, and the fierce demonic face stared up at him. He gasped, and his hand trembled. Iblis was more terrifying in death even than it was in life.

Tristan hesitated, but then he gained his resolve. Raising the stake, he plunged it into the sleeping vampire's breast. The thing shrieked loud with a noise that split the silence of the room. The scream echoed throughout every room of the tower. In final death, the vampire's hands reached to grasp the stake as if to pull it out. His eyes opened, and his mouth twisted in a frenzy of hate. But it was too late for Lord Iblis. The magical rowan wood burned the creature, and Lord Iblis's form, held together by sorcery, collapsed in on itself until it was only dust and bones, wrapped in a rich red robe.

And now it was Melusin's turn. Tristan removed the stake from the ruins of Lord Iblis's body. He examined it and found that despite the conflagration that had consumed Iblis, the wooden stake was not even scorched. Tristan walked to Melusin's tomb with deliberate tread.

The thing in the coffin was not the Melusin who had made love to him, who seemed to care about him in her own malefic way. He would end her. He had to rid the forest of her evil. He raised the stake and stood ready to plunge the rowan wood spike into her chest, but he hesitated again.

He suddenly thought of her tears when she stood regretful of the thing she had become. He thought of her innocence and how she had accepted the blood kiss from Iblis, not understanding what it was and what it would make her. Tenderness filled him. He thought of her eyes and her mouth, not dead like this, but animated and full of passion and humour, and he forgave her and lowered the stake.

"Maybe I do love you," he whispered. "Monster that you are. But I should be merciful if I would be shown mercy by others. I was no less monster than thee, Melusin. I was a vampire of kinds, not a drinker of blood, but a taker of honour, a seducer who treated all women as if they were merely prey. I owe you something for teaching me that at least."

He dropped the stake, and it clattered on the stone floor. He turned and left the room, running down the stairs to where Yann waited.

The afternoon drew on, and Melusin would wake soon, he knew. Perhaps she would forgive him for not killing her.

Tristan stood outside the Tower door and saw  Yann had fetched a wagon.

"I found it in the stables."

On the waggon, wrapped in a rich tapestry, torn down from the tower wall as a makeshift shroud, lay Arc'hantael, pale and dead.

The two horses were yoked, harnessed and ready to pull.

"Let's hurry," Tristan said. They jumped onto the wagon.

"The village should be this way," said Yann.

Yann pulled on the reins, and the horses set off. He urged them into a gallop. When they were rumbling down the path, he turned. "Did you kill them?"

Tristan studied his be-ringed fingers. "Not both."

"Not both?" said Yann. There was fear in his voice. "Which did you not kill?"

"I left Melusin."

"Why would you do that?"

"I don't know if I can explain," Tristan said.

"I can explain it — she has bewitched you."

"Maybe."

Yann was shaking. "She will come and kill us both now."

Tristan shook his head. "I don't think so." He turned and gazed back at the Dark Tower. "Though I think I will meet her again."

May time was gone, and the first flush of summer had left the Forest of Brec'helean as Tristan rode away from the the Dark Tower of Ker-Zu. They had found Yann's father out looking for him and once Tristan was sure that Yann and his dead love Arc'hantael bound for home, he took his own road, not knowing where he was going.

Drooping poppies studded the verges of the path, like a crimson army among the emerald stalks of wild grass. The sweet scent of musk rose haunted the avenues between the trees, and songbirds flitted from shade to sunshine through the undergrowth while Tristan Mab Bennog rode his bay mare Jezebel and hummed a song of his own composing. It was a song of love and loss, for he had loved, and he had lost.

# PART FOUR
# DUNGARVAN CASTLE

# CHAPTER
# ONE

On arriving at the British Club in Udagamandalam, some sixth sense made Captain William Thorpe hesitate at the door. He stepped aside, took a cigarette from the silver cigarette case, lit it with a flare of his petrol lighter, and waited.

Two men walked out, and Thorpe retreated into the shadow of a large Nigilri rhododendron so they wouldn't see him.

When he recognised the first man as William Stables, he pushed back further and cupped the glowing end of the cigarette in his fingers. When the light from the Club's door lit up the second man leaving, Thorpe grimaced and held his breath. It was Andrew Morris, a tea planter.

Thorpe stood silently while the Indian servant brought the Crossley RFC. The other two Englishmen climbed into the car after tipping the man, and Thorpe saw Stables was driving. From snatches of conversation heard through the open passenger door until it clunked shut, Morris was upset and angry.

Thorpe waited until the motorcar crunched over the gravel and down the Club's long drive. When its tail-lights were out of sight, with five minutes more thrown in for luck, he stepped into the yellow electric glow light spilling from the door of the Club.

The Indian servant started as Thorpe emerged from the shadows. Thorpe recognised the servant as Sandip and nodded. Sandip, regaining his composure, greeted him. "Are you for dinner tonight, Captain Thorpe?"

Thorpe grunted, cigarette smoke curling up. "I'm meeting Mr Thomason."

Sandip said, "Mr Thomason is already here."

At the reception desk, Thorpe dragged off his overcoat and handed it to a boy. The boy scurried off to some cloakroom with the coat. He gave Sandip a few rupees, entered the Club and, as he walked down the corridors, scanned the hall for anyone he knew. Seeing no one he knew well, he exhaled, drew on his cigarette, and stepped forward.

The Club was one of the social hotspots locally. The other place to be seen in Udagamandalam, or Ooty as the British called it, was St Andrew's Church. It was cold in here. The British Club looked like a Scottish Manor House and tonight had the climate to match.

Fires blazed in hearths in the several rooms he passed. Despite Ooty being in south-west India, it was at a height. This was why the British came: to escape the oppressive heat of the lowlands.

The strains of HMS Pinafore playing on a gramophone came from somewhere out of sight. Second-rate paintings of Cumberland and the Scottish Highlands decorated the magnolia walls. Drab plants stood in pots here and there. Thorpe passed many people he knew, but they avoided his gaze. He shrugged. What did he care about the judgement of such bores as these?

Kit Thomason sat nursing a gin and tonic, reading a month-old copy of Punch and smiling to himself at the cartoons. He glanced up when he noticed Thorpe. "Well-timed!" From the look on his face, this was a joke.

Thorpe frowned. "Well-timed?"

"You just missed Morris and Stables."

Thorpe sat, ordered a Scotch and ginger from the attentive Indian servant and said, "I saw them."

Thomason raised an eyebrow. "Pistols at dawn is it?"

Thorpe glowered. "Don't be absurd." The whisky arrived. He sipped it. "You think this is very amusing, don't you?"

Thomason laughed. "Doesn't matter what I think. You still did it."

"You don't know what I did."

Thomason grinned. "But you do."

They lapsed into silence, Thorpe scowling over his whisky. The waiter came to take their order: Mulligatawny Soup, Fillet of Sole, Mutton Curry.

As the waiter left, Thomason said, "I hear he sent Vivienne to Mysore."

Thorpe pushed his hand through his fair hair. "Makes no difference to me."

"Suppose not, now the deed is done. They do say she was distraught. They say she was going to leave him for you."

"Do they?"

"They say he wants his revenge."

"He can try to get it. I wouldn't put money on him winning though."

Thomason laughed. "They say he's burned up with jealousy."

Thorpe drew on his cigarette. "I never bothered with jealousy. It seems a pointless emotion."

"You just never loved anyone enough to feel jealous."

Thorpe sighed. He studied the tablecloth.

Thomason said, "But I think you had a little something for Vivienne—"

"—Will you please leave it?"

Thomason shrugged. "Of course, old man."

Thorpe drained his whisky and ordered another. He lit a cigarette while waiting for the drink and said, "I'm heading back to England."

Thomason seemed surprised. "Really?"

"I'm done here. These narrow-minded fools will always look down their noses at me if I stay in India."

"But what'll you do in England?"

Thorpe snorted. "Old man's got me something lined up in the City, but I thought I'd take a month or two off and do some touring first."

THORPE STROLLED through the crowded Bombay bazaar, not looking for anything special. He glanced at his watch. He had three hours to kill before he had to be on board and four before his ship departed.

He was perspiring and red-faced. This place was a maze. He stopped to get his bearings and looked around him. Today would be the last time he would see India, probably forever. Some impulse sprang into his mind that she should take home a souvenir. He hadn't come to the bazaar to buy gifts. He didn't believe anybody in England would want a gift from him. Maybe his mother, but why not buy one for himself as a memento of all he'd failed to do in India?

Thorpe wandered down the crowded bazaar alleys, but nothing caught his eye. He passed stalls piled high with spices: turmeric and coriander, cardamom and cloves. Then booths that displayed multi-coloured saris in silk and cotton.

As he walked, jostling and being jostled, the sweet scent of a flower stall replaced the aroma of spices. A dark-skinned man heaped garlands on the table in front of him. They lay like coloured snakes in piles on the counter. The stall-keeper was doing a roaring trade as men and women of all ages huddled round to buy garlands. When they'd purchased their bouquets, they pushed past Thorpe on their way to the myriad Hindu temples hereabouts. As well as offerings to the gods, young women bought sprigs of jasmine to twist in their dark hair. He smelled the jasmine as they walked by.

He walked on. The stalls repeated. They displayed spices, flowers, vegetables and fruits and then fruits, vegetables, flowers and spices, occasionally pans. He sighed and mopped his forehead with his handkerchief. The bazaar's smells and hubbub and kaleidoscopic colours disorientated him. The sudden alterations of sun and shadow were hypnotic.

Thorpe stopped to get his bearings. He was by a stall that sold small brass gods. Thorpe had been in India for five years but knew little of Hinduism. He paused to wipe his brow again.

A curl of incense floated up from a joss stick, and, in English, the bright-eyed woman behind the stall began her sales patter.

"Sir, perhaps Lord Ganesha? Lord Ganesha is very kind. He blesses beginnings and journeys." She offered him a small metal idol of the elephant god with a mouse at his feet. Thorpe didn't take the proffered icon.

"Perhaps you have a journey?"

Thorpe didn't reply.

She picked up another. "Or Lady Saraswati who brings prosperity?"

Thorpe shook his head. He started to move off, but his attention was drawn by a many-armed goddess riding a lion. She wielded swords in some of her hands, and others held severed human heads.

He smiled. "That's rather bloodthirsty."

The stall keeper gazed impassively. Maybe she didn't understand him. He pointed.

She said, "That is Kali Mata."

"Kali Mata?" Thorpe said. He looked at his watch. It was 10:30. The ship didn't sail until 3 pm, and he didn't have to be on board until 2 pm. He might buy this thing.

"You are interested in her?"

Thorpe shrugged. "I'm a soldier. It was the swords that attracted me. She looks warlike."

"Perhaps you have done wrong. Perhaps you have killed a man."

Thorpe exhaled. "I'm a soldier."

She smiled. "And a handsome man like you has broken many hearts."

He held the statuette, weighing it in his palm. "How much?"

The woman went on. "Mother Kali is very auspicious. She eats your karma."

Thorpe gave a wan smile. 'Karma, eh?"

"Your sins. Everything you have done shapes your life. That is your Karma. At death, all souls merge with Mahakali, and she purifies them, though there may be an ordeal."

Thorpe laughed. "I'm Church of England. We don't have that."

She was serious. "We all have karma, sir. We cannot outrun it, however far we flee."

Last night's whisky was making his stomach sour. He said, "I'll take it. How much?"

The woman named a tiny sum in rupees. It was such a small amount that he gave her a tip.

"Thank you, sir." She hesitated.

"What?"

"Nothing, sir."

"You were about to say something? Something about the idol?"

"No, sir. Not about the statue."

"About what then?"

"About you."

Thorpe frowned. "About me? What on earth would you want to say about me?"

"There is love and there is power. If you have one you can never have the other, and even a soldier must one day sheathe the sword."

Thorpe frowned, and without speaking walked away, but something made him look back. The woman was watching him, and she wasn't smiling.

Thorpe tucked the statue of Kali Mata into his blazer pocket. He grunted and walked on. His mouth was dry. Once out of the noise and heat of the bazaar, Thorpe clicked his fingers for a Rickshaw.

"Taj Mahal Hotel," he told the boy. '"Please."

At least, at the Taj Mahal, he'd get some English food. He planned to eat an early lunch, then head over to the port.

The ship sailed on time. Like the other passengers, he stood at the rail on deck and watched Bombay disappear into the afternoon. By the time they were out of sight of land, it was evening.

The ship was the *ss Ranchi* owned by the P&O line. The journey went via the Suez Canal rather than round the Cape of Good Hope.

It took just short of two months before Thorpe set foot on dry land at Tilbury. He made no friends on the voyage home but read a lot of books. He spent a lot of time drinking gin on his own and staring over the bow rail at the memory of places and people he'd left behind.

When he got back to England, he bought a car. When he had his car, he went touring. He headed to Scotland. He didn't know why.

CHAPTER

# TWO

The man in Glencoe that morning warned Thorpe not to take that road, but Thorpe smiled and pointed at his Aston Martin Sports. "She's a good car. She can handle anything these roads can throw at her."

The man shook his head and watched Thorpe head down the pass. At Ballachulish, when he stopped for water and told them his plans, folk repeated that the road was too dangerous for motor vehicles. Thorpe shrugged. "I'll be fine."

The woman in the hotel at Auchindarroch where he had his early lunch told him that he should keep the speed down if he insisted on taking the car on that road, but he just laughed. When he'd gone, she turned to her husband and said, "That young man has a death wish."

Captain Thorpe was confident in his driving, but he wasn't as skilled as he imagined, and he was also angry.

Coming round a sharp bend too fast he saw a woman standing in the middle of the narrow road. Thorpe yanked the Aston Martin's wheel left and then right, but lost control. Time slowed down as the car skidded and all he could do was jam his foot on the brake. He hit a rock. The sudden noise was so alien in that remote place, a blow of metal against stone. The shearing noise of the engine cowling coming off screeched like a ripped soul.

After the crash, the echo repeated against the mountain buttresses like a cannon, the sound rolling down the glen to the sea: a hundred gun salute announcing the accident.

Finally, the noise faded, leaving only the sound of steam hissing from the shattered radiator. In a curiously delayed reaction, ravens lifted in slow alarm from the crags. They circled above the stricken driver, but he wasn't yet dead. They wheeled in a leisurely circle; they were prepared to wait.

The open-topped Aston-Martin was on its side, wedged against the rock, buckled wheels still turning, and on his side in the soft moss at the side of the narrow Highland road, lay the ejected driver. The passenger seat was empty.

The July sun was not yet at its noon-day zenith but still hot. The clear water of the burn gurgled beside the road, washing over jagged rocks of grey and round stones of sparkling quartz, but he couldn't hear it. Bubbling on, the stream tumbled down the glen until it dropped in an abrupt waterfall.

The narrow road followed the burn as far as the waterfall, then it veered left to make a steep but safer descent toward the bottom of the glen and the sea loch that lay out of sight behind the mountain arm.

There was a dark stand of trees and a castle.

Captain William Thorpe lay in a dream between life and death. The sun sailed higher, and still he did not wake.

Thorpe didn't see the crofter and his son's horse and cart nor hear their rapid conversation in Gaelic as they jumped off the wagon and came running. They surveyed the crash, saw there was no one in sight but them and the stricken driver.

The Highlanders reached him, crouched over him and shook him and spoke what English they knew, but Thorpe did not move. He was somewhere far away.

The crofter got his son to unharness the horse from the cart because he knew Thorpe's condition was serious and beyond his ability to fix. He urged the lad to get on the big horse and ride it bareback, kicking its flanks into a gallop down the zig-zag road down towards Dungarvan Castle and help.

WHEN CAPTAIN THORPE AWOKE, the first thing he was aware of was his thumping head. The next thing he was aware of was that he lay in an old-fashioned bedroom in an old-fashioned bed. Standing around the bed was a small crowd of concerned faces. Thorpe's vision swam into focus. Bending over him, was a man in a three-piece tweed suit, with thin ginger hair.

To the right of this man stood a blonde woman of around forty-five. She was strikingly beautiful with wavy hair and blue-grey eyes. She had an air of great authority.

To her right was a younger woman, dark-haired, also lovely. Thorpe's gaze lingered on her. Her hazel eyes seemed to penetrate him. She had shining hair that fell in a wave to her shoulders, and she wore a cotton summer dress that emphasised her slim figure. She was just his type, and she reminded him of someone: a name just beyond memory for now.

Behind these three, a young red-headed maid peeked to see the drama between the shoulders of her betters. The blonde woman said something in Gaelic to the maid and the girl nodded and left.

"He's awake," the blonde lady said.

"At last!" the dark-haired woman said.

Thorpe got up on his elbows. "Where am I?"

"Take it easy, old chap," the doctor said.

The blonde lady smiled. "You're my guest in Dungarvan Castle."

Thorpe rubbed his eyes. His shoulder hurt. "What happened?"

"You had a car accident," the doctor said. "That road is hazardous. You shouldn't have been driving so fast."

Thorpe grunted. "And who are you?"

"I'm Dr McKinnon. I live here in the castle."

"Dr McKinnon is my husband's physician."

"Edinburgh trained," McKinnon said.

Thorpe looked at the blonde woman. "And you?"

She smiled indulgently. "I'm Gráinne McScaigh."

"Lady Gráinne McScaigh," Dr McKinnon added.

Thorpe turned to the beautiful dark-haired woman. She was so familiar, but he couldn't yet remember her name. "You?"

She stepped closer. "You silly! I'm your wife!" She reached and squeezed his hand. He shook his head. Something wasn't right.

"My wife?"

But she grinned. "I'm Mrs Vivienne Thorpe!" Then with a strange smile she said, "Who else's wife would I be?"

Dr McKinnon looked at Vivienne and said, "He's had a bang to the head. It will take a while for his memory to come back fully."

Thorpe struggled up in the bed, bedclothes tangled around him. "There's nothing wrong with me."

The doctor looked alarmed. "Steady on, they only pulled you out of a wrecked car two hours ago."

Thorpe exhaled. "How wrecked?"

Lady Gráinne said, "My mechanic says he can fix it, but it will take at least a week."

"I'm on a motoring tour of the Highlands," Thorpe said.

"We..." Vivienne said.

"For how long are you touring?" Lady Gráinne said.

"A couple more weeks."

"You see, you do remember." Vivienne stroked his arm.

Thorpe winced involuntarily. He shrugged Vivienne's hand off him, then kicked back the covers and said, "I'm fine."

They watched him as he limped a few steps and then looked down at himself. He was wearing tartan pyjamas.

"My husband's pyjamas," Lady Gráinne said.

Dr McKinnon said, "I really do think you should rest. Get back into bed, there's a good chap."

"Thank you, doctor, but I will decide what I do." Thorpe supported himself on the bedpost, but winced and sat again.

Vivienne looked at Dr McKinnon and Lady Gráinne. She grinned. "That's typical William—far too courageous and manly for his own good."

"Your husband has a private physician? I don't see your husband here, though the world and his wife seem to be present in my room. What—is he a crock?"

McKinnon frowned. He was about to say something, but Lady Gráinne silenced him with a glance. She said, "My husband has a war wound."

"A soldier?"

"He was."

"Like you." Vivienne smiled.

"Not sure what I am now." He rapped his knuckles against his forehead.

Lady Gráinne smiled. "Perhaps if you take a little nap, you'll start to remember better."

Thorpe looked around the room. Rich drapes hung all round his four-poster bed, held open by velvet ties. The floor under his bare feet was of polished wood covered with brightly-patterned Persian rugs. There was no electric light. Instead, silver candlesticks stood on the old oak dresser, and a crystal chandelier hung in the centre of the room. The candles in the chandelier were half burned, their wicks black, and fingers of wax on their flanks now solid and cold. A potpourri of dried Seville oranges, with sticks of cinnamon mixed in, lay in a China bowl on the dresser. By the China dish sat a ewer and bowl for washing.

Thorpe muttered, "Is this the twentieth century or the eighteenth?"

Lady Gráinne chuckled.

Vivienne said, "He doesn't mean to be rude."

McKinnon snorted. "Doesn't he?"

"Where are my clothes?" Thorpe said.

"I hung them in the wardrobe," said Vivienne

"We'll leave you," said Gráinne. "Dinner will be at seven pm. You will hear the gong. If you feel up to it, you can wander outside beforehand. It's still a lovely afternoon."

Dr McKinnon said, "But you'd be better off sleeping until dinner."

Thorpe watched them go to the door, the doctor, Lady Gráinne and the red-haired maid. The door clicked quietly behind them. Then he was alone with Vivienne. He looked at her as if seeing her for the first time. She stood there and smiled back. Then she turned and went to the window that looked out onto sunlit mountains. The way she walked was full of confidence, self-possessed and sinuous.

"Nice place they've got here," she said. "Very grand. Old-fashioned but splendid."

His brow furrowed. "You were in the car with me?"

She turned. "Me?"

He nodded.

Vivienne shrugged. "I'm your wife. Where else would I be if not in the car with you?"

He looked her up and down. "But you weren't hurt?"

"No, I'm fine."

He grunted. "I don't remember the crash. The last thing I remember is a woman in a hotel in some village."

"Ah, yes."

Vivienne came over, smiling. She draped her arms on his shoulders, and he let her. She stared into his eyes, and he looked away.

"You need to concentrate on getting better," she said. "But I'm really pleased we've got time to ourselves at last."

"What do you mean?"

She gestured with her slim, well-manicured hand. "Well, there were always the others to get in the way before. Now it's just we two."

"What about Gráinne and what's-his name, the doctor?"

"They don't count."

She was close. She smelled sweet and warm, like roses and sea salt. He couldn't meet her gaze. Memories crowded for attention, but they were ill-formed and faded before he could digest them. He remembered nothing. She said she was his wife: Vivienne. Thorpe rubbed his eyes.

She stepped away and went to the window. "Should we go for a walk outside?" said Vivienne. "I've hardly seen the place. It looks divine."

"I thought they wanted me to rest."

"You said you felt fine."

"Well. I'm a little sore."

"Of course, if you don't feel up to it..."

His voice was sharp. "Of course, I'm up to it"

"Well, then."

He still sat on the bed. "Where were we heading? Before the accident?" he said. "That knock on the head has done something to my memory."

"Not sure. You know I never bother about directions. I always leave it to you, darling. This trip was all your idea. I don't mind where you take me, as long as you take me with you."

He struggled to his feet and limped over to the heavy window, its mullioned glass held by diamonds of ancient-looking lead. It was open, and the air outside was warm. The scents of summer drifted in.

The stone around the window was grey and solid. Through the window, was a view of the castle terrace and then beyond the terrace, the vista led his eyes into the jaws of the glen. And on all sides stood massed ranks of mountains. The sun was still high. These were the long days of summer, and in the Highlands of Scotland, it would be light even after 11pm.

Then his eyes caught a little bronze statuette sitting on the dressing table. He pointed. "I remember that at least." It was a hideous thing—a woman with many arms, some holding swords, others severed heads.

"It's yours," Vivienne said.

"I got it in India."

"Of course."

He stared at her. "Were you with me in India?"

"You ask such silly questions." Then she said, "But it's the bang on the head. The doctor said it was to be expected."

He remembered something. "You were with me in India." He pushed his hand through his hair. "I remember."

"Do you?"

"Not all of it. But you were with me."

Vivienne smiled. "I'm your wife. I'll stay with you as long as you treat me with respect."

"Respect?"

"You must respect me. You made me promise to love, honour and obey." She laughed. "Though there won't be any obeying."

He said, "I'll settle for love and honour then."

THORPE FOUND his clothes hanging in the wardrobe, where Vivienne already told him she'd put them. He took off his pyjamas and put on his shirt then his trousers. He drew out his silk tie from the wardrobe and knotted and tightened it. Vivienne watched him but didn't speak. Then he pulled on his jacket and winced. A smile haunted Vivienne's red mouth.

"Does my pain amuse you?"

She said, "Of course not."

He snorted and shook his head.

"You're in a hurry," she said. "Do you have anywhere to be?"

Thorpe muttered. "I want to see the damage to the car."

"Of course," she said. "I'll come with you."

He shrugged. "You don't have to."

"I'd like to. I almost lost you, after all. I want to make the most of our remaining time together, darling."

"Our remaining time? What on earth do you mean?"

She went to tickle him under the chin, but he pulled back. She grinned. "What do you think I mean?"

"I have no idea."

Thorpe checked himself in the mirror. He pulled his jacket straight, buttoned it and turned to the door. Vivienne got the door for him.

"I'm not a bloody invalid."

"Of course not, darling." She laughed, took his hand and twined her fingers through his. At first, he pulled away, but she wouldn't let him go. By the time she closed the door behind them, he had let her fingers stay locked through his.

Their room was on the third floor of the castle. The walls were of grey stone panelled with dark wood. Pictures of local lakes and mountains adorned the short corridor that led to the top of the stairs.

A grand staircase descended in front of them. On the first step, Thorpe halted. The stairs were steep. He teetered and brought his free hand to his brow.

"Are you all right, darling?" Vivienne said, squeezing his fingers.

"Fine."

"You looked unsteady."

"I felt dizzy. Must be the accident."

She smiled at him. "Must be."

"What are you looking at me like that for?"

"Like what?"

"Like a moonstruck calf."

"I love you." She tilted her head. "I hope you still love me."

He sighed and shrugged.

With her free hand, Vivienne stroked his cheek. "I'm so happy to have you back. You're mine now. No one else's."

They looked down from the top of the oak staircase. Thorpe gripped the bannister. The polished treads descended to the castle's entrance hall.

Suits of armour stood in the hall, and stags' heads were mounted as trophies around the walls. Heraldic displays of tartans and coats of arms with Gaelic and Latin mottoes hung between the stag's heads.

Thorpe and Vivienne descended the staircase and, as they went down, Vivienne commented on a dark tartan. Thorpe glanced at it. The family name was McScaigh, and the motto was *De Umbris Venio*. Upon the tartan was superimposed the image of a spear.

"The lady of the place is a McScaigh. It must be the family tartan."

Taking care where he placed his feet on the wide treads, Thorpe went down, Vivienne stroking his arm.

"Don't do that."

"I thought you seemed like you might trip."

"I'm fine."

"As you like, darling."

The entrance hall was floored in tiles in red and black diamonds. A classical statue of the Roman goddess Diana and another of Venus flanked the stairs.

Leading outside was a heavy studded wooden door that looked as if it could withstand a siege. It was partly open. Thorpe felt the afternoon sun's warmth and smelled the heady scent of roses coming in from the garden.

Vivienne cast her gaze around the entrance hall and peered down the connecting passages. "No one about."

Thorpe held back, but Vivienne tugged him with her as she approached the door.

Vivienne shielded her eyes as she stepped out into the day. Thorpe scanned the rose garden for someone to ask directions from. He heard the sounds of someone working, then saw a young man. He shouted over, "You! My car, do you know where it is?"

The man, who was about twenty, stopped hoeing and looked over to Thorpe. The man spoke with an understandable accent, but whose vowels betrayed that English was not his first language.

"Yes, sir," he said. "If you take the path to the left and follow it round towards the stables, you will find Muirdeach who is fixing your car."

Thorpe saw Vivienne cast a lingering glance at the young man who had now returned to his work. He imagined her admiring his short brown hair and skin tanned by his work outside and felt an unfamiliar twinge of jealousy. "Like him, do you?" he said.

Vivienne laughed.

Thorpe sneered. "I'm going to find this Murdo, chap. You can stay with your gardener if you want."

Vivienne said, "I'm coming along with you. I told you, William. I'm going to stay with you always now."

But he set off without her.

Thorpe was walking past the stables when she caught up. He caught the familiar stink of horses. It reminded him of India and the Army. Walking past the horses with their stamping and whinnying, he found his car inside the far stable. A door sat open to let out the heat and let in the sun. Another young man with a shock of black hair was bent over the engine. He was tall, healthy, and well-muscled. He looked up as Thorpe blocked out his light.

"You're Murdo?" Thorpe said.

"Muirdeach."

"That's what I said."

Muirdeach stared back at him evenly.

Thorpe said, "You're the mechanic?"

Muirdeach opened his left hand to show the spanner he held, then the right to show the screwdriver. He grinned. "Aye, I'm the mechanic."

Thorpe scowled. "How long?"

"You mean before the car is fixed?"

Thorpe snapped. "Of course, that's what I mean. Is everyone here an idiot? Is it inbreeding or something racial?"

Vivienne stroked Thorpe's shoulder. Thorpe saw her smile at Muirdeach.

He snapped. "How long before the bloody car's fixed?"

Muirdeach was unfazed. "I am thinking it will be at least a week. I will have to send for parts to Glasgow."

"Pah". Thorpe snorted. "A week? I can't bear to be cooped up in this place that long."

"I can only do what is possible," Muirdeach said. His manner was mild, and his blue eyes unconcerned at Thorpe's abrupt manner.

Looking away from Thorpe, Muirdeach smiled at Vivienne. "I hope you are enjoying your stay here more than your husband."

Thorpe saw her smile back. Thorpe glared at her. Was she deliberately trying to humiliate him? The conversation was over. He stormed out of the stable by the open door. Vivienne lingered. He hesitated, waiting for her, but when she didn't come immediately he stalked off.

After a few yards, Vivienne caught him and took his hand.

"He's only doing what he can," she said. "These are remote parts."

Thorpe fumed. "Did you hear the way he talked to me? In the Indian army, we would have had the natives horsewhipped if they spoke like that to an officer."

She said gently, "He's not a native, William."

"Well, what is he then? He's not English. What is that bloody jabber they speak, anyway?"

Vivienne squeezed his fingers, not letting them go. "William, let's go for a walk along the terrace, then we can go back and relax before dinner."

Thorpe said coldly. "You can go where you want. I'm going back to the room."

He walked off without looking back. But as he got to the corner, about to enter a tunnel of trees, he turned. She was gazing at him, smiling. She waved and turned to walk away.

If she thought she could play him like this, she had another think coming. Thorpe's jaw tightened as he watched her stroll down the terrace. When she was out of sight, he continued back to the castle.

CHAPTER

# THREE

The sound of someone clipping hedges drifted in through the open window. Thorpe's shoulder ached, and his legs were sore. He'd taken his trousers off to inspect his bruises. They were many. Then he'd found a three-week-old London Times on the side table and was reading the sports pages as he sprawled on the four-poster bed. When Vivienne entered, he glanced up. She had caught the sun while out on her walk, and her face was flushed.

"Go back to see your boyfriend, did you?"

She shook her head. "William, please don't be silly."

He glanced back at his paper, but when she went to undress, he put the newspaper down and watched her. He followed the flicks of her fingers as she unfastened her buttons one by one.

"The terrace is lovely," she said. "What a view of the mountains! And the smell of musk rose and honeysuckle was so sweet it was almost overpowering."

He still didn't speak.

She continued talking, taking off her dress and standing now in her slip. "There's a strange cave at the end of the terrace, with a deep old hole in the floor. It looks ancient."

He shrugged. "Places like this always have things like that."

Her eyes flashed. "But I bet this castle is haunted!"

"I don't believe in ghosts."

"You wait until you see one."

He grunted. "I'll be waiting for a long time."

"You old sceptic. By the way, did you find out where the bath-room is?"

"No, but it won't be far. Down the corridor, I suppose."

His eyes devoured her curves as she stood there in her underwear.

"I'm going to bathe," she said and walked over to the pile of clean white towels. Stooping she picked one up and wrapped the bath sheet around her. She strolled to the door.

He snapped. "You can't go out of the room like that. It's not decent."

She chuckled. "For your eyes only am I, William?"

"You're my wife. Only I get to see you like this."

"I can do what I want, William, walk where I want, dressed as I want. Be who I want," she said.

He glared. "Of course you can't. Not if you're my wife; you'll do what I damn well tell you."

"Not if I'm your wife? What a strange thing to say: of course I'm your wife. But, remember, I do as I wish, not what a man tells me."

Vivienne cocked her head, grinned and turned. She opened the door and wandered half-naked down the corridor while he watched.

Thorpe crumpled the newspaper in two hands and hurled it against the wall.

As she walked away, he could even hear her humming. Anyone might hear her humming, and they might go find out who it was, and if they did, they'd see her. They'd see her like that.

As she turned out of sight, Thorpe stood up as if to go to the door. He should grab her, twist her arm and drag her back. But he stopped himself. He wouldn't give her the satisfaction of thinking he cared that much. He went to the window and stared out. There was the brown-haired boy still clipping the rose bushes. Thorpe gripped the sill hard, fingers whitening. He spat. "Bloody, peasant." Then more quietly: "Bitch."

Composing himself, he bent down to pick the crumpled newspaper and tried to pull the pages straight. Then he sat in the window seat to read them. His eyes followed the lines of print, but the words wouldn't go in and he had to re-visit every passage. His eyes kept flicking to the door. Finally, with a grunt, he threw down the paper and drummed his fingers on the windowsill. Listening to the click of the shears and the twittering of sparrows in the eaves, he clamped his hand to his eyes and swore. Then he looked at his watch again. After another minute, he got up and opened the room door to stare down the empty corridor. He slammed the door shut and threw himself on the four-poster bed.

The clicking of the shears outside stopped.

Lying on the bed, Thorpe stared at the plaster moulding of the ceiling. His eyes traced it all around the corners and the edges of the room. When that was done for the third time, he blew out air, swung his legs from the bed and jumped up. Landing on his sore foot, he winced.

Then a memory returned. It was of Ooty and a tea-planter named Morris. This Morris was connected to Vivienne. He chewed his thumb. Had Vivienne had an affair with Morris? He remembered that Morris had been scared of him, that was one thing. But Thorpe knew he intimidated other men. He relished the power his violent reputation gave him. That's how he'd managed his Company in the Army.

But that was in India. It all seemed like a dream now.

His eye caught the statue of Kali Mata where it sat on Vivienne's dresser. He snatched the statuette and thrust Kali Ma beneath the socks and shoved the drawer shut.

She still wasn't back. He checked his watch again. What was she doing? Who was she with? Perhaps she'd made an assignation to meet the mechanic. She'd liked him, that damned Scottish Murdo. He stared at himself in the mirror. He needed to get a grip.

This was stupid. He balled his fists so tight that the fingernails dug into the palms. This was absurd. It was ridiculous. Thorpe stared at himself in Vivienne's mirror. No woman had made him feel like this before.

But he would not dignify her games by letting her know how agitated her teasing made him.

He started to get ready for dinner. He took off his tweeds and hung them in the wardrobe. Then he washed with the ewer and shaved in cold water with the cut-throat razor from his shaving kit. He had on his shirt and underwear but not his trousers.

Halfway through his shave, Vivienne returned, her dark hair wet and shining. She stood, still swathed in towels and nothing else. "I had a lovely bath," she said.

Scraping the lather from his cheek, he grunted.

Vivienne unwound the towels and dropped them in damp heaps on the floor. Thorpe watched her in the mirror as he shaved. He saw the dark triangle between her legs and the soft shake of her breasts. He moved slightly to see her better and nicked himself. A bead of bright blood rose up at the wound.

Vivienne went to her wardrobe and got her black-sequinned dress. She held it up by the window to admire it.

He stopped shaving. "Someone might see you." He said.

"I don't think so. We're too high up for them to see in."

She ambled across the room to her dressing table.

Thorpe put down his pearl-handled razor beside the bowl. He wiped the remaining soap suds from his face with the blue towel. Then he dabbed the blood away and put the towel down.

He reached for the matching pearl-backed hairbrush and brushed his blonde hair, still watching her.

Vivienne sat on the chair by her dressing table. She rolled on her stockings and clipped them to the suspender belt. Her skin was olive. He thought about how succulent and yielding it would be.

He turned to face her. He wanted her, and he wanted to punish her as well. He would teach her who her master was. He would teach her to respect him. He couldn't remember when they'd last made love. "Vivienne," he said.

She looked at the swollen state of him and raised an eyebrow. Then she smiled and kept on dressing.

"Vivienne," he repeated.

Her long elegant legs were now encased in silk. She pulled black French knickers up round her soft buttocks then stooped for the black brassiere. As she moved, he saw her swaying breasts: white and round, topped with the nipples like dark cherries.

He stepped over to her and snatched her elbow to jerk her towards him. "Don't tease me." He hissed.

She grinned.

His mouth twisted, and he yanked her up from her seat.

Vivienne tried to resist, but Thorpe was stronger. He pulled her to him and gripped her hips. He pressed himself against her and shoved her to the wall. With her back to the plaster, he pushed himself into her so she could feel him. His right hand was on her breasts, and his left tangled through her wet hair.

At first, she let him kiss her. He could feel the smile in her mouth as she played with his teeth and tongue. He wound his fist in her black hair, and she didn't prevent him. He cupped her full breasts, but then she said, "No."

Thorpe didn't stop; he couldn't stop.

She put her fingertips against his chest and pushed him away.

He staggered back, astounded. Then he moved forward again.

She took his shoulders forcibly and pushed him away. "I said— no." She was still smiling.

His mouth twisted in a snarl. "But you're my wife."

She met his stare with eyes as black as a snake's. Her mouth was half-open and amused, but she shook her head. "There's a lot you need to learn about women, William."

He spluttered. "I'm your husband. I have rights."

Vivienne touched the tip of her finger on his bottom lip. Her hazel eyes stared into him. "I am my own mistress. I decide when and who I want to fuck."

The Anglo-Saxon word stung him like a whip. He stepped back. "What did you say?"

"You heard. Get dressed," she said. "And put that away."

She reached down and playfully twisted the end of his hard penis. Then she let it go. "If I have a use for it later, I'll let you know."

He raised his hand.

She shook her head. "You wouldn't hit a woman, William. That's not in your code."

He lowered his hand but spat. "You bitch."

She moved away and picked up her slip. "Now hurry. They'll be ringing the gong soon, and I still have to dress."

DINNER WAS SET out on the long table in the Baronial Hall. The room was huge, with a high ceiling and a gallery running around it. Someone standing on the gallery could look down on the diners unobserved, but, glancing up, Thorpe didn't see anyone this evening.

More heraldic designs adorned the walls. A crisp white linen cloth covered a long table of dark wood, and crystal glasses were set by each dinner place. Silver cutlery lay on three sides of each setting. Gleaming six-armed candelabras stood along the middle of the table, candles already burning. The thick walls and small windows of the Baronial Hall meant the room stayed dim, even though outside the summer still light lingered and the candle flames flickered in an unfelt draught.

Thorpe and Vivienne were not the first to arrive. As they entered, a handsome, patrician-looking man with clipped greying hair and beard that had once been fiery red sat at the head of the table. He wore a black dinner-suit with a white tie. At the opposite end of the long table, sat the blond-haired woman Thorpe recognised from when he woke. He remembered she called herself Gráinne.

The man rose and came to greet them as they came in. First, he greeted Vivienne by kissing her hand, saying. "Mrs Thorpe. You are as lovely as my wife led me to believe."

Then he extended his hand for Thorpe. Thorpe shook it. The man had a grip as firm as Thorpe's own.

"Captain Thorpe," he said, "How delightful to meet you. I'm only sorry about your car. I hope we can make up for the inconvenience."

Thorpe dropped the handshake. "This is your castle?"

Vivienne glared at Thorpe. "Darling, you shouldn't—"

The man nodded. "I am Eachann McScaigh. I have the honour of being Laird of Dungarvan and its estate."

His wife, Lady Gráinne, nodded at Vivienne as she took her seat. Thorpe sat down beside her.

Next to Lady Gráinne, Thorpe recognised the quack-doctor, McKinnon.

Lord Eachann said, "Captain Thorpe, this is Dr McKinnon—"

"—we've met," Thorpe said.

"And this," Lady Gráinne said, "is Mr Alastair McDonald."

She indicated a fresh-faced young man with blond hair. The young man's eyes darted between Thorpe and Vivienne. He clasped his hands on the table before him as if he didn't know where to put them. He didn't speak, he just blinked.

Lady Gráinne said," Alastair is our guest here while he does some academic research. He's a local boy but belongs now to the University of Edinburgh."

The young man stammered. "Pleased to meet you, Captain Thorpe, Mrs Thorpe. Lady Gráinne is a wonderful hostess. I'm sure you'll enjoy your stay here. Dungarvan has a marvellous library. Lord Eachann has collected many volumes on Highland and Gaelic myths and folk tales. That's my subject."

His speech frothed forth, jumping from subject to subject. Thorpe thought this Alastair McDonald wouldn't last long in the Army.

As McDonald prattled, Thorpe surveyed the room. Nothing he

saw attracted his attention until his eyes rested on the maid. He recognised her as being in his room with the others when he woke. She stood in the corner of the hall. She was pretty. Noticing the direction of his gaze, Vivienne slipped her hand over to cover his. Thorpe let it stay. For a second he thought a secretive glance passed between the two women, but of course they didn't know each other. Women knew things anyway, some kind of sisterhood they shared, keeping men out.

Now everyone had sat down, the male waiter with dark hair and the pretty maid brought the soup. He looked familiar. Vivienne was very friendly with him, how she smiled.

When the soup was served, steaming before him, Thorpe stared at the dish. "Cock a' Leekie," he said. "At least we can never accuse the Scotch of breaking with tradition."

Lord Eachann beamed. "Tradition is everything here," he said. "I hope you enjoy your meal."

Thorpe realised that the waiters were the staff that he'd already seen. The rose clipper, the mechanic, and the red-haired maid all wore different clothes for their different roles..

Lady Gráinne watched as Thorpe's studied her servants. She said, "Yes, we are so remote here that we have such a small staff. You will recognise Muirdeach from the garage, and this is Calum, whom you may have seen among the roses."

Calum poured white wine into Thorpe's glass.

"You've forgotten the prettiest one," Thorpe said.

"You mean Màiri?"

Thorpe raised his glass at the maid. She blushed. Lady Gráinne nodded at them, and the staff withdrew.

"Very gallant, William," Vivienne said. "To salute the maid."

Lady Gráinne said, "She's taken, I'm afraid—promised already to Muirdeach."

"The mechanic?"

Eachann nodded. "He's a fine lad. He could have had his choice, but he and Màiri are to be married in the Autumn."

Thorpe laughed and took a gulp of wine.

Conversation was sporadic around the table as they drank their soup.

Dr McKinnon was engaging Lady Gráinne in conversation. She looked bored. A few minutes into the meal, Lady Gráinne said, "I hear you were decorated for gallantry in the War, Captain Thorpe?"

Thorpe nodded but didn't look up.

"He doesn't like to talk about it," Vivienne said, "But yes, he was fearless."

Thorpe muttered. "Any officer would have done what I did."

Lord Eachann said, "Few men win the Military Cross."

Thorpe glanced at the older man. "You looked me up?"

"I hope you don't mind. I peeked in Who's Who."

Lady Gráinne said, "Tell us the story, Captain Thorpe."

"It's not very interesting."

"I'm sure it is," Dr McKinnon said.

Vivienne squeezed Thorpe's hand. He pulled his fingers away.

"Please tell us," Lady Gráinne said.

Thorpe grunted. "The Boche were pinning down my men, picking them off. Someone had to go and clear out the machine gun nest. I was best placed. That's all there is to it."

Lady Gráinne said, "You are lucky to have such a courageous husband, Mrs Thorpe. And such a handsome one. I'll wager you had a fight on your hands to land the brave Captain."

"I certainly did. But please call me Vivienne."

"And please call me Gráinne."

Vivienne patted Thorpe's hand. "But yes, there was some stiff competition. Lots of the other girls had their eye on him. I was lucky enough to be the one he finally chose. Though I believe he did do some extensive research."

"I can see why you're together," said Lord Eachann. "You are a very handsome couple."

"Yes, he's mine now," smiled Vivienne, taking Thorpe's hand again. "Mine forever."

Thorpe frowned.

The servants came in to collect the dishes and returned shortly afterwards to bring the main course. The main course was roast venison with a red wine jus. Màiri went around the table, pouring red wine to accompany it. Thorpe shook himself free of Vivienne.

Spearing a piece of venison, Thorpe said, "The mechanic told me it would be a week or so before my car was fixed."

"The problem is," Dr McKinnon said, "that everything has to come from Fort William, or if it's more specialised, even from Glasgow."

Thorpe nodded. "I understand that. I'm not dense."

Vivienne said, "You're very gracious, Lord Eachann, for putting us up."

"It's my pleasure," said Eachann. "Is your father in the military, Captain Thorpe?"

Thorpe shook his head. "He's a merchant banker."

"But you didn't want to follow in his footsteps? I would imagine that it would be quite lucrative."

"He wanted me to, but I prefer a life with more action."

"Preferred," Vivienne said. "William will be going into the family firm when we return to London. I need him to be safe now."

At the end of the main course, Lady Gráinne said, "Captain Thorpe, did you enjoy the War?"

Thorpe dabbed his mouth. "I don't think 'enjoy' is the right word, but it gave me a sense of purpose. I suppose I was suited to it in a way I'm not suited to peace."

"You must have seen some dreadful things," Gráinne said.

"I think sometimes difficult situations cause us to make choices. And good choices can ultimately make us better people," Vivienne said.

Eachann said, "Ah, Mrs Thorpe. How wise! You remind me of my ancestor—the one after whom I'm named. Alastair can tell the story better than me. Go on, Alastair."

Alastair McDonald blushed. "Oh, I don't know..."

"Please Alastair, you're the expert," Gráinne said.

"Oh very well," he said. He sat back and cleared his throat, looking pleased but nervous to be performing his party piece. "Once upon a time, as they say—but probably back in the ninth century, or so—no one really knows, but from my research, I think that's about it."

Everyone listened in polite silence. Thorpe followed the maid round the room with his eyes, watching her top up glasses.

"Well, in those days, Eachann Dubh Mac Scathaich: they called him 'Black Eachann son of the Shadow,' as it could be rendered, was Lord of Dungarvan. It's said that one day when he was hunting, he saw a dark snake of a type he'd never seen before. He followed the snake to the entrance of a cave he'd never noticed before. He went into it hoping to catch the snake, skin it, and add it to his many hunting trophies."

Alastair glanced around the table. They were all listening.

"They say he was a man who knew no fear. But at the end of cave there was no snake, only a pool of water, but water so deep that he could not see the bottom. By the light of his torch, he gazed down into it, and then he realised he was not alone. He turned round, and he saw a beautiful dark-haired maiden wearing a cloak of silk."

Even though they'd heard it many times, Lady Gráinne and Lord Eachann were gazing on with rapt attention. Dr McKinnon was smiling at the performance, and Vivienne seemed enthralled.

When the maid, Màiri, came close to Thorpe, she stood very close to him. He felt her thigh against the back of his hand. He was sure she pressed herself against him. He looked up at her but she was busy serving. Màiri stepped away and carried on with her work. Thorpe glanced at his wife who had not taken her eyes off Alastair.

Alastair continued, "So... the Lady of the Fountain, as she is called in the story, became Eachann's wife. But she had two sisters, each as beautiful as she was. She was dark but one sister was blonde and the other red-headed. Eachann was the kind of man who thought that anything he could take was his and he thought he could take his wife's two beautiful sisters. But his wife watched him with them, and she went to her sisters in secret. The women swore never to betray each other."

Alastair cleared his throat and went on. "It was clear to all that the Lady of the Fountain was of faery kind. She knew that Black Eachann was tempted by her beautiful sisters. She commanded him to be faithful to her, but he, like all men, took his own counsel on that."

Alastair blinked. "You will know that Celtic women were often powerful and rivalled their husbands in prestige. The Lady of the Fountain and Eachann Dubh were engaged in a war between the sheets."

"Go on," Lady Gráinne said.

Alastair continued. "At first he recognised that everything he had came from the magical success granted to him by his wife, and he was grateful. But he grew proud and thought he could fool her. She warned him that if he was unfaithful, she would punish him. He swore he was true, but she sent her sisters to tempt him..."

"Ah," said Eachann. "Here's the pudding!"

Black-haired Muirdeach served to the end of the table to Thorpe's right. He saw him talking to Vivienne as he put down the plate and thought Muirdeach lingered with Vivienne longer than he needed to. Thorpe watched him laugh and joke and saw Vivienne touch the young man's arm as she joked back. Then William saw Màiri standing by the door glaring at Muirdeach as he flirted with Vivienne. Her eyes were full of poison as she stared at her man.

The servants withdrew, and the guests ate.

Alastair said, "Well, to finish the story quickly—the Lady of the Fountain told Eachann if he was ever unfaithful to her she'd leave him."

"You told us that already." Thorpe said.

Alastair blinked. "Yes, but he was unfaithful with her red-headed sister. He denied it at first, but she knew. She gave him another chance and—"

"—and?" Thorpe asked.

"She said she'd kill him if he did it again."

Vivienne said, "And did he?"

"What?"

Thorpe rolled his eyes. "Did he go with another woman?"

"Yes."

"And?"

"The Lady punished him."

"How?"

"She cut off his..." Alastair's cheeks blushed beet red.

Thorpe snorted.

"Thingy." Alastair said.

"God give me strength," Thorpe muttered.

Vivienne laughed. "And that's it?"

Alastair frowned. "It was quite serious. He became an outcast and a wanderer for the rest of his life, which was short and brutal."

Vivienne turned to Thorpe. "So, you see, darling, the moral of the story is don't take your fairy wife for granted."

Thorpe raised an eyebrow. "Really?"

Vivienne said, "The Indians call it karma."

Lady Gráinne said, "And the Gaels call it geas."

"Superstitious peasants the lot of them," Thorpe said.

No one spoke. The silence grew strained, then Dr McKinnon said, "I hear young Calum's in trouble, eh?"

Lord and Lady McScaigh ate on in studied silence.

The doctor went on. "He is though isn't he? He's got the Fraser girl from the village in the family way. I hear he isn't going to stand by her and her father is gunning for him—literally, probably."

"We don't approve of what Calum did," said Gráinne, without looking up.

"I've spoken to him," said Eachann. "Told him to do his duty, but he has other ideas."

Gráinne's expression and her grave, grey eyes suggested the subject was now closed.

McKinnon went back to his pudding.

When he had finished his dessert, Thorpe put down his spoon said, "Is there a gymnasium here? I will need some exercise if I am to be here a week."

"There is no gymnasium," said Gráinne. "But you could walk the mountains?"

Thorpe said, "Walking's fine, but I will need something to get rid of my frustration." He looked at Vivienne, but she was talking to Dr McKinnon.

"We do have a fencing room," said Lord Eachann. "Though it hasn't been used for months."

Thorpe said, "That sounds perfect. I was a good swordsman in the Regiment." He looked over at Alastair, "But I'll need an opponent. You're the only one of roughly similar age. I fear Lord Eachann and Dr McKinnon are rather too old."

Alastair blustered. "I'm not really a fencer."

Thorpe said, "I'll show you. I won't take no for an answer. I'll see you down there after breakfast."

As Thorpe made his way out of the dining room after the meal, Vivienne walked a few paces behind. From ahead in the Entrance Hall, Thorpe heard the low voices of people arguing. They sounded angry but trying to keep their disagreement quiet.

As they got closer, Thorpe saw it was Muirdeach and the red-haired maid, Màiri. They looked over and saw William and Vivienne. They went quiet. Màiri looked at Thorpe and half-smiled. Vivienne saw the look and glanced at Thorpe, one eyebrow raised. Màiri glared at Vivienne, turned and went through the servants' door, slamming it after her.

Muirdeach looked over and grinned, but he was grinning at Vivienne, not William. Vivienne smiled back at him. "Good night, Muirdeach. Will you be serving us breakfast tomorrow?"

"I will, madam."

Vivienne said, "I will look forward to seeing you then. Good night."

. . .

LATER, in their room, Vivienne said, "I think you frightened Alastair with your fencing challenge. He's not really a fighter."

Thorpe laughed. "No, he likes stories and reading. But I could see that you took to him."

"I love stories and legends. That's why you got me that statue of Kali Mata."

Thorpe frowned. He'd forgotten that he got it for her. He said, "Don't worry, I won't rough him up too much."

Vivienne said, "What did you think of his story?"

"Wasn't listening."

"No, you were too busy looking at the maid."

Thorpe gave a derisory snort. "Well, you weren't paying me much attention."

"Don't be a baby."

Thorpe bit his lip. "I'm going out for a smoke."

THORPE STROLLED DOWN the staircase and out through the main door. Was she trying to drive him crazy with jealousy and desire? He walked without knowing where he was going. It was now dark, and the air was heavy with night-scented stock. He looked back at the castle, silhouetted against a clear sky that was still red with the fingers of day. All around the dark bulk of the mountains towered. Thorpe lit his cigarette. He drew on it, and the ember flared in the dark.

As he stood by himself and smoked, the warm evening air calmed his anger. He was by the servant's entrance.

Màiri started as she came out of the door and saw Thorpe in the shadows.

"Don't be frightened," Thorpe said.

He saw her grin in the light from the small window. "I'm not frightened, not by a handsome gentleman like you who would never do a girl any harm."

"Wouldn't I?"

"No." She studied him. "You seem upset."

"It's nothing."

"Affairs of the heart?"

He shrugged. "I just don't understand feelings, really."

"I've been upset too," she said abruptly.

"Oh?"

"Muirdeach. He has a roving eye."

"He neglects you then?"

"Oh, yes. He runs after every pretty girl he hasn't had, then he comes back to me."

"That's a pity. But you are still going to marry him?"

"I love him."

"Yes, it's a bit of a rum do, love,' Thorpe said. "I've never been much good at it."

Màiri said, "I was just going home. You can walk with me a way if you like."

"Do you live far?"

"Just on a farm in the valley."

"Do you live alone there?"

She shook her head. "No, with my father and mother and brothers."

There was something very sweet about her. She was attractive too, and she knew she was, but beauty isn't a crime, he thought, nor is knowing you're beautiful. He smiled at her.

"What?" she grinned. She was flirting now.

"You're a lovely young woman, you know. He doesn't deserve you."

"No, he doesn't. But that is my fate."

He said, "You're Mary, aren't you?

"Màiri, sir."

They strolled together. "I've just come from India. In India, in wild places like this, there are tigers."

"We don't have tigers here."

He laughed.

"There are the wolves. But they don't come close to the castle unless they are hungry. They sometimes take lambs and the wild deer."

He raised an eyebrow. "Wolves? I thought they were extinct in Scotland."

She shook her head. "Not here, sir. We have lots of things at Dungarvan that have gone from other places."

Thorpe thought her mention of wolves was an encouragement, a way of giving him an excuse to walk with her. Then he walked close enough so he could smell her clean hair and feel the heat of her skin.

"Want a cigarette?" he said.

"I'll have one, sir." He gave her one from his cigarette case and leaned in to light it from his. Màiri laughed. She smelled of warmth and life and night flowers.

"Let's walk then," she said.

"This way?"

She nodded.

"Are you sure you want me to?"

"It would be rude of you not to," she said. "With the wolves, and all."

"Ah, yes, the wolves."

She smiled. "Maybe tigers too. You never know."

They walked down the main pathway from the castle with its high box hedges. Then they came to a stile.

"Will you help me over, sir?"

Thorpe said, "Don't you normally manage it yourself?"

She smiled. "I just thought it would be nice for you to help me since you're here."

At her direction, Thorpe put his hands on her waist and lifted her over. Then he stepped over himself. They walked in silence until they came to the shadow of a field barn.

Màiri said, "I feel a bit tired. Do you mind if we stop for a rest?"

"A rest? We've only just started walking."

She laughed softly and leaned back onto the wall of the barn. Thorpe put his hands on the stones which were still warm from the day's sun.

She took his hand, and he let her take it. She put it on her breast. He felt it firm and yielding. "I like that," she said.

Thorpe cleared his throat. He smelled her sweet skin. He could almost feel her laugh in the dark. She put her arm on his shoulders and pulled him in. He hesitated.

"What if we kissed?" she said.

"We probably shouldn't."

"But you want to."

He sighed heavily. She was intoxicating. His lips were dry.

She said, "I want to pay Muirdeach back. And you are very handsome."

His arms were still round her waist.

She said, "Why should't you?"

"Well, I'm married."

"Are you?"

"Of course."

"I didn't know."

He frowned.

She said, "Wherever she is, she need never know."

Instinct was taking Thorpe over.

Màiri leaned in close. He felt her warm breath on his cheek. She smelled of summer and salt and flowers. She said, "I don't think you're a stranger to this kind of thing. I know your type."

His hands dropped to her hips. She knew his type.

"I can feel you're enjoying yourself." She stroked his arm. "You really are a very handsome man. And very brave." Màiri pulled him in. "It'll be fun."

He knew she was doing it out of jealousy to get back at her flirtatious boyfriend. He knew he shouldn't but she was attractive and clever and Thorpe's resistance melted, and he bent to kiss her. She returned his kiss with a hunger that threatened to eat him up.

They grew more passionate. He unbuttoned her blouse, kneaded her breasts then stooped to shower them with kisses. His lust raged in his loins and his urgency to have her almost overwhelmed him. He hitched up her skirt and pushed her against the wall of the barn. Then he unbuttoned his trousers and when they were round his ankles, she took him in her hand and guided him into her.

Màiri wasn't a virgin. She moaned in rapture as they coupled and kissed him back, passionately. With his hands grasping her buttocks, it took minutes until he finished with a grunt. He brushed her damp hair from her face.

She kissed him tenderly. "That was nice. I don't regret doing it with you."

Thorpe sighed. He bit his bottom lip. He dressed while she lingered.

"What's sauce for the goose is sauce for the gander too," Màiri said. "Remember that."

She turned to go but stopped. "And remember, this is our little secret," she said. He thought he heard her laughing as she disappeared into the darkness.

WHEN HE GOT BACK to the room, Vivienne was in bed. The moon had now risen. He undressed by its light and put his clothes on the back of a chair.

Vivienne stirred and said, "Where've you been?"

He whispered. "I couldn't settle. I went for a walk. Go back to sleep."

He got in bed beside her. He was starting to doze when Vivienne sat up.

"What?" he said.

"Where have you been?"

He rolled over and muttered. "I just went for a walk."

Vivienne didn't speak again, and within minutes he was asleep. Much later, he woke from a dark dream of snakes in the depths and quiet of the night inside the grey stone castle.

Then he fell asleep again. Later, he was aware of his wife's smell, the feel of her damp hair and the firmness of her sinuous body pressed into his.

Just before dawn, she was gone.

CHAPTER

# FOUR

In the morning, when Thorpe woke, Vivienne was not in the room. The day was bright outside, and he heard the small birds cheeping in the ivy around the stone window. Thorpe presumed she'd got up early and gone for a walk in the garden. She might be hoping to bump into that gardener again.

Thorpe glanced over to the dressing table. The little bronze statue of Kali Mata sat in pride of place on the centre of the dressing table, grinning at him with arms full of swords and severed heads. He'd put it away. Vivienne must have got it back out. He got up, snatched it and stuffed it back in the drawer. There was no sign of Vivienne's things. He frowned. Neither was there any sight nor sound of Vivienne herself.

Breakfast was laid out down in the dining room, but there was no one else there. It seemed everyone had either eaten earlier or was still slumbering. Thorpe selected devilled kidneys with scrambled eggs and toast. There was one waiter there—the mechanic, Muirdeach. Thorpe felt momentarily uncomfortable and to cover it up made conversation. "On your own?"

"Calum has not turned in this morning."

Thorpe snorted. "Must be serious. I don't imagine you strong Highland men ail for much." He turned around. "By the way, have you seen my wife?"

"No, sir," said Muirdeach.

Thorpe said nothing more, and when he had finished his breakfast, he made his way to the fencing room. The Fencing Room was past the Library and then through the Orangery. Lord Eachann had given him directions the previous night.

He walked through the Orangery and found Eachann tending the trees.

"Good morning, my Lord."

"Call me Eachann please."

Thorpe gave a small bow and said, "And please call me William."

Eachann said, "The sleep seems to have evened out your temper. But perhaps you were in pain. How are the aches and pains today?"

Thorpe moved his shoulders and his arms. "Seems fine."

"Must be the healing Highland air."

"I'm sure it is."

The Orangery was glazed over and hot already. Thorpe pulled at his collar.

Eachann pointed to the dark-leaved trees in their pots. "I love the citrus scent. It's very refreshing. We have apple trees outside of course, though you've missed the glory of the blossom. I take it you're on your way to fence Alastair?"

Thorpe nodded.

"He's been there for an hour," the older man smiled. "I think he's a little nervous."

"I won't humiliate him," Thorpe said.

"Of course not. He's a gentle soul."

"If you'd excuse me," Thorpe said.

Eachann looked at him as if trying to work out what kind of man he was. "Of course," he said.

As he was about to leave, Thorpe turned and said, "Have you seen my wife?"

Eachann frowned.

"Yes, Vivienne."

Eachann's frown grew deeper. "Erm, no. I haven't seen her."

"She won't be far," Thorpe said, and left to find Alastair.

WHEN HE ARRIVED in the fencing room, Thorpe found Alastair already practising with the dummy. He was wearing his lamé and gloves, but not his mask. He held a rapier.

"Good morning," Thorpe said.

Alastair looked hot and sweaty. He studied his sword and muttered, "Morning." He didn't meet Thorpe's gaze.

Thorpe went over and began to dress in his protective lamé and took his gloves. He spent some time examining the swords in the rack.

Alastair went back to his practice with the dummy.

"Done much fencing?" called Thorpe over his shoulder as he hefted the sabre he had taken from the rack, testing it for balance.

"A little. I was in the Naval Cadets. We did a little then as one of the senior officers was keen on it."

"It's a damned fine sport," said Thorpe. "I don't believe in exercise for its own sake—dumbbells and the like. A man needs exercise that will remove his aggression."

"I'm not very aggressive," Alastair said.

Thorpe grunted. "Nature built men to fight."

"Yes, if you believe in Evolution and all that. But what purpose has fighting now?"

"You need to be able to take what you want in this world."

Alastair laughed. "Not sure the Law is too keen on that—the 'taking what you want' stuff."

Thorpe ran his thumb along the sabre's edge. "Ah, the Law. I bet you obey all the laws, don't you? Anyway, here."

He reached out the sabre to Alastair who looked at it but didn't take it. "It's a little too heavy for me. I've only ever fought with rapiers."

"The sabre is a manlier weapon," Thorpe said. "Don't worry; I won't hurt you."

Alastair's eyes darted to the proffered blade. Thorpe still held it out to him. Alastair hesitated but then went forward and took the heavier sword.

"You'd better put your mask on," Thorpe said.

Alastair fiddled with it, taking three attempts to close the catch.

Thorpe called "Ready?"

Alastair's voice was muffled behind the mesh of the mask. "I suppose."

Thorpe shouted, "*En garde!*"

They began to fence. Thorpe tested his opponent. Alastair's technique was poor, and his stamina was poorer. But Thorpe went easy on him, checking him now and again with a touch to the mask or lamé. He even allowed Alastair some advantage so that he wouldn't be too discouraged. They fought for fifteen minutes or so. Thorpe prided himself on his physical fitness. He wasn't tired, but he could hear Alastair's ragged breathing.

"Do much exercise?" Thorpe shouted. "It's important."

"I walk," said Alastair.

"I didn't mean walking. Old women can walk. What about boxing? I was a member of a gentleman's boxing club in Mysore, and of course, I fence ."

Alastair was out of breath. He couldn't talk and fence at the same time.

Thorpe decided to be merciful and end it. With a flurry of flicks from his sabre and a lunge, he had Alastair against the far wall. He went inside Alastair's guard and touched the tip of his blade on his chest. "Yield?"

Without a word, Alastair struck at Thorpe's sword and knocked it away. Snarling behind his wire mask, Alastair slashed and swung. His attack was ill-timed and worse executed, but the speed and anger of his whirling blade set Thorpe back a step. Thorpe retreated, measured up his opponent, blocking slashes and cuts but then recovered his composure, and with deft use of his sword, cut left and right and came from underneath making Alastair recoil and stagger off balance. Thorpe pressed the advantage, jumped forward and pushed Alastair back further. With determined strokes, he drove the younger man to give ground until they were halfway down the hall, the only sounds now the grunting and the harsh clash of steel, then, after a weak slash from Alastair, Thorpe's lightning-fast riposte knocked the sabre from the young man's hand and sent it clattering across the wooden floor.

"Very plucky," Thorpe said, laughing.

Alastair went to retrieve the sword from where it had fallen, but Thorpe kicked it away.

Alastair lunged for the sword and would have come round to attack again.

"Enough," Thorpe said, removing his mask. "Bravo for your spirit," he said. "But remember not to lose your temper. That's how you lose the fight."

Alastair pulled off his mask. His face was sweaty and red, flushed and angry, and his eyes were raw with tears. Thorpe went up and offered his hand, but Alastair wouldn't take it.

"I meant it," said Thorpe. "Well played."

Alastair took off his fencing gear with his back to Thorpe.

"Suit yourself," Thorpe said.

Alastair turned, still breathing lightly. "Thank you."

"No problem. I enjoyed it. We'll have to do it again," said Thorpe. "You might win next time."

Alastair laughed. "I'll get the better of you eventually."

Thorpe clapped him on his shoulder. "Well said."

Alastair breathed out, nodded to no one in particular then rubbed his face with the towel. "I'm off for a quick wash. Will you be coming to the Drawing Room for coffee with Lady Gráinne? That's the normal morning routine."

Thorpe shrugged. "Why not? There's damn all else to do around here."

"You're on the third floor?" said Alastair.

"Yes."

"I'll show you a short cut. This place is enormous, and it takes time to know your way around."

Thorpe followed Alastair out of the fencing room and up a back staircase panelled in dark wood. There was a Turkey pattern carpet with brass stair rods on the stairs. Busts of Roman Emperors glared from alcoves every few steps.

Alastair pointed. "You see that door?"

It was a nondescript door. "Yes."

"That's a quick way to the Rose Garden if you don't want to have to come in through the Entrance Hall."

As they mounted the stairs, Thorpe said, "Have you seen my wife by the way? Damned if I know where she's got to."

Alastair was a stair ahead of him. He said, "Your wife?"

"Vivienne."

"Is she here with you?"

Thorpe frowned. "Of course she is. You were talking to her at dinner last night."

"Oh," said Alastair. He appeared to be about to say something else but stopped. Then he said in a very considered way, "No, I haven't seen your wife."

Alastair pointed out Thorpe's room. "I'll see you in the Drawing Room for coffee in about twenty minutes. Can you find your way?"

"I'll manage," said Thorpe. "Thanks for showing me the short cut. Doubt I'll remember it again though."

When he got back to his room, there was still no sign of Vivienne, or that she'd ever been there.

When Thorpe went down, Lady Gráinne was already in the drawing-room with Dr McKinnon. Alastair came in behind him.

Muirdeach served the coffee from silver pots, and they took it in bone china cups with cream and sugar. Comfortable chairs and sofas furnished the drawing-room. A black and white cat wound itself round the legs of Lady Gráinne's chair. Wide French windows gave a view down through the castle gardens, and beyond the castle terrace stood the mountains and past them, a faint glitter of blue water.

"I haven't seen this side of the castle before," Thorpe said. "I didn't realise you were so close to the sea."

"Technically the Atlantic Ocean," said Dr McKinnon.

Thorpe smiled thinly. "The sea's the sea to me," he said.

"Ah, but you're an army man, not navy! I should say a navy man would not have the same view—eh, Alastair?"

"I'm not in the navy any more," Alastair said.

Dr McKinnon chuckled. "No, you're an academic now, and a very promising one too, if what Lady Gráinne says is true. I was quite respected too in my time at Edinburgh, you know. I could have had a career at the University. I'd be a professor by now. But the ocean it is though. You of all people should know the sea from the ocean!"

"Does it matter?" Thorpe said.

Gráinne gazed out of the window. "I was brought up by the Atlantic in my youth."

"Where was that? If you don't mind me asking."

"In the southwest of Ireland. A long time ago." She sipped her coffee. "So I'm used to the wild Atlantic."

"I visited County Kerry once," Thorpe said.

"Near there."

"Charming place, I thought. Nice people too."

Gráinne smiled. "Thank you. You do have a hidden grace, I see."

Thorpe grunted.

"It's a compliment!" said Dr McKinnon. "Accept it!"

"It's such a nice day," Gráinne said, "I think we should open these windows. Though I fear they're a little stiff. Would you, Captain Thorpe?"

"Of course." He put his coffee down on the occasional table and stood up. With a slight effort, he had the French Windows open, and the outside breeze blew in with a refreshing tang of salt.

"Would you care to walk with me a while, Captain Thorpe?" she said.

Thorpe frowned. "Are the others not coming?"

Lady Gráinne smiled. "Just we two, for now. Would you?"

He nodded. "Of course."

THEY STEPPED through the French Windows and into the garden. Lady Gráinne led him through an orchard where there were stands of trees: apples, cherries and espaliered pears against the walls.

Thorpe gestured to the apple trees. "I should think these are beautiful when they're in blossom."

She smiled. "Yes, they are. But you've missed them this year."

They turned and walked down a gravel path along a terrace above the gardens.

"Have you seen Vivienne by the way?" he said as they walked.

Gráinne pursed her lips. "Vivienne?"

"My wife."

"I didn't know she was here."

Thorpe furrowed his brow. He stared at Lady Gráinne as if trying to see whether she was playing a joke on him. Finally, he said, "This is damned strange. She was at dinner yesterday, and you all spoke to her, and now I can't find her, and everyone says they haven't seen her."

Lady Gráinne gave a slight shrug. "As far as I knew, Captain Thorpe, you were on your own."

"No," he said, starting to become angry. "I was with Vivienne. If this is some kind of practical joke that you and she have cooked to teach me a lesson or something, then I must say I don't find it funny."

Gráinne was serious. "You were alone when we found you after your car crash. There was no one with you."

"That's absurd. Vivienne ate with us all last night. She slept in the same bed as me."

Gráinne shook her head. "I don't think so. Perhaps you should see Dr McKinnon again. You did have rather a bang to your head."

"That old quack? I don't think so. There's nothing wrong with my head, I can assure you."

Gráinne looked sympathetic. "People can act out of character after a head injury."

"Out of character?"

She kept on walking. "Or it can change their character. Sometimes people feel they are given a second chance after a serious accident—an opportunity to change."

They continued to walk. There was a silence, and then Thorpe said, "From your tone of voice, I think there's an implication in what you've just said. But I can't tell you what it is."

"Can't you?"

He shook his head.

She said, "I spoke to Màiri this morning."

"Ah."

"The maid."

"Yes, I know her."

Gráinne said, "The women of this castle are not here for your amusement, Captain Thorpe."

"Of course not." Thorpe frowned. In fact it was Màiri who had created the opportunity rather than him, but to say so would be ungallant, so he kept quiet.

Gráinne said, "I understand Màiri fell out with Muirdeach. Muirdeach is a ladies' man. She probably wanted to make him jealous."

"It's not for me to say."

"In any case, this matter is now closed, but I would be very displeased to hear of you abusing my hospitality again."

Thorpe stopped, about to defend himself, but he couldn't without casting a poor light on Màiri. Lady Gráinne seemed to think she was an innocent, and Thorpe didn't want to be responsible for damaging Màiri's reputation.

Lady Gráinne turned. "You are going to say something?"

Thorpe shook his head. "Nothing. Point taken. That's the end of it."

They came to the end of the terrace and stopped a while to take in the view. Gráinne seemed entranced by the scenery and stood in silence, admiring the mighty hills.

Thorpe was quiet. His cheeks were red.

After five minutes, Gráinne turned and offered her arm. "Would you lead me back? I want us to be friends."

"I just want to get my car fixed and be on my way."

"Without your wife?"

He frowned and rubbed his eyes. "You admit she is here then?"

Lady Gráinne said, "I'm sorry. I was teasing you. I shouldn't have. I know no one here called Vivienne."

He exhaled. "I assure you I am married and that she is here with me."

Gráinne pursed her lips. "It's important for you to make the correct moral decision."

"About Vivienne?"

"About everything. About how you deal with people."

"Women?"

"If you like." She continued. "People will make allowances for you. But there are only so many allowances anyone will make. Do you understand me?"

He didn't meet her gaze.

She said, "I don't think you're a bad man, Captain Thorpe. But it's not good for a man to always get his way; because then he doesn't know how to make difficult choices."

Thorpe cleared his throat. "A man gets his way if he has the strength and determination. I had it drummed into me at school and then in the Army."

"But the true knight mixes fearlessness and strength with compassion and mercy."

He snorted. "It sounds like the tales of King Arthur. I used to read those when I was a boy. Pity they're not real."

Gráinne said, "Let's go back to the others."

CHAPTER

# FIVE

When they got to the Castle's front door, a young woman emerged who Thorpe had not seen before. She wore a long cream dress, and her blonde hair was up. She was pretty, but she was not smiling.

"Oh, mother," she said.

"What is it, Fiona?" Gráinne said.

"Something terrible has happened. They've found Calum on the Terrace, near the Well."

"What do you mean?" Gráinne said, taking her daughter's hands in hers.

"He's taken very ill. I don't know what's the matter, but he's hardly moving, just muttering nonsense."

"Goodness me."

"Muirdeach found him. He hadn't turned up for work and wasn't in their lodgings. Muirdeach went looking for him when he'd finished serving coffee. Dr McKinnon's gone over. Will you come?"

"Of course." Gráinne paused. "This is Captain Thorpe, Fiona."

"The automobile accident man?" she said, hardly looking at him.

"Pleased to meet you." He gave her his hand. She shook it briefly. Thorpe said. "I'm sorry it has to be in this situation."

Fiona nodded but looked to Lady Gráinne. "Come with me, mother. It's awful."

Gráinne was halfway toward the door with her daughter. She turned and said to Thorpe, "Are you coming with us?"

"No," he said. "I'm going to search for Vivienne."

Lady Gráinne looked at him for a minute then turned away and went after Fiona.

THORPE WENT BACK to his bedroom. He checked in the wardrobe and found her clothes were gone. Her perfume was gone. Her shoes were gone. There were no effects by the washstand to indicate she'd ever been there.

He put his head against the pillow where she'd laid her head the night before, but instead of her perfume or the scent of her flesh, he smelled only fresh linen.

He yanked out each drawer with increasing violence and found nothing: no sign of Vivienne at all.

And then on the dresser—he didn't know how he hadn't seen it before—was a folded note. The bronze statuette of Kali Mata sat on it like a paperweight.

He recognised Vivienne's handwriting as he pushed the bronze figure away and grabbed the note. He flicked it open. It said simply:

I warned you not to be unfaithful to me, or I would leave. The next time you are unfaithful, you will have to pay a heavy price.

Pay a price? What the hell did that mean? He knew what had happened. Vivienne had stomped off in a jealous rage: somebody had told her about Màiri, and that someone was probably Gráinne. And that after denying Vivienne even existed. They were at some game, he knew it, but he couldn't fathom why.

But Vivienne was gone. A sudden agony wracked Thorpe and he was pierced by an unfamiliar emotion so strange that he didn't even recognise it at first. What was it: Remorse, regret, anger? He knew anger—but anger wasn't it all or even most of it.

He dashed around the room thinking of new places to look and then searching places he'd already searched. Between his frantic turning over every paper and opening every drawer just in the hope they might contain a clue to where she was, he kept looking at the door, as if Vivienne might push it open and walk in, smiling.

If she did, they would have a row, and then it would all be all right again. He would apologise and say he'd never do it again. She would be his again and not gone. He recognised finally that the feeling rushing through him was panic — panic that she might be gone forever.

Not having anywhere else to look, he stepped out of the room. He hurried down the short corridor to the top of the staircase they'd descended together the previous night. He took the stairs two at a time, getting to the bottom as fast as he could, then he half-ran through the whole castle. He rushed from the Drawing Room to the Dining Room, to the Library and to the Orangery.

Pulling open a heavy door, he found an unfamiliar room. It was a chapel. The room was quiet and cool with the air of damp and musty books. On the altar stood a strange symbol. He had presumed that the Lord and Lady were Roman Catholics, as many of the old Highland families were. But this was not a crucifix bearing the figure of Jesus. Instead, it was a slate slab with three women carved into it. The women were blank-faced with lentil-shaped eyes and lines for mouths. The carving looked ancient, and it looked primitive.

Thorpe stared at the image, then left, hurrying on in his search for Vivienne.

He stalked down the great hall flanked by classical statues, his feet echoing on the wooden floor. Despair flooded him. He could not see Vivienne; he could not hear her; he could not touch her; he could not smell her. She was gone.

Finally, Thorpe leaned on his arms against the wall and dropped his head. Whatever they said, he knew Vivienne had been with him. Then he'd done that stupid thing with the maid, and now she'd left him. When would he ever learn? When would he ever stop running after women? It wasn't love that made him do it, it wasn't even lust, it was always to prove he could, to collect women like beads on a string.

He stood upright and slowly walked on until, in a daze, he found himself back in the Drawing Room.

He slumped into one of the chairs and stared through the open French Windows. He felt the sea breeze on his cheeks. The sea tang mixed with that of honeysuckle and roses as the summer day drifted towards noon. He lost track of time. It was as if his grief had emptied him out.

He did not notice Lord Eachann enter and he started as Eachann put his hand on the top of his chair. "A wonderful view," Eachann said. "I never tire of it."

"No. It is lovely," Thorpe's mouth was dry.

Eachann walked over to the chair nearest to Thorpe's and turned it so that he too faced the open doors. Thorpe noticed Eachann walking with a limp. He remembered that Dr McKinnon was Lord Eachann's personal physician. The old man was either a hypochondriac or the injury was serious and long-standing.

They sat in silence for a while, Eachann gazing out. Thorpe saw him looking past the cultivated castle terrace, past the rocky green fields of sheep and cattle, until his eyes seemed to rest at last on the sparkling sliver of the sea.

Thorpe covered his eyes with his hand.

"You seem troubled," said Eachann finally, without turning his head.

"My wife."

"Ah."

Thorpe started. "You remember her?"

Eachann shook his head. "I haven't had the pleasure of meeting your wife. I'd presumed you'd left her in London. Though to be honest, in Who's Who, it doesn't mention you're married."

"Ah yes, you looked me up. Don't you remember her commenting on my war record when you raised it at dinner last night?"

Eachann said, "I'm sorry I don't. This is all probably the injury. Do you think perhaps you left your wife in London? We can send a telegram."

"No, she's not in London."

"You seem very certain of that."

Thorpe put his head in his hands. "Vivienne was at dinner last night here at Dungarvan Castle."

Eachann shook his head, still without looking at Thorpe. "No, I fear not. At dinner were myself, Lady Gráinne, Dr McKinnon, young Alastair and yourself. That is all. My daughter Fiona only came back from Edinburgh today."

Thorpe remembered suddenly. He patted his jacket pocket. "I have a note." He reached into the pocket where he'd put it.

"You have a note?" Eachann said.

"Yes." Thorpe rummaged through his pockets, but even though he turned them all out, there was no note.

Eachann looked sadly on.

Thorpe snapped. "She was here."

Eachann went back to staring out of the French Windows. "Perhaps you saw the ghost."

"She's no ghost. Vivienne is as real as you or me."

Eachann said, "But there is a ghost, you know. This castle is haunted by the spirit of a woman."

Thorpe said sharply. "I know my own wife."

Eachann said, "I'll ask Dr McKinnon to take a better look at you."

"She was here."

"I don't mean to offend you, but what do you remember about her?"

"What do I remember? Everything. Her smell, the way she walks, the colour of her eyes. Her voice. Her black hair. Everything."

Eachann ran a finger over his bottom lip. "Your black-haired wife?"

"Yes, black-hair with hazel eyes."

"She sounds pretty. Do you love her very much—this wife of yours?"

"Yes. I do love her." He paused. "I don't always show it, but I'm not demonstrative; that's not my way."

"Does she know you love her?"

"Of course she knows I love her."

Eachann said thoughtfully, "Perhaps it's lucky she didn't come with you. That accident was very serious. If she'd been with you in that car, she could have been killed. So could you in fact."

"I'm fine. I haven't come to any harm."

Eachann looked at him for a second, then said, "Would you care for a whisky? From the local distillery? I know it's early but what with poor Calum, I think I need one."

Thorpe rubbed his eyes. "Thank you. That's very kind."

Eachann stood, his limp evident. "The servants are all busy. I'll fetch it myself."

Eachann came back with a bottle and two crystal glasses. He poured a good measure of the golden liquid for Thorpe who took a mouthful and felt the soft burn of the old whisky settle on his mouth and throat.

Whisky poured, Eachann sat. "Tell me, and I don't mean to be rude, but where were you married?"

"Where were we married?" asked Thorpe. He sat in silence as the grandfather clock ticked the minutes by. "Where were we married...?" He forced a laugh. "Mysore? Ooty? Surrey?" He took another sip of whisky. "Ask me another."

"Very well—where are her people from?"

Thorpe shrugged. "London, I think. Or Surrey. I don't think I've ever met them."

"You haven't met your father and mother-in-law?"

Thorpe smiled without any humour. "It seems odd when you put it like that, but I don't think I have."

"They can't have been at the wedding then."

"No, I suppose not." He sat forward. "It was in Ooty—in St Andrew's Church. They were in England. They couldn't make it."

"Couldn't you wait for them?"

"No, we couldn't."

"Do you remember why not?"

Thorpe rubbed his forehead. He took a sip of whisky. "No. I can't."

Eachann said, "Does she have brothers and sisters?"

Thorpe shook his head. "I don't think so."

"What's her favourite colour?"

Thorpe smiled. "Ah, I know that—gold. She loves gold: golden flecks in the gravel of a clear mountain stream."

Eachann pursed his lips.

"You ask a lot of questions," Thorpe said.

Eachann laughed.

The door opened, and the young blonde woman entered.

"Ah, Fiona. This is Captain Thorpe."

"I know, Daddy. We met earlier."

"Father," said Fiona. "Dr McKinnon is with Calum. He's still making no sense, but he seems to be out of danger. The doctor wants to see you about him."

Eachann rose stiffly from his seat. "Very well. I won't be long. Will you entertain Captain Thorpe in my absence?"

"Of course." She smiled. "Could I have a whisky too?"

"It's not really a lady's drink. Your mother wouldn't approve."

Fiona winked. "Don't tell her then, pop."

Eachann grinned. "Oh, Fiona, you are incorrigible." He waved at the bottle. "Help yourself."

Eachann walked out of the room, using his stick.

"Terrible about the boy," Thorpe said.

"Goodness, I know. I grew up with him. He is a bit of a philanderer, but he has a good heart really." Her eyes were red, and it was apparent she'd been upset. She had taken her father's whisky glass. Her hand trembled slightly.

Silence ensued. Then Thorpe said, "So, you've just come back from Edinburgh?"

"I was staying with friends. I need to get away from Dungarvan sometimes—beautiful as it is." She took a sip of whisky. "There's just something about the atmosphere that's too heady."

"Must be the ghost," Thorpe said.

Fiona raised her eyebrows. "You're a believer?"

"Not really."

"But you know the story."

"Only that there's supposed to be a ghost."

Fiona said, "Alastair has a theory that the ghost is an old Celtic mother goddess. There's a cave in the grounds with a well that's called *Tobar na Màthar*: the Well of the Mothers, not just any old mothers either—the divine feminine."

"Not really my thing, mythology."

After a silence, Fiona said, "I understand you've not been well either."

"No, I'm fine."

"Oh, I thought my mother said..."

"What?"

Fiona laughed. "You'd had some funny ideas—you'd been seeing things."

"My wife? Or as you all here would have it—my hallucination?"

Fiona gave an awkward grin. "Some of the best people are crazy."

"You're very forthright," Thorpe said.

"I didn't mean to be insensitive. It must seem terribly real. I've read about such things."

"Vivienne isn't a hallucination. She's real. I just don't know where she is. Perhaps the bang on my head did make me a little confused, but the woman I love is real."

"Of course. Sorry." Fiona stood up and knocked back her whisky. "I'm going to find my father and mother, but afterwards, do you fancy a little walk after lunch? Up Beinn a' Choire?"

"Up what?"

"The mountain behind the castle. Not the biggest. But it's a nice walk and a lovely view from the top."

"Yes, I'll come. I have nothing else to do."

AFTER LUNCH, Thorpe met Fiona on the terrace. She had changed into clothes more suitable for hiking—a white shirt, trousers and sturdy boots. He had walking clothes amongst his things and had pulled them on to come down and meet her for the walk. Fiona had a backpack, and she handed him a stout walking stick. He took it and waved it around.

"It's not a sword!"

Thorpe laughed.

Fiona looked at the ridge line in the summer sun. "Not too hot— just pleasant."

They set off through the castle garden, and out by an almost hidden wooden gate. From then, it was a walk across the fields until the path started to rise. Ahead of them was the mountain called Beinn a' Choire. There were white clouds high up, and the sky was full of swallows, swooping and chattering as they flew.

She walked well.

"I noticed your father has a limp," said Thorpe as they started to climb.

Fiona called back over her shoulder. "Yes, he was wounded in the South African War at Mujaba Hill by a sniper."

"Lucky he wasn't killed. What outfit was he with?"

"The Gordon Highlanders."

They were climbing the first steep slopes of the mountain now, coming out of the bracken and into the heather. Next month he guessed the heather would bloom in a glorious sea of purple all over the mountain's flanks. It would be quite nice to see that.

Thorpe got into the lead so that he could help Fiona up the craggier parts, extending his hand. At first, she hesitated as if wary of him, and he wondered whether her mother had told her about Màiri. But then she took his hand, and he pulled her up.

"Nice view even though we're not at the top!" she said, shielding her eyes from the sun. Thorpe admired her shining blond hair, her smooth young skin and the curve of her bosom. He liked how she sucked her bottom lip while climbing as if she were concentrating on where to place her feet. She started going up again without waiting for him. She was a few steps ahead now, so he hurried to catch her and then, without it being too obvious, place himself in the lead once again.

"Not married then?" he said, out of breath.

She laughed, panting too. "Nearly. Lucky escape really."

"Oh?"

"He was an advocate. Very well connected. We almost got engaged, and then he broke it off."

"Foolish man," said Thorpe, now in front, helping her up a scramble of rock.

She grinned. "He said I was too opinionated. But he didn't really want someone like me. He wanted a maid and a mother for his beautiful children to be and someone to impress his friends."

"I'm sure you'd do that."

"How gallant you are Captain Thorpe." She flashed a smile at him. "Trouble is I can't keep quiet if someone says something foolish."

"That's a good quality, in my opinion. At least—"

" —'in a man', were you going to add?"

Thorpe shook his head. "I was going to say 'at least if you don't mind not being liked.'"

"No, I don't mind not being liked. I prefer to do the right thing rather than keep people happy all the time.

Thorpe said, "Did you bring some water? I'm parched."

"I have both water and whisky."

"Water, please. Whisky will dehydrate us."

"Goodness me, I thought you were the wild man, and you're worried about your health."

He blushed. Then he said, "Somewhere like this looks kind in the sunshine, but if the weather turns, it can turn nasty."

"These are my mountains," Fiona said. "I know them well. But you are right. Even so, when we get to the top, I am planning on a dram."

Thorpe looked around. The weather looked fixed to stay fair. "We'll probably be fine."

"Thanks for letting me know. Now, you've reassured me, I can relax."

Thorpe checked to see whether she was teasing him. She handed him the water bottle and took out a silver hip flask herself. "Think I'll have a nip now."

"You shouldn't, not yet anyway."

She uncorked the hip flask. "I told you I don't take advice well."

They both laughed.

Thorpe said, "Neither do I. I've been accused of being pig-headed, as well as self-centred."

She sipped the whisky, corked the flask again then took back the water bottle from Thorpe and put it in her pack. "I don't think you can be so very self-centred," she said.

"How's that then?"

"Well, what you did in the War—the medal—cleaning out the machine gun nest. My mother told me."

He looked at her, trying to work out whether she was flattering him. He couldn't gauge her so decided to take her at her word. He said, "People say I did it for the glory. But that's not true."

"You did it to save your men."

"I honestly didn't even think of what I was doing. It was just my duty. But as I say, some people don't take to me."

"They don't take to you?" she was smiling. Thorpe didn't know how to respond.

They continued up a craggy face of scree, picking their way through the broken rock.

"I hope Calum's going to be all right," she said.

"Any idea what happened yet?"

"The gossip is that it's punishment because he got a girl pregnant in the next village and wouldn't stand by her. They say the girl asked the wise woman to cast a spell on him."

"A wise woman? Like a witch?"

"A '*cailleach*' they call them in Gaelic."

Thorpe snorted. "But what really happened?"

"No one knows. He's gone back to his parents' croft to recuperate."

They were walking across the shoulder of the mountain now. From this high, they saw the ocean sparkling down to the west. Dungarvan Castle nestled below them between the arms of the mountain, cut off from the road by a dark wood.

"No one would know the castle was there," he said.

"We're very secluded. That's why it's nice to get visitors—even by accident."

"And what an accident!"

The grass opened, as a viper curled out of the heather and raised its head to strike Fiona's leg. Thorpe hurled his walking stick, and it hit the snake, which recoiled but then reared again. He grabbed Fiona's arm and yanked her out of the way of the serpent's strike. He snatched his stick and clubbed at the snake but missed it. The beast thought better of the fight and slithered away into the undergrowth.

Fiona was breathing heavily. Thorpe felt her pulse in the wrist he still gripped tight.

She clung onto him. "Oh my God," she said, shaking. "Thank you."

He let her go. "You're welcome. I wouldn't have liked to have had to carry you all the way down."

She laughed. "I'm not sure Dr McKinnon is such a whizz with snakebites either." Then her expression changed and softened.

"What is it?" he said frowning.

"Just that I'm enjoying your company."

"Are you surprised? Didn't you expect to?"

"Daddy told me to entertain you. He thought you were bored."

"He thinks I'm mad."

She said, "Not as such."

"Not as such? What then?"

"He thinks you're bewitched too."

"Bewitched? Seriously?"

She nodded. "He is a Highlander after all. And he's married to my mother."

"She's a formidable woman."

Fiona laughed. "Indeed, and I hope I take after her."

"I think you do. Anyway, I'm glad you took him up on his offer of entertaining me."

"So am I. But I felt wary."

"Why?"

She gave him a strange look. "Because you're a bad man."

"You just said I was a good man."

"I mean you are a heroic good man, but I think you're a bad man with women."

His mouth tightened. "Did your mother tell you that?"

"Yes, but I'd know anyway. I know your type."

"Ah," he said. "My type."

"There's no point being offended," she said. "You either like being like that, or you change the way you are."

"A leopard can't change its spots," he said.

"You're not a leopard."

They carried on climbing, and the path became steeper. The fresh mountain air cheered them both. In some places, they had to scramble up rock staircases. Then they waded or skipped over the clear mountain burns using rocks as stepping stones. The mountain was deceiving. They thought they saw the summit ahead, but when they crested each ridge, they saw another in front of them. They were sweating and out of breath as they finally reached the cairn on the top.

It was very high, and Thorpe stood there, enjoying the vast expanse of mountains and sea and islands. "What a place!" he said.

Fiona lay down on a large flat rock. "I need a rest," she said.

He looked around for somewhere to sit. He said, "You've got the best rock. The rest are all sharp."

She patted the rock beside her. "There's enough room here. Come on. I won't bite."

"Unlike the viper."

"Yes, thank you again for my rescue, Captain Thorpe."

"You're very welcome."

He regarded her, wondering what her invitation meant. She looked pretty sitting there, and it had never been in his nature to look a gift horse in the mouth. He went and sat down close to her. The stone was wide and flat, after a moment's hesitation, he lay. The stone was warm under Thorpe's back. He gazed at the blue sky over-head and then looked down to the mountains stretching on either side of the glen and all the way down to the glittering sea. There was a slight breeze that ruffled Fiona's hair as she sat gazing silently over the sea. Thorpe smelled the heather and the peat and heard the staccato call of a peregrine falcon as it made its way home to its nest in the crags that fell steeply away to the east.

"More water?" Fiona said.

"I'll try a whisky now," he said.

She reached and got the hip flask, which she handed to him. "You see—you did take my advice eventually."

He took a mouthful, got a mouthful of the burning spirit and handed the flask back to her. He turned and looked at her, propping his head on his arm. He was alone with a beautiful woman, and one who was giving him signals that she didn't mind being alone with him.

"I have more goodies," she said. "Here." She delved into her back-pack and pulled out a loaf of bread." Fresh-baked at the castle this morning."

"Very nice!"

"And..." She rummaged further in the bag and came out with a lump of cheese. "Highland cheese from our home farm."

He laughed. "A veritable feast. No cutlery? Do we just rip lumps off them like savages?"

She flashed a smile and from her belt, pulled a black-handled knife. He hadn't noticed it before. "I have my *sgian dubh*!"

"Your skiing what?"

She prodded him with a finger. "You know so little about our Highland ways. All good Highlanders carry the 'black knife.'"

"Even the Highland women?"

"This Highland woman does. I can't speak for the others." She cut him a portion of bread and cheese. The meal was simple but good. He ate, staring at the sea. Then he watched her eat.

"What are you looking at?" she said.

"You."

"Oh?"

"I was thinking about how beautiful you are."

She grinned. "Lots of people tell me that, so it must be true."

"How immodest of you, though honest," he said but smiled. "I admire that."

"Anything could happen up here," she said.

"Could it?"

She shrugged.

"You hardly know me," he said. "Do you feel safe?"

"I feel as safe as I want to be."

She was lovely: bright and bold and beautiful.

She turned and looked at him; her eyes different hues of blue like a stained glass window. "I always seem to get involved with men who aren't good for me," she said.

He glanced away. "I'd like to be good for a woman. I got myself a bit of a reputation in India. It was too easy, all the bored wives. You can imagine."

"And none of them stole your heart."

He shook his head.

"Until your wife, Vivienne, of course."

He nodded. "Until Vivienne."

'So, despite you being that kind of man, I'm safe from your advances?" She was lying on her side, head propped on her arm. She was looking at him, half-teasing, but half-serious.

He flushed. "But whatever they say I was, I would never force myself on a woman."

"Of course not," she said. Still, she looked at him. "And, in any case, there's Vivienne."

"Yes, there's Vivienne."

CHAPTER

# SIX

That night, at dinner, they talked about dogs and fishing and after they'd eaten, they retired to the Drawing Room. Thorpe sat in a leather chair drinking malt whisky. The room was warm from the blazing log fire.

The grand piano stood towards the window, and a gilt candelabra with four candles burned on top of it. Seated on the stool, Fiona prepared to play. As Thorpe listened, the gentle notes of Debussy's *Clair de Lune* arose and rolled through the room. Fiona played well.

Lady Gráinne watched her daughter. She drank red wine, and Lord Eachann sipped his whisky while he too gazed adoringly at his talented girl.

When Fiona finished Clair de Lune, the audience gave a ripple of applause. Then Alastair stood to give a rendition of the Highland Lament, *Cha Till Mac Cruimein*.

He glanced at Fiona, who sat ready to accompany him. Lord Eachann smiled indulgently at the two of them.

"This is a song about the famous piper Dòmhnall Bàn Mac Cruimein who was killed in the 1745 rebellion."

Alastair's voice was light but carried with it all the grief of the clansmen who lamented the death of their piper in that long-ago war.

*Cha till, cha till, cha till Mac Cruimein*
*An cogadh no sìth cha till e tuille*

It was a song of war and honour. Thorpe's eyes moistened with his own memories, and he took a gulp of whisky and blinked the grief away. He was embarrassed at his tears, and extinguished them with the heel of his hand.

After he finished singing, Alastair translated the song. "Basically, it says that MacCrimmon would not return ever to the mountains and farms of his people. Neither in war nor in peace, he would return nevermore."

"I'm sorry," said Thorpe, softened by the wine and whisky he'd drunk.

"What for?" said Alastair, genuinely puzzled.

"You know—for the wrongs my people did here."

Eachann said, "Not your people; it was all governments and politics. Not your fault, Captain Thorpe."

"In fact, MacCrimmon and his Lord MacLeod were fighting for the British government," Lady Gráinne said.

Thorpe laughed. "Really? Even more complicated then."

Lady Gráinne said, "Situations aren't always what you first think them to be, Captain Thorpe."

The absurd idea that he was here at Dungarvan to prove himself in some way came into his mind. Then he dismissed it. This strange feeling of guilt and unease arose from the whisky and the car accident. That was all. He would feel better soon.

Eachann came to sit in the leather chair beside Thorpe, a crystal decanter of whisky in his hand. "Would you like another dram?"

Thorpe said, "Why not?"

Eachann poured a generous measure. As they drank, Eachann indicated with his glass. "They're a lovely couple, don't you think?"

Thorpe followed where he was pointing. "Those two?"

"Yes, Alastair and Fiona. They grew up together. His father was my solicitor, but he died young, and I took Alastair under my wing. In the past, Fiona's taken it into her head to run around with different kinds of men, but she needs a kinder soul—a man with a soft heart like Alastair's."

Thorpe shrugged. "Depends on what she wants."

"I think if she runs after a soldier, she'll regret it."

"You were a soldier, weren't you?" Thorpe said.

"I was."

"So you don't want her to have a man like you?"

Eachann laughed softly. "No. That's my point. They would quarrel all the time. She's too strong-willed to have a man equally as strong-willed."

Thorpe smiled. "So, she would dominate Alastair, tell him what to do all the time. Is that what you want for her?"

"Better that than he dominates her."

Thorpe drained his glass, then stood. "I'm tired. I think I'll retire to bed."

As he stood, Dr McKinnon said, "I hope you sleep well." He'd probably been eavesdropping.

"I hope you don't dream too much. This place is famous for making people dream," Lord Eachann said.

Thorpe nodded. "Thanks for the meal, Lady Gráinne." He bowed toward Fiona and Alastair. "And for the music."

"You're very welcome, Captain Thorpe," said Gráinne. "Sleep well."

As he went out past the piano, Fiona caught his fingers. "William," she said. "I enjoyed our walk today. Perhaps we could do another tomorrow. Or go down to the sea in the horse and trap?"

"Yes, I'd like that," he said.

She dropped his hand and smiled.

Thorpe saw Gráinne look at her husband and raise her eyebrows. Eachann took a puff of his pipe and shook his head.

As he left the room, the last thing Thorpe saw was Alastair gazing doe-eyed at Fiona.

Ah, that's it then, he thought.

ONCE IN BED, Thorpe slipped into a deep sleep, but somewhere in the middle of the night, he stirred. He felt Vivienne come into the room. He knew it was her because he smelled her scent and heard her bare feet on the wooden floor. Thorpe sat up in bed and looked around the darkened room. The bed was warm beside him as if someone had been lying there. Vivienne wasn't in the room, but he still smelled her lingering scent.

Her laughter came from outside the door. He was so convinced it was her laughing that he swung his legs out of bed and pulled on the dressing gown he'd been lent. Moonlight pooled in through the window, but everything else was draped in deep shadow.

Thorpe fumbled for a match and from that lit the candle. By candlelight, he opened the door of the bedroom and went out onto the landing. No one was there either.

He saw from his wristwatch that it was 3 am. The house sat in profound silence. He walked to the top of the wooden staircase. There was still no one. He couldn't even hear the wind outside. The whole castle seemed asleep.

He was about to go back to bed, thinking he had indeed dreamt Vivienne's return when he heard voices. He stepped down the stairs, one tread at a time. Her laughter rose up the stairwell. It was her, he was sure of it. And she was with someone else.

He was stealthy so he would catch Vivienne and whoever was there with her. He heard them laughing. He heard Vivienne's voice again, and a low, lustful moan. He stopped. He thought his heart would burst with anger and grief. The sound made him nauseous.

There was no doubt it was the sound of a woman in pleasure. There was a man's voice too. The man laughed softly, and Vivienne cried out again.

He hurried down the stairs and turned down the corridor. He didn't care about being quiet now. He wanted to confront them. She was his wife. Whoever this man was, he would fight him for Vivienne.

Thorpe came to the long corridor that led to the library. At the end of it, he saw a dark-haired woman, leaning back against the wall with her dress hem around her waist. Her pale thighs were wrapped around the legs of a man whose trousers were round his ankles. She looked when she saw Thorpe's candle, and Thorpe recognised her dark beauty.

"Vivienne!" he yelled and ran to them. The woman broke away from her lover and, hooting with laughter, opened the door into the library and ran through it. The man hitched up his trousers as he went. Thorpe saw only the back of the man's head, but he was sure it was Muirdeach.

By the time Thorpe reached the end of the corridor and followed them into the library, they were gone.

Nothing stirred. There was only the silence of the dark leather-bound books in their shelves. His candle fluttered and threw shadows that made it seem that people were hiding behind the shelves. He searched, but there was no one.

In despair, he shouted out. "Vivienne! Come back to me! I love you."

His voice died away. The shadows the candle cast danced and shifted. The place seemed to listen as if the castle was keen to know the next scene in this unfolding drama. It was like he was in a play, not in reality at all.

The atmosphere was so odd and dreamlike that Thorpe wasn't sure whether he was fully awake. Was it really the blow to the head that made him think he saw Vivienne?

He walked back to his room. Vivienne had not returned there

either. But what was there was the small statue of Kali Mata, sitting on Vivienne's dressing table. He knew he'd put it in the drawer and no servant would have taken it out. It was Vivienne who'd taken out the Indian goddess of karma. It was meant as a sign for him.

Thorpe didn't sleep. He watched just in case Vivienne returned. After long hours, the early dawn lightened the sky with grey. Then the sunrise slowly flooded the room with warm yellow. The growing light revealed the patina of the wooden floor. The warm rays highlighted the motes of dust swirling in the air. The yellow beams picked out the gold and blue of his borrowed dressing gown that hung over the back of the chair where he'd thrown it. Doves started cooing outside his window.

But Vivienne did not come back. He wondered whether he'd dreamed her completely. He even wondered whether he'd left her in India, whether she'd ever existed. All the details of his life swam together like goldfish in castle's pond and everything that happened before the accident was vague. He wasn't sure what he remembered anymore.

CHAPTER

# SEVEN

D r McKinnon was already in the Dining Room at breakfast. "Good morning, Captain," he said as he bent over his kippers and the morning sun shone equally on his silver fish knife and his shiny forehead.

"Good morning, Doctor," Thorpe replied and then turned to Muirdeach to ask for bacon and eggs.

How smug Muirdeach looked standing there. Thorpe scowled and went to sit. Around ten minutes later, Màiri brought his breakfast, though she avoided his eye and gave a brief nod to his greeting.

"How's your patient?" Thorpe asked McKinnon sitting opposite.

"Calum? Back home with his parents. He's somewhat better but has not recovered his senses. He's quite delirious; keeps talking about a woman with eyes like a snake."

"Poor man," said Thorpe. "I hope he gets better soon." He poured himself tea from the antique silver teapot. After a minute, he said, "I saw my wife last night."

"Oh," said McKinnon, obviously embarrassed.

"It's all right. I know you don't believe me."

"It's not that..." blustered the doctor, still not meeting Thorpe's

215

eye. "There are just other explanations for what we sometimes think we see."

Thorpe nodded, accepting but not agreeing what McKinnon said. He bit some bacon. "Lord Eachann said he was going to ask you to examine my head."

McKinnon nodded wisely. "He did mention something of the sort to me. But really, there's very little I can do. You have no obvious injuries, and I think if you had a contusion on your brain, you would be a lot more ill than you are. For example, I would expect your balance to be off and your cognitions disturbed."

"My cognitions disturbed?"

"Yes, you would have lost contact with reality."

Thorpe met McKinnon's eyes. "So you don't think I'm crazy?"

McKinnon looked embarrassed and took a fishbone from his mouth with the flat of his knife. "Psychiatry is not my field."

"She was with Muirdeach."

McKinnon raised his eyebrows. "Who was?"

"They were outside the library."

"Who? Your wife?"

"He was making love to her."

"Come now. You shouldn't be slandering the poor man."

"I'm sure it was him with Vivienne."

"And when was this?"

"In the middle of the night."

"Are you sure? It seems unlikely."

"I'm sure."

They didn't speak any more about it. Thorpe waited until McKinnon had gone and he was alone with Muirdeach. He stood and went over to the servant.

"You don't have the guilty air of an adulterer, I'll give you that," said Thorpe.

"I'm sorry, sir?"

"Do you know my wife?"

Muirdeach looked puzzled. "I didn't know you had a wife, sir."

"You met her the other night when she came with me to look at the car. You said it would take a week to get fixed."

Muirdeach shook his head. "No, sir. You were on your own."

"You damned-well smiled at her. Then you flirted with her at dinner. That's why Màiri was angry with you."

Muirdeach held his tongue.

"I tell you, I saw you last night - with my wife."

Muirdeach stared down the breakfast room, ignoring Thorpe. He looked as if he wanted to leave, but couldn't.

"Outside the Library at about 3 am," continued Thorpe.

"Not me. I was fast asleep."

"I saw you. At least I saw the back of your head."

"I'm afraid you must be mistaken, sir."

Thorpe went and perched on the edge of a heavy wooden table, still between Muirdeach and the door. He pushed a Chinese jade elephant out of the way so he could sit. "Well if it wasn't you; who was it? It looked like you."

Muirdeach said, "I've never met your wife."

"Vivienne. I saw how you looked at her the first night. The way all men look at her."

"I'm sorry, sir, but I've never met your wife."

Thorpe raised a warning finger. "If I catch you with her; I swear I'll kill you. She would eat a man like you for breakfast. She's clever as a snake—you wouldn't stand a chance against her, you Highland peasant."

Muirdeach's jaw clenched.

THORPE TURNED and walked out of the breakfast room. He stalked the long corridor towards the Baronial Hall, marching as if he had some-where to be. Or, as if he was looking for someone, but now he didn't cxpcct to find Vivienne. She had retreated from him. He found himself outside and went and sat on one of the stone benches in the Rose Garden.

He lit a cigarette, taking three attempts because he couldn't hold his lighter steady. And then he breathed out smoke as the bees and hover-flies went around their business with the roses. Ants crawled over the stone flagstones in a line carrying the body of a bumblebee back to their nest. He lost track of time. He was there almost an hour, maybe more.

Not knowing what do to with Vivienne gone, not knowing what to believe and why they would lie to him, he decided to check on his car. The sun was still not at its zenith, but it was hot. He stood in the shadow of the high box hedge and wiped the sweat from his brow with the back of his left hand. He had a cigarette held in his right.

He smelled the horses and heard them stamp and turn in their dark stalls. The converted stable that Muirdeach used as his makeshift mechanic's shop was past these stables. Thorpe heard Muirdeach's voice before he saw him. It was nearly an hour since breakfast finished and the mechanic was back at his other job. Muirdeach was telling someone an amusing story, and a woman was laughing. At first, Thorpe thought Màiri had gone back to him. That's what happened, lovers tiffs were soon mended. Poor Màiri. She had spirit. What was she doing making up with this faithless lout?

But then he slowed. He heard the woman's voice clearly. They were speaking English, not Gaelic. And the woman had a well-spoken English accent. It wasn't Màiri—it was Vivienne. He balled his fists and stepped out of the shadow into the stable. But only Muirdeach was there. He wasn't bent over the car. Instead, the mechanic was standing by the door as if he'd just said goodbye to someone.

He looked at Thorpe. "You again. Why don't you leave me alone? I have work to do."

Muirdeach looked pleased with himself. He must think he had the better of Thorpe, that he'd cuckolded him. Thorpe had forced many husbands to wear the horns of the cuckold, but he'd never felt that raw betrayal himself.

Thorpe gripped the wooden post by the stable door to steady

himself—damn Vivienne for making him feel so weak.

Muirdeach looked at him with his steady, confident gaze. "Are you well?" the mechanic said.

Thorpe tried to steady himself. "I've come about the car." No, it was Vivienne. He heard her. She was real.

Muirdeach nodded. "I guessed."

"How long now?" Thorpe asked. He struggled to focus. He kept imagining Vivienne was outside the stable, peering in, mocking him. His forehead broke out in a rash of sweat.

Oblivious to Thorpe's inner turmoil, Muirdeach nodded. "As I said before—it will be a week."

Thorpe stammered, "Was Màiri here just now?"

Muirdeach shook his head.

"Who was the woman you were talking to?"

"A woman? No woman here."

"Don't lie to me. I heard you as I was walking up."

"I was talking to one of the horses earlier. Maybe that's what you heard."

Thorpe's mouth twisted. "I'm not a fool. I know she was here."

"I don't know what you're talking about, sir." He said the last word with an emphasis to make it sound like a sneer.

"I know your type," said Thorpe.

"And what type is that?" said Muirdeach, putting down his spanner and wiping his hand with the oily cloth.

Thorpe said, "I know your every trick. I know your every little insincere compliment and every little way you wheedle your way into a woman's affections."

Muirdeach laughed. "I think you're losing your mind, sir."

Thorpe turned. The world span round. He felt off-balance, and his mouth was dry. He loosened his tie and stepped out of the stable into the cooler air.

Muirdeach watched him as he walked away. When he'd got about ten yards, Thorpe stopped and said, "You treat Màiri well. She deserves better than you."

Muirdeach said, "Màiri knows what I'm like, and she doesn't mind."

Thorpe stood, supporting himself on a stone wall. After ten minutes, he was steady enough to go back to the castle. Though when he got there, he had no idea what he would do.

THORPE WAS WALKING by the high grey walls of the west side, when Fiona and Gráinne appeared, walking down the gravel path from the vegetable garden back to the castle.

"Hello you," said Fiona. "I was wondering where you got to."

"Nowhere much," said Thorpe.

"Are you all right, William?" Fiona said.

"You sound glum," Gráinne said.

"Been to see the car. It's a long way off being fixed."

"That's good—it means you'll be our guest for longer," Fiona said.

Thorpe looked at her, squinting in the sun. She looked radiant, her tanned skin brought out the blue of her eyes.

"Captain Thorpe looks bored," said Gráinne. "You should entertain him, Fiona."

"Everyone thinks I'm bored."

Fiona said, "Well, we could play tennis. Do you play?"

"A little," he said.

"Let's have a match before lunch."

"I have no suitable kit."

"You can borrow some shorts from Alastair, I'm sure."

"Ah, Alastair," said Thorpe.

"He won't mind lending you something. He's a lovely chap. Very kind. Well-meaning." said Fiona.

Gráinne just looked at them both and said nothing.

"I'll ask someone to bring them up to your room," said Fiona. "Not Murdo."

"Oh. You don't like Muirdeach? Someone else then. How about an hour? After tennis, we can have lunch."

"I will just be a minute here. I'll make my way back shortly," said Thorpe.

Lady Gráinne studied him. "You don't look well, William. Are you quite yourself?"

Thorpe nodded. "I'm fine. Not used to your whisky." He forced a grin.

Fiona said, "Fine. See you later. You know where the tennis court is?"

"I'll find it."

"It's easy," said Fiona.

Lady Gráinne said," Come on, Fiona. I want to get some flowers for the Drawing Room."

The two women walked off. Thorpe watched them go. Before they turned the corner and went out of sight, Fiona looked back over her shoulder. She smiled, and he smiled back. When she'd gone, he shook his head and sighed.

Thorpe went up to his bedroom. He found the tennis shirt and shorts laid out on the bed for him. He dressed in them, and as he opened his door, he saw Màiri coming along the landing. She looked down. He felt himself redden but said, "Hello."

She didn't speak at first. As they passed, he said, "I know it was jealousy and rather hot-headed of me, but..."

She said, "You didn't force me."

"I was just enraged about Vivienne and Muirdeach flirting."

Màiri looked concerned. "Who is Vivienne?"

"My wife. We spoke of her last night. You were angry with Muirdeach because he paid her too much attention when he was serving her at dinner."

Màiri shook her head. "No, I was angry because of him going with that Cameron lass."

"No, it was Vivienne; we spoke about her. You served her soup at dinner last night."

Màiri said, "You were not with your wife at dinner last night. You were on your own. You have no wife here."

Thorpe sat heavily on the bed, crumpling the tennis shirt. He had his head in his hands. 'What on earth is going on here? What trick are you all trying to play on me?"

Màiri came over. "I am sorry for you, Captain Thorpe. I think you are under the spell of the *bean sìth*."

Then he saw that she was carrying white flowers. The flowers had long shiny leaves of dark green with white flower heads in bunches. They were pungent.

"What are those?" he said.

"Garlic."

"Oh. Bit smelly."

"I was going to put them up at your window."

He frowned. "Why?"

"For protection."

He raised an eyebrow. "Protection? From whom?"

Màiri didn't meet his eye. "The spirit of a woman haunts the castle. Something has woken her. All men are at risk from her. She's taken Calum. Garlic and iron will keep her away."

"Is this the woman of the story that Alastair told—the so-called Lady of the Fountain?"

Màiri said, "She ha other names."

Thorpe said, "So you really believe in these legends?"

"I do. We all do. They come again and again. Dungarvan is a place where the story must repeat itself time and again.”

Thorpe glanced over at the statuette of Kali Mata. Like a bad joke, she sat again on the dresser.

Thorpe said, “So, this Lady of the Fountain doesn't like men."

Màiri shook her head. “The *bean sìth* likes men well enough. But she also punishes them. She told her husband Eachann Dubh never to be unfaithful to her. If he did, he would pay a heavy price."

"If that means what I think it does, it sounds unpleasant."

She gave a laugh. "I think it was meant to be."

"So if he knew he would be punished like that, why did he do it?"

"He was a man, and men can't help themselves."

Thorpe remembered himself and Màiri and how he'd been overcome by his own passions, lust certainly, but anger at Vivienne too for her flirting, and resentment that she went against his wishes. He regretted all of that now. He had been no better than an animal in his behaviour, no better than a fool in his emotions.

"Keep the garlic in the window," Màiri said.

As she stepped into the light of the window, Thorpe saw a bruise on her cheek. He stopped and almost reached out to touch it. "How did you get that?" He asked.

"I walked into a door."

"A door? It looks like someone hit you."

Mairi shook her head quickly. "No. I walked into a door."

"Did he hit you?"

"No."

She put the garlic around the window and hurried out. "I'm sorry. I must get on."

Thorpe nodded, but his mouth tightened. He disliked the man even more now.

THORPE WENT OUT via the short cut Alastair had shown him, pleased he remembered it because it saved him walking all the way to the front entrance when the tennis court was by the rose garden.

Fiona seemed pleased to see him. She commented on his tennis gear. "Very fetching. Sad to say for poor Alastair, but you look better in his tennis kit than he does."

Thorpe shrugged. "Come on then, let the thrashing begin."

Fiona winked. "Yes, I hope you aren't a bad loser."

They began to play on the hard court surrounded by high box

hedges. Fiona wasn't going to let him win easily, but still, he pulled ahead. The tennis took his mind off Vivienne. Playing tennis was a return to normality after the strangeness of the dream he'd felt immersed in lately.

After he won the first two sets, he said, "30 - Love."

He waited while she wiped her brow with a towel. "Phew, it's hot. I thought you said you only played a little."

Thorpe grinned. "I may have downplayed that. There's not much to do in the Army other than shoot people and play sports. You're good, though."

Fiona smiled back. "I was champion at my school. I'm ready. Do your worst Captain Thorpe."

Soon the court resounded again to the sound of the tennis ball hitting the strung rackets. There was a rally. Then Fiona suddenly volleyed, wrong-footing Thorpe who lost the point. "30 -15," he said.

Fiona grinned. "Your serve."

He served, but she hit it back once and then again. The ball shot across the net, and she scored another point. "30 all," she shouted, waving her racket triumphantly.

He smiled back at her. "You haven't won yet."

"It's only a matter of time." She laughed.

Then they began again. Thorpe served strongly, but Fiona deftly caught it in mid-air and whacked it back. The ball ricocheted between them back and forth. Then Thorpe stumbled and let the ball through.

"Match!" she yelled. "Match! I beat the great Captain Thorpe!"

He grinned back at her. "Yes, you did. Well played."

Fiona danced with joy. She came up to him and hugged him. He stiffened but didn't pull away.

"I'm so happy!" Then she frowned and looked up at him, still in a half embrace. "Hey, did you let me win?"

He cocked his head to one side. "Would I do that? Don't you know my reputation? I never let anyone beat me."

· · ·

Fiona was still teasing Thorpe about her beating him at tennis when Gráinne appeared from the direction of the house. She was walking fast, and her face looked troubled.

"Mother?" said Fiona, stepping back from Thorpe and walking towards Gráinne. "What's wrong?"

"It's Muirdeach," she said. "He's dead."

Fiona's face drained of blood, and she dropped her racket. "Oh my God," she said. "What is happening in this place?"

Gráinne said, "He's over by the terrace. We need to move the body into the house. Will you help, William?"

"Of course," Thorpe said. Even he felt stunned and guilty—as if his dislike for the man had killed him.

They laid down their rackets and went at a half-run over to the Long Terrace. They still wore their tennis whites. The sun blazed overhead; it was a perfect summer day. Birds sang from the hedges, bees buzzed around the flowers, but someone was dead. They hurried along in silence. Gráinne strode ahead, lost in her own thoughts, Fiona lingered beside Thorpe. "He was only twenty-three."

Gráinne said in a soft voice. "Please. Hurry."

They found Muirdeach lying by the entrance to the cave Vivienne had spoken of. He was on his back, his eyes open—staring at something. He was soaking wet—his shirt was open and drenched. His trousers and shoes were wringing.

Dr McKinnon was kneeling by him.

"Looks like he drowned," Thorpe said.

McKinnon said, "If he did, how did he get back out here?" He bent down and touched Muirdeach's shirt then he tasted his fingers. "It's seawater."

"How on earth does that happen?" Thorpe said.

Lady Gráinne said, "The old well in the cave–*Tobar Na Màthar*; it goes down to some tunnels that eventually connect to the sea. When the tide is high, it comes up the well and floods over the cave."

Thorpe walked forward towards the cave. "A saltwater well?"

"Careful," said Fiona, grabbing his arm.

"What's there to be frightened of?" Thorpe said.

"Whatever killed Muirdeach."

Thorpe said, "Nothing killed him. It was most likely an accident. That's the way it looks. Maybe he fell into the water, managed to drag himself out, but died of shock or inhalation or something."

"I don't think that's possible," said Dr McKinnon.

Just then, Alastair arrived. He had run down the Terrace and was sweating, his blonde hair plastered over his forehead.

Alastair stared at the corpse. "That's horrible. Poor Muirdeach."

"Yes, poor Muirdeach," Fiona said.

Behind them loomed the vast mountains. Swallows and swifts darted through the air above them. Thorpe stepped into the cave.

"No, William!" shouted Fiona. Thorpe turned and raised a hand to reassure her. The cave was cool, dark, and damp. It wasn't deep, and he could see a hole that led down to unknown depths. From it, he could smell the sea and see the froth of the waves.

The women entered in after him. Alastair stayed outside. "The tide's coming in," Gráinne said. "Be careful. If you fall down there, the tunnels will fill with water, and you'll be stuck."

The cave floor was wet. There were wet footmarks, but Thorpe couldn't tell whether they were Muirdeach's.

Fiona said, "It's cold in here," She held his arm.

Thorpe indicated a trail of water. "Someone's dragged him out of the pool."

"Dragged? Who?"

"I don't know. We'd better get the police."

The three of them stepped back out into the sunshine. Gráinne said she would arrange for the police. "They'll have to come from Fort William so they won't arrive until tomorrow at the earliest."

"Let's carry him," Thorpe said. Alastair and Dr McKinnon helped him, and they bore Muirdeach's body back to the castle.

# EIGHT

Later, after he had washed and changed, Màiri came with a message. She said Lady Gráinne wanted to see him in the Drawing Room for coffee. Before she left, he told Màiri he was sorry about Muirdeach. Màiri began to weep but stopped herself as if she would not let him see her crying, brushed the tears away and turned and hurried down the corridor.

When Thorpe arrived at the Drawing Room, Lady Gráinne sat with her black and white cat on her knee. It purred as she stroked it, looking up warily as Thorpe came in.

Lady Gráinne said, "Coffee, William?"

He nodded. There were no servants, so he poured himself coffee and cream. He took two cubes of brown sugar with the sugar tongs and sat where she indicated. He felt he had come for an interview with the headmistress. She watched him while he drank his coffee, all the while stroking the cat.

"It's all very distressing," Gráinne said.

"I didn't like him. But any death is to be regretted."

She raised an eyebrow. "Why didn't you like him? I'm surprised you even knew him."

"I don't like his type."

Gráinne evidently decided not to pursue the subject. "You're getting on well with Fiona," she said. It was a statement, not a question.

"We seem to be."

"I think she's taken a shine to you."

He shrugged. "She's a beautiful young woman — intelligent and spirited too. She'll make someone a good wife."

Lady Gráinne laughed. "I think she may be a little spirited for most men. They prefer a wife to be more pliable, and she'll never be that."

"More fool them," Thorpe said.

Gráinne took a genteel sip of coffee from her fine porcelain cup. "What are your feelings towards her? I only ask because I don't want my daughter to be hurt. She's been hurt enough already by thoughtless men. And we've spoken before about—"

"—about my taking liberties with your women?"

"I wouldn't put it so crudely."

"I wouldn't hurt Fiona for the world. Anyway, I'm not in the market for weddings. I'm married already."

Gráinne nodded slightly. "You know we disagree on that. But when you come to yourself and realise you aren't married, what then? Is Fiona safe?"

"Safe? That's an extraordinary thing to say. And, whatever you think, Vivienne is not a figment of my imagination. She's real."

"Real? I wonder."

"I know you all think I'm insane. Either that, or somehow Vivienne planned all this with you and that I'm somehow the victim of some monstrous practical joke.

"The victim of something maybe. Possibly yourself."

Thorpe sat back. He felt her scrutinising gaze on him.

She said, "You know they say power is the opposite of love?"

"Do they?"

"If you love someone, you submit to them and give them all your power. You make yourself vulnerable."

Thorpe shrugged. "Perhaps."

She sipped her coffee. "But you've never had the experience?"

He looked at his cup. It was white porcelain with blue Chinese willow pattern. After a while he said. "It sounds an unpleasant experience—to make yourself vulnerable to someone."

"Of course the opposite is true too. If you want power, you have no room left inside you for love."

"You're quite a philosopher, Lady Gráinne."

"And I'm your friend, though you don't realise it."

He changed the subject. "Tell me, what's all this nonsense with the maid Màiri putting garlic flowers around the place?"

Gráinne said, "We are very superstitious in the Highlands. The old beliefs remain. Things like garlic preserve things from rotting. It's because of this that they have authority against the powers of corruption like evil spirits or ghosts. Garlic is powerful against the *bean sìth*: the female spirit feared all over the Gaelic world."

"Banshees? I've heard of them of course. I thought they were in Ireland."

"We have them in Ireland, but here too."

Conversation lapsed.

He surveyed the view. "You've been very kind to me here, but I'll be glad when I leave."

"I wonder when that will be."

"Longer now with Muirdeach gone."

Lady Gráinne said, "I don't think your coming here was a coincidence. Not for you, nor for us." The cat stretched and jumped from her lap onto the floor. It sat there, staring at Thorpe with amber eyes.

He said, "Of course that's exactly what it was: a coincidence."

"I think what was waiting here, was waiting for you. Some old story is being retold, and it needs you to take the main part."

"You can't really believe that."

"I think I do."

"If I'm involved in some kind of play, I suspect you also take a lead part."

Lady Gráinne chuckled. "I played Queen Titania at our outdoor Shakespeare a few years ago."

Thorpe said, "She played tricks on her husband too. Women always want to punish men because they don't imagine their men care enough about them. It's like the story Alastair told."

"I thought you weren't listening?"

"I listened enough."

"'A war between the sheets', he said. Sometimes it seems that men and women always vie for power over the other. But it needn't be that way."

"No?"

Gráinne said, "Men and women can be equals."

"I don't know. I sometimes imagine that women think men have had it too good for too long. They don't want to be the equals of men, they want their turn on top."

"Then the power struggle would reverse, not resolve."

Thorpe said. "In your story, Lord Eachann's ancestor had his manhood removed. That's pretty sour."

"For the man."

He tutted.

She said, "In all of the versions of the story I know, he did. But maybe there's another version where he manages not to betray her trust?"

At that point, the cook entered. "Milady, I was wondering about tonight's menu. Could I have a word with you?"

Gráinne rose. "If you'll excuse me. So nice to have the chance to talk to you, William."

The cat followed her out of the room, and Thorpe was left alone.

THORPE LEFT the castle and went to the stable. Muirdeach was dead, but his car still lingered there, broken, but Thorpe was desperate to be gone. He felt with Calum's illness, and Muirdeach's death things were closing in on him. Màiri had said that all men were at risk here.

He saw his car sitting there. Muirdeach had done some of the work, and now Thorpe had half an idea that he might be able to fix the rest himself. He lifted the bonnet, stared at the engine for ten minutes. He fiddled with hoses and poked around the cylinders, but in the end, shook his head. He slammed the bonnet shut and stalked out.

He had nowhere to go: it seemed he was imprisoned in this place. Thorpe walked through the Castle's park, head down, taking little notice of where he went.

He reached the river and walked along its banks, wandering some miles beside the willows and wild yellow flag iris. Clouds covered the sky above. Curlews called their bubbling cry from the damp meadows. He saw a heron standing stock still as a prehistoric creature by the river bank. Eventually, he looked back and saw Dungarvan a distant dot behind him. He could walk away, but ahead were the mountains and wilder country. This country could kill a man. There was no escape on foot. No escape by car. Perhaps he could borrow a pony and trap? But then he was never one for running away. He would stay and play out the fate Dungarvan offered him.

With a sigh, Thorpe turned and retraced his steps. When he got back to the castle, he didn't see any of the inhabitants, which suited him fine. He went in by the main door. There was no one about. He trotted up the staircase and opened his room where he threw himself on the bed and slept within minutes.

NIGHT FELL. He missed dinner. Someone knocked to call him down, but he didn't answer. Eventually, they left. He didn't know how many hours had passed before something made him waken. Thorpe knew she was in the room, even with his eyes closed. Hardly daring to breathe, he opened his eyes. She stood in the corner. He sat up on the bed, and she didn't vanish. She was there, clothed only in shadows. He saw her white flesh, her round thighs and flaring hips. His gaze travelled over her soft belly and the swelling of her breasts. He took in the dark hair between her legs, and like every time he saw Vivienne, he wanted her.

"William," she said. Her face was half-hidden, but he saw her long black hair, rose-red lips, white teeth that glistened as she smiled. Her eyes seemed to have their own luminescence, gold and black like those of a serpent.

His throat was dry. "Vivienne. I love you."

She whispered, "I know you do."

He wanted her. His grief that he'd lost her and his anger that she'd left him both threatened his self-control. He stood up from the bed and walked to her. She welcomed him, took him in her arms and folded him to her. He caressed her full breasts. He bent his mouth to hers, and as she kissed him, the boundaries between them blurred and blended. He felt the heat of her sex and smelled the perfume of her lust. He ran his hand in her long hair, twisting it and pulling her to him. He felt her hands rake his back, but then she stopped. He was befuddled by his desire. He couldn't think straight, but she whispered, "No."

He gripped her tightly. "Vivienne, I love you. I want only you. From the first minute I saw you in India, I only wanted you."

"William, how many hearts have you broken without a thought? I will give you one more chance to show you can be truly faithful to me."

HE WOKE AGAIN on his bed. Day shone through a gap in the curtains he hadn't drawn properly the night before. He looked frantically around him, but Vivienne wasn't there. If it was all a dream, it was a dream of what he wanted most.

He went down for breakfast which was served by a servant he didn't recognise. He ate in silence, then went back to his room where he stayed all day. He smoked too much and sat in the chair by the window staring at the clouds and mountains. He picked up one of the books left in the room for guests. He sat slumped in his seat and turned over pages one by one, reading but not remembering a word. He flicked thumbfuls of pages, then riffled pages a hundred at a time, picking up book after book. But he found nothing to take his mind off Vivienne.

Trying to shake off the bleakness that weighed him down, he decided he would join the life of the castle. Another day had gone by. He dressed for dinner and went down before the gong was sounded. Màiri was acting as a waitress, and there was a young servant man he didn't recognise. The mood was sombre. He was surprised that Màiri was at work after Muirdeach's death. Candles were lit on the table, the wine was poured, but the conversation was sparse. Fiona was staring at him. He knew it, but he was wary of returning her gaze in light of what her mother had told him.

In avoiding Fiona, he looked too much at the others. He saw Alastair gazing at Fiona. His eyes were dreamy like those of young men who read too much poetry. Fiona was why Alastair spent so much time at Dungarvan, but Alastair was in no way good enough for Fiona. He had no courage, and she needed a man with sufficient bravery to match her own.

The meal continued with stilted conversation about the weather. Then Fiona chipped in about an exhibition she'd seen at the National Gallery in Edinburgh. Thorpe pretended to be interested. He picked at his food. The pheasant was well cooked, but the sauce was too creamy for his palate. More wine was poured.

"It's a Claret," said Lord Eachann. "I'm not a wine expert, I'm afraid; I take my instructions on what to buy from Gráinne."

"And I submit to your superior knowledge about dogs, horses

and shooting," said Gráinne.

Eachann reached out and put his hand on hers. Those two were the perfect symbol of enduring love—from youth to age and still devoted to each other. Thorpe didn't know if he believed in things like that. Could two people love each other all their lives? It was just another myth. They were smiling liars. This whole place was full of myths and stories and things that couldn't really be true.

Eachann said, "It's been a long and unpleasant day, I hope no one will mind if I retire to do a bit of reading."

Gráinne got up with him, leaving the doctor and the three younger people. The doctor then excused himself. He was an old fool. Good riddance. That left Thorpe with Alastair and Fiona. She was wearing a blue gown that matched her eyes and pearls that looked old and valuable.

"I'll go up too, I think," Thorpe said.

"No—stay. Please?" Fiona said. "We're going to retire to the Baronial Hall and put some records on the gramophone. I'd like to dance."

"I'm quite tired," Thorpe said. "I'm not much of a dancer, and I know little about music."

"Stay for me?" She said.

Thorpe sighed but said, "Who could resist such a gracious request?"

"Good!" Fiona said, clapping her hands.

She was thoughtful and kind. She had ideas and opinions, but it was easy to delight her, and when she was pleased, she had all the wonder and charm of a child.

"Let's go through," she said. She came over and took his hand, pulling him after her. Over her shoulder, she called, "Hurry up, Alastair!"

Alastair came through behind them without speaking. He just watched them as Fiona chatted away to Thorpe.

"Just before I went to Edinburgh, a lot of records I'd ordered from New York arrived, but I had to leave, so I haven't had the opportunity to listen to them. Do you want me to put a few on now?"

Thorpe shrugged. "I wouldn't know the good from the bad."

In the Baronial Hall, Thorpe glanced up the balcony above. Fiona told the two men to move the chairs to clear a space for dancing. Alastair set up the gramophone, and Fiona stood there, lost in thought reading the sleeve notes to herself, her finger tracing the words as she did so. He smiled. She really was a delight.

Alastair stood in the shadow saying nothing. Thorpe looked at Fiona and smiled. She would indeed make someone a good wife.

"This one is good," she said finally. Putting a record on the turntable and placing the needle on the groove as it spun around, she said, "This is 'A Cup of Coffee, a Sandwich and You,' by Billy Rose."

Thorpe shook his head. "Never heard of any of them."

"Dance?" she said, extending her hands.

He shook his head. "Alastair will make a better companion than me."

Alastair's face blossomed into a smile when Fiona's attention turned to him. He blustered something about not being very good at this, but she grabbed him anyway.

Thorpe watched as she had to teach him some of the steps. He was not a good pupil, as graceless at dancing as he had been at fencing. Then the music stopped, and he stopped, standing awkwardly in the middle of the floor.

Fiona went over to the gramophone again. "And this," she said, "is 'Brown Eyes, Why Are You Blue?'"

She smiled at Thorpe. "Dance now?"

He shook his head. "I'll sit this one out."

"Lucky Alastair then," she said, smiling, but she was looking at Thorpe.

"Indeed," he said.

Alastair watched her every move. He was smiling now, a soft-mouthed smile like he'd never learned how to do that properly either. He stepped forward and snatched at her hands. Then, as the music started, he was an ungainly jig of gangly arms and swinging knees as they did some American-style dance.

After that song finished, Fiona said, "I want a rest now." She came and sat on the chair close to Thorpe's. She cocked her head and said, "You seem blue. Are you?"

He frowned. "Blue?"

"Melancholy."

He laughed. "A little."

She put a hand on his where it rested on the arm of the chair. She stroked it, playing the part of a concerned friend. Thorpe squeezed her hand, then dropped it.

Alastair stood by the gramophone watching them. "Do you want to dance again, Fiona?"

She waved him down, "Not yet, Ally."

She turned back to Thorpe. He felt uncomfortable with Fiona. He didn't want to lead her on. Alastair had probably loved her secretly since they were children, and he was Eachann's choice, as misplaced an idea as that almost certainly was. Fiona wouldn't settle for someone like Alastair. Alastair was going to get his heart broken, but that was none of Thorpe's business.

Thorpe stood. "Listen, I'll be off now. I'm not very good company tonight."

It was dark now, and a ring of gas mantles illuminated the hall. The door to the Entrance Hall was half open.

She got up from her seat and snatched at his hand. "No, William, you spoilsport. I insist you stay!" She had the look of a little girl used to getting her own way. Then with a beatific smile said, "At least for one dance."

Alastair still hadn't sat down. He had a record in his hand. "What about this one, Fiona?" He showed her the sleeve. "I think it's one you like."

"Just a second, Alastair," she said, not looking at him.

"I really must go," Thorpe said.

"I want you to stay," she said.

Alastair threw down the record. It smashed as it hit the wooden floor. Without a word, he turned and stalked out of the hall.

"Oh dear," Fiona said, raising her eyebrows.

After he was sure Alastair was out of earshot, Thorpe said, "You realise he loves you?"

"I suppose."

"You should go after him."

"I don't want to. It'll give him the wrong idea. I'd rather stay here with you."

She took his hands again. He didn't want to pull them away, but he was uncomfortable. "I'm not right for you," he said.

She whispered, "I'll decide that."

She moved in closer so that her knees pressed against his.

"Do you still think you're married?" she asked.

He shook his head. "No. I don't know. Maybe I dreamed Vivienne. There was a real Vivienne. In India. She wasn't mine though I wanted her to be."

"Do you want to tell me about it?"

"Not really." He rubbed his forehead. "I don't think I'm very well."

"No, you're not." She stroked his hair. "But you will be well."

He put his hand over his eyes. "You're very lovely," he said. "But how can this work out between us?"

"Why don't you kiss me?"

"For all sorts of reasons—" Some prescient impulse made Thorpe look around.

At the door of the Baronial Hall, standing half in shadow was a figure. Thorpe snapped his head round to see who it was. She wore a black dress and had long dark hair. It was Vivienne.

He started up and went towards the door.

"Don't follow her!" yelled Fiona.

He turned. "I have to know who she really is. I have to break her hold on me."

Fiona called after him, "If you go, she will prove you are her slave."

CHAPTER

# NINE

Vivienne fled from the hall door back into the passage, and without waiting for Fiona, Thorpe rushed after her. Her footsteps echoed through the castle in front of him and he chased her. He hunted her along the corridors and through room after room, seeing only her back, hearing only her laughter as she drew him on.

He realised she was heading outside. Panting, he reached the entrance hall and stood to catch his breath, hands on thighs, still without catching another glimpse of her. He hadn't seen her since that first glimpse, but he'd heard her footsteps. This was the way she must have come.

The oak entrance door swung open, and from the widening gap, summer fog seeped inside. Vivienne must have left it unlatched to show him she'd come this way and to tempt him to follow her. Aerial and tenuous, like the fronds of ghostly ferns, the fog's tendrils felt their way into the room. Thorpe put his hand to the door handle, damp with condensation, and looked. It was dark out there. The warm air had condensed on the ocean's edge and drifted inland to surround the castle, so Dungarvan was now an illuminated island cocooned in mist. Thorpe stepped out. Where was she? The damp air wrapped him, cutting him off from the castle door behind and making the world dreamlike. It made sounds muffled, and the cries of birds echoed eerie and strange.

Thorpe's footprints crunched on gravel, but he could see nothing. Vivienne wasn't there. How could he find her in this fog?

"Vivienne!" He called, but only the dull echo of his own voice came back from the castle walls. Why had she summoned him if only to disappear? She must mean him to follow her and perhaps now he would be reunited with her, whoever she was.

As he stood, looking every way around him, Fiona stepped from the castle door behind. She wore a jacket and had an old tweed overcoat in her hands. "Here, put this on," she said.

Thorpe shivered and let her help him with it. Fiona leaned close to fasten the buttons and turned up his collar. "That's better. If you must go on a fool's errand, you might as well be warm."

She switched on the electric torch she held and waved it around, but the beam hardly cut the fog.

Thorpe had still not spoken.

She said, "So you still want to follow your dream?"

Thorpe said, "Where can she have gone?"

Fiona said, "You shouldn't go after her, you know."

He stared at Fiona. "So, you saw her?"

Fiona said, "I saw something."

"It was Vivienne."

Fiona said, "She isn't what you think she is."

Thorpe rubbed his mouth. "She says she's my wife."

She said, "Maybe finding her will help you shake off this obsession: get rid of this spell before it destroys you. I only hope that is possible."

"So what is she if she isn't my wife?"

"Do you even have a wife?"

He threw his head back and stared at the fog-bound sky. "I don't know what's real anymore, Fiona."

"I just hope you realise that you can never have her. If anything, it will be her that has you."

He faltered. "What is she?"

"A spirit. Maybe a woman. Their names change. Their faces change."

"So I'm not mad?"

Fiona gestured. "It's this place. It's my father's story, and now it's your story too. It seems men like you are fated to replay it time after time until finally, maybe one of them gets the ending right, and then it can stop. I wish I could stop it myself, but she's not interested in me. I'm not the hero. I'm only a supporting actor in this troupe of players."

"What is happening here?"

"Dungarvan isn't an ordinary place. Myth soaks the ground and we sink deeper with every step. I hoped you wouldn't be caught up in it. You are the first one I've liked. But it seems you'll have to play it to the end."

"Whatever she is, do you know where she has gone?"

Fiona said, "Do you have a cigarette?"

Thorpe reached inside his jacket and pulled out a pack of Egyptian cigarettes. He took out one for her and one for him.

"Does your father know you smoke?" he said.

She laughed. "Of course not. There are lots of things about me that my father doesn't know."

The lighter flared, first once then twice. They each lit a cigarette and then they were serious again, suddenly quiet.

"So what happens in this story to men like me?"

"We'll have to see," she said. "Maybe it won't end so badly."

And then they heard a sound. It was someone's feet in the gravel coming from about ten yards away.

Thorpe spun round. "She's over there." He went to go towards the noise.

Fiona grabbed at his hand and gripped it tight. "You'll get lost. You don't know the place like me."

"Let me go to her, Fiona. I need to know what she wants from me."

"Let me come with you."

He sighed and nodded. As they stepped down the stone steps, away from the light of the door, it was as if they descended into a dark sea. They dropped fathoms deep, wrapped in a garment made of mist and night.

More footsteps.

"Over there," Fiona said.

It was someone walking, but the sound was both magnified and muffled by the fog. Fiona pointed the torch. The beam cut a small way into the mist, but not far enough to be useful.

"We'll only to see someone if we actually walk into them in this," Thorpe said.

The footsteps sounded again. Whoever was walking had speeded up.

"They must have heard us," Thorpe said.

"Whoever it is is walking away. Must be going into the rose garden."

They went after the footsteps, Thorpe leading, Fiona hanging back. They entered the rose garden, and in his haste, Thorpe tripped over some stonework. "Ouch."

She shone the torch. "You've cut your hand."

The footsteps hurried away. "Quick, she's getting away," he said.

"Let me clean the wound."

"It's nothing. Go back to the castle. This is something for me to fix. I don't expect you to come with me."

"I want to."

"You're very brave—"

—For a woman?" she said.

"For anyone!"

She chuckled. "I suppose that's a compliment coming from you."

"Fiona, I know you think I'm crazy, but you're a good friend to me."

"A chum? Like you had in the Army?"

"I didn't have any chums in the Army. I never had any really."

Fiona said, "I think she's going towards the Terrace, but once she's off the gravel, we won't hear her footsteps. Let's hurry."

They hurried. The sound of their own steps drowned out the sound of anyone else's. Now and again, they stopped. They strained to hear and only moved when they heard the footsteps walking away.

"The Terrace is a straight walk from here, though?" he asked.

"More or less."

"Where's she heading?" He said.

Fiona laughed. "Where she always goes in the story."

"The Well?"

"The Well of the Mothers."

"Then we'll go there."

Fiona said, "I only wish you didn't want to."

They walked on. All went quiet.

"We've lost her," he said.

"Keep on to the Well."

A sound came from nearby. Thorpe halted, turning his head to catch it. "That sounded like a person."

"Vivienne?"

"No, she was ahead. This noise is to the right."

They heard footsteps on gravel, then on stone, then on gravel again. Whoever was walking was in the rose garden.

"That's definitely someone—just to the right of us."

"But—someone else?"

He frowned. "Must be. But who?"

Fiona shone the torch into the wet grey mist. "Who's that?" She yelled.

No answer came.

"It might be her," Thorpe said.

"I thought you said it was someone else."

"I don't know. I'll go and see."

"Wait!"

Thorpe ran into the fog. His feet echoed in the damp air. He went right then ahead. Then he stopped. He wasn't even sure he heard anything any more. He had no torch. The fog surrounded him. He could see nothing.

Behind him, he heard Fiona calling that she didn't know where he was.

"Vivienne?" he shouted.

He remembered Fiona was on her own in the mist. He shouted back to her that he would come and find her, and then something smashed into his head, and he stumbled.


THORPE FELL TO HIS KNEES, the darkness around him illuminated by the bright stars of concussion. He staggered to get up and touched his head to feel blood seeping from the wound. He half-rose then was hit again. A heavy log smacked him on the shoulder, sending him reeling into the hedge. He tumbled into the rose bush's spiky fingers that scratched his face but stopped him tumbling over completely. Thorpe pushed back out of the bush and spun round to face his attacker.

"Vivienne, is that you?" he hissed.

But it wasn't Vivienne's voice that answered; it was Alastair's.

Alastair said, "You bastard."

Thorpe made out a shadow in front of him, darker than the surrounding grey. "What are you doing? Why did you hit me?"

Alastair sneered. "You think you can take her from me. She's mine; she's promised to me."

"What are you talking about?"

"You took Fiona from me."

"I didn't take Fiona from anyone."

Alastair brandished the heavy piece of wood. "Men like you think they can take what they want without giving a damn for anyone else, but her father has given her to me."

Thorpe's palm was sticky with blood. He backed off. "Her father can't give her to you. Fiona will choose who she wants."

"She will choose me!"

Thorpe laughed. "I actually don't think so."

"You pig!" Alastair held the log ready, ready to swing it again, but he held back.

Thorpe heard Fiona's voice calling from somewhere in the fog. "William, what's going on? Are you all right?"

Thorpe looked over his shoulder and shouted, "Fiona, go back to the castle."

Alastair swung the branch at Thorpe's head. Thorpe dodged, but the branch caught him a glancing blow on his left shoulder. Thorpe leapt at Alastair and swung a punch into his face with his right fist. As Alastair recoiled, Thorpe followed with a left then another right to the stomach.

Alastair went down, gasping in pain and dropped the heavy log.

Thorpe snarled, lurched forward and snatched Alastair by his hair. He yanked Alastair's head forward and pulled him close to bring up his knee and smash Alastair's nose. Then Thorpe stopped. He breathed heavily, and let go of the fistful of hair. Alastair was on his knees gasping in the grassy mud, and Thorpe grabbed his opponent's left lapel and stood with his right first clenched, ready to hit Alastair if he kept fighting.

Alastair pulled himself free, and Thorpe let him go.

Alastair said, "I only ever wanted Fiona. But you had to take her from me."

"I've not taken Fiona from you. Don't be stupid."

"Of course you have. Don't you see the way she looks at you? She has no time for me."

"She doesn't love you."

"She did."

"No, she didn't. You've been fooling yourself all these years. You've been a victim of your own imagination."

"You liar!"

Thorpe said, "Fiona's only fault was that she should have told you straight she had no interest in you and put you out of your puppy-dog misery. But she was too soft-hearted to do it."

Alastair backed away from him. "I'll make all of you sorry. You'll all regret underestimating me." Alastair wiped his face with a muddy hand, blood streaming from his nose. Then he turned and ran into the fog.

Thorpe stood alone, touching his head. When he concluded he wouldn't die of the wound, he let it be. He called out for Fiona, but no answer came. He hoped she was all right. She was a sensible girl, she'd have gone back to the castle, of that he had no doubt. He had no idea where Alastair had gone, and he didn't care.

Any idea of finding Vivienne had ebbed away. Whatever this apparition was, she wasn't his wife. She had convinced him they were married, but he remembered nothing of their life together. He did remember a Vivienne, but that was thousands of miles away. A day in Ooty Botanical Gardens came back to him. He remembered her telling him that she wouldn't leave her husband. He remembered begging her, imploring to go with him, telling her they would make a new life together in Australia. But she had turned and walked away. This thing at Dungarvan, this banshee had used his feelings for the real Vivienne and twisted them against him.

He started to walk back to the Castle. The fog was still thick, but he found his way. As he stepped through the massive door, he saw himself in the glass of a painting. He was wet from falling against the hedge, and his head was plastered in blood. His hand was smeared with red, and his nose was bruised and cut. He was a mess.

As he came into the Baronial Hall. Eachann was standing there, leaning on his stick and looking as if he had been waiting. He saw the state Thorpe was in and his face twisted in rage. "What have you done? Where's Alastair?"

Thorpe shrugged. "It was a misunderstanding."

"Look at the state of you! You've been fighting. You come to my house, and you fight like a thug."

"Alastair attacked me."

"And where is he now? Have you left him for dead?"

Thorpe sighed wearily. "No, he went off into the dark. Where's Fiona? Did she come in?"

Eachann exploded. He pointed his stick at Thorpe. "What? You tell me that my daughter has been out there with you, watching you brawl?"

"She came back to the Castle. I've come to find her. I need to apologise for running off."

"What have you done to her?" said Eachann, his voice shaking.

Thorpe frowned. "I haven't done anything to her."

"I know what kind of a man you are. I know about Màiri."

"Màiri wasn't what you think, and I assure you I've never touched Fiona."

Eachann was still shaking. "Keep away from my daughter."

"I assure you I only want to make sure she's safe."

Eachann shook his head. "I want you to go. Leave in the morning."

"What about my car?"

"Take it with you. Or walk. I don't care. I want you gone. You've done enough damage here. You woke the *Bean Sìth*. I put it to sleep, but you woke it again."

Eachann turned and began to walk away. Thorpe gripped his elbow and pulled the older man back. "It's time you told me what's going on here."

Eachann glared.

Thorpe said, "Fiona said something about this being like your story. What did she mean?"

Eachann was cold-eyed. "It means that you have woken her, as I woke her long ago. And I paid the price to quiet her again. She's feeds on the energy of men: men like I was; men like you are. She felt you coming along the road and knew what you were, so she caused the accident and brought you here."

"So what about Vivienne? Who is she?"

"Whoever the real Vivienne was, this creature is not her. Vivienne is your dream, and the Bean Sìth used the shape you provided."

"But why me? Why you?"

"Because I was like you, a soldier, a womaniser. We made a fetish of our masculinity. You, Captain Thorpe, you fight, you win, and you take. You have no care for others. You treat women as if they were objects for your pleasure. The Bean Sìth will punish you for the way you mistreat women. As strong and cruel as you are, she is stronger."

"But you beat her."

"I did not."

"But you said you put her back to sleep."

Eachann exhaled. "She came to me. She haunted me. I was married to Gráinne, but I was a terrible rake. My mistreatment of women woke the woman spirit of this place. Only I could see her, and I couldn't beat her. In the end, I gave in and paid her price."

"How?"

"I sacrificed myself to her."

Thorpe's brow furrowed. "What do you mean?"

"You're familiar with the Classical Goddess Cybele? Whom the Romans called Magna Mater—the Great Mother?"

"No."

"The pagan Gaels had a similar goddess: a terrible, devouring mother. They pictured her as three women in one: *Na Mathaireachan*: The Mothers."

"That well's called The Well of the Mothers."

Eachann said, "Yes. *Tobair na Màthar*. Sometimes they call these wells *Tobair Maire*: Mary's Well, but Mary too is a version of the mother goddess. She gives birth and takes back at death. She creates us and destroys us."

"Like the Indian Kali?"

Eachann laughed. "Yes, like Mother Kali, the little statue you have in your room."

"But how did you stop her?"

Eachann looked to the floor. "Cybele's priests were castrated. They offered their masculinity as a tribute to her."

"Good God," Thorpe said, stepping back. "No man should have to do that to himself."

Eachann lifted his eyes and met Thorpe's gaze. "And no woman should have to submit to a man's violence."

Thorpe felt sick. "Surely we're not doomed to an endless war between men and women, each vying for power over the other. Surely there is a middle ground."

"I never found it."

Thorpe shook his head. "I won't do what you did."

"It is the only way you can stop her. You will have to pay the *Bean Sìth*'s price. Offer yourself to her as her eunuch servant, or she will destroy you."

"I need to check on Fiona," Thorpe said. He turned and left Eachann in the Great Hall and ran up the stairs and along the passage. As he knocked on Fiona's door, he felt guilty for knocking when she'd gone to bed, but he wanted to make sure she was safe. The rapping echoed down the passage. No reply came. Thorpe knocked again, and then he listened at the door for sounds of movement inside. All was silent. Perhaps it was that she had just fallen asleep.

"Fiona," he whispered, then louder: "Fiona, it's me—William. I just came to say I'm sorry for running off and make sure you got back safely." His voice died away without an answer. He steeled himself for her righteous anger and turned the handle of the door. It was locked.

He heard Dr McKinnon's door open from down the corridor, and the shiny forehead with its strands of ginger hair poked out. "What the hell are you doing, Thorpe?"

"I'm just making sure Fiona got back safely."

"Do you realise how late it is?"

"Oh, go and hang yourself you boring little man," snapped Thorpe and knocked on the door, again "Fiona! Are you all right?"

McKinnon hissed. "She's not there."

"What? Where is she?"

"She's gone with Alastair."

"Gone with Alastair? When?"

"About five minutes ago. I heard him coming up the back way, so I looked out. I don't think they saw me."

No, I bet they didn't, you little spy, Thorpe thought.

McKinnon continued, "No, and he seemed very serious, but she followed him out. She was always too soft-hearted, that girl, but I can't see her settling for Alastair. He's too weak."

CHAPTER

# TEN

Thorpe made his way down the stairs. He did a quick tour of the castle's room on the ground floor and saw one of the maids. He asked her if she'd seen Alastair and Fiona.

"Yes, sir. They went outside."

"They went outside into the fog at this time of night. Didn't you think that was strange?"

She looked blankly at him. It wasn't her place to question the decisions of her betters, no matter how ill-advised they seemed.

Eachann was nowhere to be seen, and Thorpe guessed he had gone to bed. He couldn't remember which was the door that was the short cut to the Rose Garden though that must be the way Alastair got in without coming past Eachann and himself talking. Thorpe went to the Entrance Hall and hesitated by the castle's door. There was a rack of electric torches there. He took one and clicked the on button. It stuck, and it didn't work at first. But then he hit it, and it did. He stepped out into the fog, as impenetrable now as it had been before.

Alastair had told him he was going to make them all sorry. What the hell did he mean by that? Thorpe's mouth went dry with

250

anxiety for Fiona. As he got further into the gardens, he heard someone. He gripped the metal torch tight. The grass was bent here as if something had been dragged through it. He dipped the beam and saw the grass was stained red. He leaned down and touched the red liquid, examining it in the yellow light, and saw it was blood.

Thorpe's heart beat faster. Whose blood was this? He followed the tracks in the grass. Though he could hardly see his way, he knew where he was going. He hurried past the rose bushes dripping in the night's dew, and broke into a run on the gravel path, jogging along the box hedge walk until he arrived on the Terrace.

His shoes were soaked from the wet grass, and his ragged breath issued forth in billows. He took a moment then went on, the torch beam swaying and conjuring demonic faces from the fog. It took longer to walk the terrace in the dark than he remembered from journeys during daylight. In this murky weather, he couldn't smell the honeysuckle or musk rose. The fog had drowned them.

He went along the terrace, down the dip he remembered, his feet slipping on the muddy grass. There was still a trail of blood. He was near the end of the Terrace now, and the cave was ahead. He paused outside. His throat was dry, and his voice nearly failed him. Clearing his throat, he shouted, "Fiona."

No answer came. Thorpe went closer to the cave mouth and called, "Fiona?"

His heart was hammering. What if she was hurt?

In response to his call, he heard a weak, gasping voice. He had heard enough wounded men to know that someone was in terrible pain. But it was a man's voice, not Fiona's. "Alastair, if that's you, come out."

From the cave entrance, Thorpe flicked the torch beam in front of him like a probe. Walls of fog reflected it back, but he could see the walls of the cave. They were slick, and the smell of the sea rose up.

He knew where the hole in the ground was where the well had been, but it took him a second to locate it with the torch.

By the gaping hole of the well, lay Alastair. His shirt and trousers were soaked in blood.

Thorpe said, "Where's Fiona?"

"Help me, Thorpe. I'm wounded."

"What did you do to Fiona?"

Alastair shook his head. "I just wanted to talk to her to apologise for running out. I needed to tell her I loved her."

Thorpe narrowed his eyes. "Why didn't you talk inside the castle? Why bring her outside?"

"Please, help me. I'm bleeding to death here."

Thorpe flicked the torch beam around. Blood pooled on the cave floor. Alastair was wounded, but how? A thought occurred to him. "Did Vivienne do this?"

"Vivienne?" Alastair frowned then nodded. "Yes, It was Vivienne."

Alastair turned to look where Thorpe gestured at the well. The tide was out and at the cavern below was empty of water. "I don't know Thorpe. But please, you need to help me. I'm bleeding."

"And you need to be honest with me—for the first time, you all need to be straight with me. I don't know whether I'm coming or going. Where is Fiona?"

"I don't know. When I told her I loved her, she left me."

Thorpe went silent. "But you think she's safe?"

"She must have gone back to the castle after our argument."

"How come I didn't see her?"

"You must have missed her in the fog."

"And then you ran into Vivienne—or the banshee or whatever she is."

Alastair nodded. He was very pale. Sweat beaded on his upper lip and forehead. Thorpe felt sorry for him. It was possible that Fiona had left Alastair and made her way back to the castle and he'd missed her in the fog. The banshee might have hurt Alastair. After all, she'd hurt Calum and killed Muirdeach for their crimes against women.

"Please take me back to the castle," Alastair said. He was crying.

Thorpe looked at the hole in the cave. In the light of his torch, he could see blood, but it was Alastair's. The cave was dank and dangerous. No one would go there of their own free will.

Alastair moaned. "Please help me. I'll die here if you leave me."

Up until now, they had all denied seeing Vivienne. But perhaps now they could see her. Thorpe closed his eyes. Then he decided. He reached down and took Alastair's hand. Alastair's bloody fingers slipped through his, but he grabbed again and got a solid grip around the wrist. Thorpe helped him up then Alastair was on his feet with his hand nursing his wounded groin. Blood was only seeping from the wound, but Thorpe didn't have a bandage. He hoped there would be something to clean up the injury in the castle. He guessed it would need sutures. He'd stitched men up when necessary in the War. The main thing was to get Alastair somewhere dry and warm and light so he could treat him.

Thorpe retreated, pulling Alastair with him and they made their way out of the cave back into the fog-bound night. When they were clear of the cave, Thorpe supporting Alastair as he limped along, Thorpe said, "How badly are you wounded?"

Alastair said, "The bleeding has stopped. But it hurts so much."

"All right, let's take you back to the castle. You'll have to bear the pain."

It took more time than he wanted for Thorpe to help the limping Alastair back to the castle door.

EACHANN WAS BACK in the Baronial Hall when they entered. The clock's hands showed it was 3 a.m.

"What have you done to him?" said Eachann, coming over, leaning on his stick, his face melting in concern for Alastair, then a quick look of anger at Thorpe.

"It wasn't me," Thorpe said.

Alastair said nothing.

"But you're hurt," Eachann said, staring at Alastair's ripped groin. "My God."

Alastair grimaced.

"Do you have a bandage?" Thorpe said. "We need to clean the wound."

"I'll get Màiri," said Eachann. "She can help."

Alastair stood, blood dripping onto the floor from where it seeped through his trousers. There was a clean slash mark in the groin. It looked like it had been made by a sharp knife.

"Don't worry," Thorpe said. "We'll get you cleaned up. I've done lots of field dressings."

Màiri came. She saw the blood and where the wound was and her eyes filled with horror.

Thorpe told her, "I need you to clean as best you can. Use warm water. But first, can you get me a needle and thread?"

Màiri nodded and went off. When she returned, she had what was needed. She had brought a bowl of warm, clear water and the thread and needle. She cleaned Alastair's wound while he shuddered and moaned with the pain. When she had mopped away the congealing blood, Thorpe could see what he was working with. He began to suture it closed. Alastair put one hand on Thorpe's shoulder, and Màiri took his other as Thorpe worked. He didn't bear the pain well. And then Thorpe put down the needle and bloodied thread.

He said, "I've done what I can to repair it."

"Thank you," Alastair whispered. "I don't deserve your help."

"You're damned right, you don't. You're lucky I've got this sense of honour that won't let me leave a wounded man behind."

"Who did this?" Eachann said.

Alastair's eyes closed. He didn't speak.

Thorpe offered. "He said Vivienne did it."

Eachann's eyes widened. "Your imaginary wife? I doubt that."

Thorpe said, "You told me about the banshee. You know it's true. You know what she did to you."

"I think there is a less supernatural explanation. I think you did this."

Thorpe looked from Alastair to Eachann. "You think this is my fault?"

Eachann's eyes were cold. "Who else's?"

Thorpe said, "Alastair says that Fiona came back to the castle after she left him. Did you see her?"

Eachann shook his head. He looked at Màiri. He spoke in Gaelic, and Màiri turned to go.

Alastair was very quiet. Tears seeped from the corners of his eyes.

Thorpe said, "Why are you crying?"

Alastair brought his bloodied hand to his face.

Thorpe said, "Alastair, where's Fiona?"

Alastair shook his head. "I'm sorry."

"Sorry? What for?"

"I think she's out in the garden still," Alastair said.

Thorpe shook his head, puzzled. "What? But you said she came back here."

"No," repeated Alastair. "She's in the garden."

He was horrified. "She's out there? Why did you lie to me?"

Alastair said, "I just ran. When I couldn't run anymore because of the wound, I crawled. I didn't know where I was going, but I ended up at the cave."

"So Fiona's still out there?"

"Yes."

Eachann said, "Out there? In this weather, after this monster has terrified her to death." He pointed at Thorpe.

Alastair grimaced.

Thorpe said, "I'll go and find her. I'll bring her back safely."

Eachann said, "She doesn't need your help. I will find her. She's my daughter."

Thorpe sighed. "With all due respect."

"What? You think I'm a cripple? You think I can't protect my own daughter?"

Thorpe shrugged. "At least let me help you."

Eachann scowled at him then said, "Very well."

Thorpe nodded then went back out of the door. Eachann followed him, limping. He slowed Thorpe up, but he couldn't leave him, so they went slowly, Thorpe having to remember, stopping and waiting for Lord Eachann. All the time, tension grew, nearly choking him. Fiona was out here with the banshee. Though she'd never harmed a woman before, perhaps she might now. If only because Thorpe cared for her.

He and Eachann walked through the garden, searching. The fog was still as thick as it had been. The night lay so heavy on the place that he doubted it would ever be dawn. It was cold.

"Anything?" said Eachann from over his shoulder. "Is Fiona there?"

"No," Thorpe said.

Then Eachann said, "Shine the torch over there."

Eachann gripped Thorpe's hand and yanked it so the beam shone on a stone bench that would provide a private little spot for a summer's day. Tonight it was sinister.

"What's that?" Thorpe said. He stepped closer, bent down, touching it to make sure.

It was a woman's dress.

Eachann said, "It's hers."

The dress was ripped as if it had been torn off her. Something had made so great a rent in it that it would have fallen off her. It was stained in blood.

"Oh my God," said Eachann. His hand went to his throat. "My Fiona"

"We need more people," Thorpe said. "The banshee might have her. The thing that is playing the role of Vivienne."

Eachann stared at him then said, "Let me go back to the Castle. We need to have weapons."

"Will weapons hurt her? Is she human?" Thorpe said.

But Eachann was already walking off. Hurrying and stumbling, Eachann hastened to the castle. Thorpe followed behind.

BACK AT THE CASTLE, Alastair and Màiri were sitting where they had been before Thorpe went out. The gas lamps were still burning, hissing faintly. They both looked up when Eachann and Thorpe entered.

Eachann had Fiona's ripped dress in his arms as he entered. Màiri wailed. Alastair's mouth tightened.

"Oh my Lord," said Màiri. "Where is Miss Fiona?"

"We think Vivienne has her," Thorpe said.

"The *bean sìth*?"

Thorpe nodded.

"Oh, no."

Eachann said, "Màiri, do you know where the key to the gun case is?"

She nodded.

"Go and fetch my shotgun from the gun room and cartridges. Hurry Màiri please."

When she'd left, Eachann turned to Alastair. His strained face gave a kind smile. "How are you now?"

Alastair closed his eyes. He said nothing.

"I know how much Fiona means to you. Nearly as much as she means to me. I know you probably blame yourself for letting her leave, but she's a wilful girl; you couldn't have stopped her. You weren't to know."

Alastair gave a weak smile.

"He's very quiet," Thorpe said. His jaw was set, and his voice grim. He fished Alastair's bloody and slashed trousers from where they'd been thrown on the back of a chair when they were cleaning his wound. Even at arm's length, he confirmed what he'd seen before. The cut that had caused the injury was straight and clean.

Did a banshee use a knife? He remembered climbing the mountain with Fiona when she'd produced her Highland dagger, her *sgian dubh*.

Eachann nodded. "He's been through a lot."

Thorpe shook his head. "But did he deserve it?"

Eachann's eyes blazed with anger. "What do you mean? You wait here."

He turned and yelled into the castle, "Màiri!"

Thorpe said, "And the banshee ripped her dress?"

"Hmm."

Thorpe prodded Alastair with his foot. "Don't pretend to be asleep."

Eachann glared at him. "Leave him alone."

Thorpe said, "He knows something about this."

Alastair's eyes flicked open. "What?" he muttered. He stared at Thorpe and when Thorpe met his gaze, glanced away.

Thorpe said, "I think it's time you told the truth."

Alastair licked his lips. It was as if he was about to say something, but he stopped. He stared at the ceiling.

Thorpe said, "You've never seen Vivienne, have you? You were just humouring me."

Alastair gave a bitter laugh. "I just needed you to bring me back here. If I had to go along with your madness, then that's what it took. There is no Vivienne. There never was."

"So who hurt you, and who ripped Fiona's dress?"

Alastair closed his eyes again.

Thorpe snarled. "If you don't tell me where you put her, I will break every bone on your body."

Eachann lifted a warning finger. "Do not speak to Alastair like that. He knows nothing about what happened to Fiona." He turned. "Màiri, hurry!"

Thorpe said, "Because Alastair sings and tells stories, because he prefers music to fighting, you think he's not capable of behaving as the worst men do."

Eachann said, "He's not the same kind of man as you."

"We're all the same kind of man—all of us. Unless we choose differently."

Eachann shook his head. "He's not like you."

Thorpe turned back to Alastair. "Where's Fiona? I'm warning you. Speak!"

Eachann's face twisted. "What are you accusing him of? How dare you? He adored Fiona. They were children together."

Thorpe said, "And after all these years, he finally decided to take what she wouldn't give."

Eachann screamed. "Get out while you still can!"

Thorpe said, "You need to think straight."

Eachann raised his stick and brought it down, aiming for Thorpe's head. With a twist of his shoulder, Thorpe avoided the blow, then he grabbed the stick, yanked it and threw it away. It landed with a clatter on the wooden floor.

When Thorpe's back was turned, Alastair raised himself and stumbled over to the fire. Thorpe tried to reason with Eachann, while behind his back, Alastair picked up the heavy iron poker. He covered the yards between them while Thorpe was still turned the other way, then he brought the poker down across Thorpe's back.

The pain ripped through Thorpe like a jolt of electricity and he fell forward, gasping. He shouted out, turned, jumped at Alastair and pounded his fist into Alastair's face.

Alastair's nose exploded, and he screamed, falling back to put his a hand up to his nose, blood streaming through his fingers.

Màiri entered carrying a shotgun.

Thorpe saw the gun. He yelled at Eachann. "You old fool, I would never hurt Fiona,"

Eachann hobbled towards her and reached out for the gun. "Give it to me! Hurry, Màiri!"

The girl looked terrified and confused.

"Give it to me!" commanded Eachann and Màiri handed the gun to him, her eyes darting to Thorpe then back to her master as if trying to work out what had happened.

"Cartridges!" he snapped.

Thorpe turned to Alastair who stood, one hand to his face, the other still holding the poker. Alastair stared over Thorpe's shoulder, watching Eachann scrabbling to load the gun. Thorpe had only seconds to get the truth.

"Tell me!" he snapped. "Where is she?"

Alastair screamed like an animal and brandished the poker but had no intent and no courage. He was like a cornered cur dog: he would bite if pushed, but Alastair was counting on Eachann to shoot Thorpe.

There was a click, then another click as Eachann pushed the cartridges into the shotgun.

"Lord Eachann," Thorpe shouted. "He knows where Fiona is. He put her there."

As Thorpe turned to face Eachann, Alastair lunged with the poker.

Thorpe spun round, sidestepped and swung. His fists met only air, but Alastair fell back, and Thorpe advanced. He ducked under the waving poker and came up to punch Alastair once then twice in rapid succession. Alastair stumbled. Thorpe snarled and went for him, losing his head in a red mist. Then out of the corner of his eye, he saw Eachann level the shotgun and jumped out of the way of the deafening double blast.

His ears rang, and a jolt of pain came from his left shoulder. But the bulk of the shot had gone past, embedding itself in the wood panelling. Màiri put her hands to her cheeks and screamed.

Eachann yelled. "Give me more cartridges!"

Alastair was weeping, his face smeared with blood, tears and snot. His mouth twisted in a snarl. "Fiona threw herself at you, but you didn't want her. So I tried to take her. How dare she scorn me all these years?"

Thorpe's hand was on his wound. He felt the sticky warm blood soaking through the tweed. But in his rage, he felt no pain. "You little shit," he said.

"After you hurt me, she was on my side. She tried to be nice to me, so I asked her who she wanted most. And she cried and said she wanted to be my friend, but she didn't love me. She said she loved you. How could she love you? She hardly knows you."

"So you raped her."

"I would have. If she hadn't done this." He pointed to his wound. "But either way, I beat you."

"You beat me? You vile beast, you misunderstand everything." Thorpe grabbed Alastair's jacket with both hands and head-butted him, breaking his nose. He heard and felt the crunch of the bone, and Alastair's blood ran down his face. Thorpe dropped him onto the floor and turned back.

Behind him, even with his fumbling fingers, Eachann had succeeded in reloading the shotgun. He pointed it at Thorpe. He hadn't heard Alastair's confession. From the other side of the Baronial Hall, he yelled at Thorpe, "Men like you should be locked up."

Thorpe turned, "He tried to rape your daughter. It's she who stabbed him in self-defence."

Eachann faltered. He went white. But he firmed his mouth and shook his head. "I don't believe you. He's a good man. I've known him since he was a boy. If anyone hurt Fiona, it was you."

Eachann's fingers curled around the double triggers. He was about to fire both barrels.

Màiri said, "Don't shoot the Captain. You all need to go for Miss Fiona. She's not safe."

Thorpe looked at her. She seemed to be taking his side. He frowned.

Màiri said, "Fiona is not safe out there. You're the only one who is fit and able. You must go and find her."

But Eachann had already made his mind up who the villain was.

He'd fired the first shot in anger. The second would be with unshakable determination.

When he saw Eachann's eye narrow, Thorpe ducked right and rolled on the floor towards the door.

There was a roar and a flash. With his ears ringing and heart thumping, Thorpe thought he had received his death-wound.

He looked back at Eachann, and he saw Màiri's face screaming "Go!" From Eachann's rage, it appeared Màiri had pushed him, causing him to miss.

Thorpe took Màiri's advice and ran.

THORPE FLED FROM THE CASTLE, blood drying and matting through his jacket and shirt. Outside, the fog had thinned, and points of starlight littered the sky between high ragged clouds. The moon was up, pale and sick, and over in the east behind the mountains was a hint of grey. Dawn would be here soon.

He guessed Eachann was reloading and would be out after him before long. He had to find Fiona. Just because her dress was in the Rose Garden didn't mean that's where Alastair had finished his attack. Thorpe guessed he'd taken her to the cave because he thought that would be away from any chance of discovery while he assaulted her. His nose had been bleeding from Thorpe hitting him earlier, hence the trail of blood on the grass.

He hadn't seen her around the cave entrance or down the drop into the Well of the Mothers. Even though she'd stabbed Alastair he could have hurt her. She could still be somewhere round there. Thorpe started to jog in the direction of the Terrace. Where the poker had hit him was throbbing agony. It bent all his mind towards it, and he found it hard to think of anything else, but he had to focus. The few shotgun pellets that had penetrated his coat were nothing—like a stinging of nettles. Madness infected the castle. Lust and rage, rape and violence, filled the place, and it came from Vivienne.

He ran on until running hurt too much, and he had to slow. He walked through the garden, in pain and bleeding still heading for the Well.

In the dark, he heard someone call his name. It was a woman's voice. He looked through the dawn light and, coming through the garden, saw Màiri and her mistress, Lady Gráinne. He stopped, stood his ground and was ready for more hatred from them. But when Gráinne called his name, her voice was kind. "William, you must help us. You must save Fiona."

"Have you seen her?"

Gráinne shook her head. "Alastair took her down into the cave. "

He nodded. "That's what I think too."

Gráinne said, "You must save her."

"She could die down there," Màiri said.

Gráinne took his hand and gripped it. "No one else here is strong enough to help her." Then as she got closer, she put her hand to her mouth. "You're covered in blood."

"Where's Lord Eachann?" he said. "Is he following me?"

They both looked blankly at him.

"He shot me. Màiri, you were there. You made him miss."

Màiri smiled gently. "I did it for you."

"Thank you. He thinks I attacked Fiona and that Alastair is innocent."

Gráinne said, "Alastair got what he deserved. But you must prove your courage, sir knight."

Màiri nodded. "You must risk your life to save Fiona."

"You're our only hope now," Gráinne said. "We brought you something." She nodded at Màiri, who was carrying a bundle wrapped in a blanket. She offered it to him.

"What is it?" he said, not taking it.

"Look," Gráinne said.

He hesitated then took it from Màiri's arms. He knew what it was through the blanket. He unwrapped it and there in the faint dawn light was a great Highland claymore.

"We took it off the wall," offered Gráinne.

"We covered it," Màiri said. "It's steel. Iron and steel are poisonous to the *Sìth*. They can't touch them."

He took the great basket hilt of the claymore. With his left hand, he gave Màiri back the blanket and then wrapped both of his hands around the claymore's hilt.

"Do you think I will meet the banshee down there?"

Màiri said, "Certainly you will. This is her test for you."

Thorpe held the claymore in front of him. "I'm not so confident this will work," he said. "I'm not sure Vivienne is made of flesh and blood."

"Don't lose your nerve," Màiri said. "You must go into the cave. You must keep your courage. Rescue Fiona."

"I will. I won't let her down."

"We like you," Gráinne said.

"We admire your courage and strength," Màiri said.

"We have some other things to help," Gráinne said. She showed him a rope and an oil lamp.

"Thank you," he said.

Màiri said, "Let us walk with you to the cave entrance."

"Are the caves explored?"

"Only partly. They go down to the sea, but they flood. Once you're in, you must keep going forward. You have to be careful the tide doesn't catch you, or you will drown," Gráinne said.

They started to walk in silence. After a few minutes, they arrived at the entrance to the cave. In the pale dawn light, he could see into it. He saw the rocky hole in the floor that led down to the sea caves. The water had receded; the tide must be out. There was no sign of Fiona, but there was a smear of blood on the rock. Previously, he'd thought it was Alastair's, but it could easily be Fiona's.

"Do you think that Alastair took her down there?" He said.

Gráinne and Màiri said together, "She is down there. So is danger. Hurry now."

Thorpe touched the blood. It came up wet on his fingertips. Alastair could have hurt her before she stabbed him. She may be grievously wounded. Who knew what he would do to her in his feeble rage?

"Is this the only way down?" he said to Gráinne.

She nodded.

"Be bold. Let not your courage fail you," Màiri said.

Gráinne said, "We are counting on your bravery and your will.".

Thorpe smiled grimly. "I hope I prove worthy of your trust."

He went to the edge of the hole. He knelt, then turned and lowered his feet down, then his belly until he was hanging by his fingertips. Unsure of the depth, but guessing it wasn't more than eight feet, he lowered himself as far as he could, then he released his fingertips and he dropped into the dark. He landed on the rock floor and shouted back up. "I'm down."

He saw the women's faces appear above him, orange in the lamplight. Màiri tied the lamp to the rope and lowered it down. When he had the light in his hands, she drew the rope up again and retied it to the claymore. She let that down too. When he had the sword, she released the rope that slithered down and fell in a coil on the damp rock floor. He couldn't get back up now even if he wanted to.

He put the lantern down on the floor while he wrapped the rope around his middle like a belt. Then he picked the lamp up in his left, and in his right hand he held the heavy sword.

Gráinne shouted down. "Please take care."

He looked up at their worried faces. "I will."

"Hurry to save Fiona," Gráinne said. "Be brave."

"Choose well," Màiri said. Then they were out of sight.

CHAPTER

# ELEVEN

Thorpe made his way into the cave like a blind worm tunnelling into the earth. The light of the day world was lost far behind. Faint as it had been, that light had anchored him. Now the anchor was gone, and he wandered a netherworld of spirits and dreams.

As he went into the earth, it was as if he had entered an ancient and primitive realm of rock and water. Things moved out of sight. Imagination rose up to disorientate him. Dreams were more potent than in the daylight here. Things emerged from the depths of the earth and from nightmare in these nether caves. He smelled salt water, and he remembered Gráinne's warning about the tide. He wondered when it would be at its fullest and hurried to find Fiona before it rose.

Deeper and deeper he went, stumbling and almost losing his footing on the slippery rocks. At times, the path was level but tended always down. He came across a place that was frothing and boiling with seawater and jumped from one rock to another to avoid falling in.

Another time, slipping on weed, he teetered, unable to use his hands. He lurched backwards, balancing the steel claymore in one hand and his lantern in the other. Then, throwing himself forward, he lumbered one step after another onto a bank of sand. Oil sloshed in the bottom of the lantern as he stumbled. He shook it to work out how much was left and hoped he had enough to light his way down and light their way back.

It was cold in the cave. He seemed to go deeper and deeper. It was hard to believe that ordinary caves could be so labyrinthine. He had lost all sense of time. It must have been more than an hour, but it could have been minutes.

In the distance, he heard the primordial swelling of the ocean, a deep rhythmic beat of waves. The rock path led beside a flooded cavern, a finger of the sea. Thorpe looked down into the green water, and in the weak yellow light of the hissing lamp, saw creatures beneath the waves. Colossal fish flicked too and fro, agitated by his presence. There were white eels there also and things worse than those moving in the lightless deep.

Turning a corner, he nearly slipped and flung his arm around a stalactite to save himself. Breathing raggedly, he imagined falling into the water. Mind racing, he thought about going under and churning among the slithering things that lived there.

After that, he walked more carefully, choosing his footholds in the dim light of the lamp. He would be no use to Fiona if haste drowned him, but as he slowed, he cursed himself. He listened to the water and did not know how far yet he had to go. Then he saw blood against a rock. Examining it in the lamplight, he saw it was still wet.

He went on. He thought the flame burned lower and fainter. He grew frightened the light would die, and he would be left in the dark down here. Without light, he knew he would never leave. He would never leave and never find Fiona, and neither of them would ever see daylight again. He could have cursed Alastair, but what use was cursing now?

There were noises down here. Strange noises made by things that had never seen the sun. His heart skipped and his eyes darted to every shadow.

"Get a grip on yourself, man," he muttered.

The rock galleries flickered in the lamplight, and a thousand shadows fluttered suggesting someone was there. He felt people watching him, and things other than people. He imagined them breathing. Sometimes he thought he heard the chuckling of their old voices. He saw shapes out of the corner of his eyes, ahead, below and in front. The sea was rising. He had to hurry, so he put safety to one side and went at a jolting pace, until he slipped, almost fell in the water, and stopped to catch his breath and calm his jumping nerves.

To keep up courage, Thorpe began to mutter to himself. He told himself to be strong; he told himself to be brave. At one point he even sang snatches of the nursery rhyme his nanny used to sing him when he was small.

The sword was a terrible burden in his hand. The lamp heavy as lead.

DOWN IN THE SEA CAVES, he heard a noise. It was definitely someone, not something. The noise came out of the darkness ahead. Thorpe stopped to listen. The waves slapped, the water dripped and the gusting air moaned in the deeps and whistled through dark holes in unseen walls.

But the noise he'd heard was not those. He listened harder until it came again. Yes, somebody was there.

Thorpe cleared his throat. "Who is that?" he said.

At first, there was no reply. He peered, lifting the lamp to see better. There was a thicker shadow ahead. It was different from the shadows around it. He couldn't make it out clearly.

A voice called: "William."

He stammered, "Who's that?"

A laugh.

His mouth was dry. "Don't play games. Who is that?"

"Màiri."

"Màiri?" The light was so poor. He couldn't see. But how could Màiri have got ahead of him? Unless there was another way down, and they had all played a trick on him. Unless they were all in it together

"It's Màiri; it's me," she said again.

"But how?"

She didn't reply.

"Come out," he said. "Step into the light."

He put down the lantern on the rock by his feet and held the claymore with both hands in front of him.

"Do you like me, William?" The voice came from behind now. The same voice. But how the hell could she have got behind him?

He spun around, sword pointed forward. "Màiri, what are you doing?" He felt the hilt of the claymore. Sweat made his fingers sticky. He closed his left hand over his right to get a more secure grip.

Màiri appeared from the shadows, coming out behind him. Her face flickered in the lamplight, but it was Màiri's face. And how young and fresh and beautiful she was; her red hair and her moss green eyes. But she wasn't wearing the same dress he'd seen her in when she'd knocked Eachann's shotgun. Instead, she wore a kirtle of green silk, far grander than a maid ever owned.

As he watched, she unfastened it and let it drop. She stood there in her underwear: pearl white against her pale skin.

"Màiri, I don't understand how you got here."

She unclipped her bra and took it off. Her white breasts swung free, and she stared at him with lustful eyes. "We can do it here," she said. "I know you want to do it with me. You liked it last time, didn't you?"

"I have to find Fiona."

Màiri stepped out of her knickers and stood there naked. The downy hair on her pubis was pale red. "I'm ready," she said. "Come and feel how wet I am for you."

He shook. He felt like he used to feel when he wanted a woman.

He remembered the pleasure he'd taken in making a girl want him, holding her down and making her moan. It had all been about power over women, all about being their master. Now he shook his head.

"Do you think I'm beautiful?" She whispered in his ear.

"Yes, but please put your clothes on."

She laughed. "Come and be a man. Where's your courage, little boy?"

"Put your clothes on, please."

She came close until she stood only a breath away. He felt her warmth in that cold place. Her nipples puckered pink like rosebuds, and she pushed herself into him, grinding her pubis onto his thigh. Then she reached down and squeezed his crotch.

"See," she said. "I knew you wanted me."

"It's not right," he said. "I need to find Fiona."

She walked her fingers up his back and into his hair.

Thorpe stood there, the sword still in his right hand, but trailing now, almost touching the floor.

He balled his left hand into a fist to stop himself from grabbing her flesh.

She kissed him. She was like spring sunshine. He felt her naked body against him. He smelled her musk. His resistance to her was failing. He wanted to throw her down on the ground and push her knees apart with his so he could have her.

Through gritted teeth, he said, "No."

"A real man would take me here and now."

He shook his head. His hands ached with tension as he kept them away from her.

"I don't love you," he said.

She said, "What's love got to do with it?" But it wasn't her voice, it was Vivienne's.

He recoiled. And instead of Màiri's red hair and pale skin, it was Vivienne. She stood, dark-haired and olive-skinned as a Greek priestess. The hair between her legs was sable and perfumed with her lust. Her nipples were dark red as wine where Màiri's had been rose pink.

His hand tightened on the sword. She sensed his thoughts. "You'd never hurt me, William. I am your Queen. I'm the only one you ever loved. Of all the women you took, it was only me you loved. You will never be free. Nor do you ever want to be."

And then she melted like a black mist.

VIVIENNE WAS GONE. Màiri was gone. But he was still there. Water lapped around his shoes. The tide was coming in.

He stood there, dazed. The lantern still burned. He gripped the sword tighter to give him confidence and he then he picked up the lantern and went on. He wouldn't be able to get back this way. He would have to find another way out.

He walked with greater urgency. Vivienne filled his mind. It was true the real Vivienne, of all the women he had seduced, was the only one he had feelings for. With her, he was the biter, bit: the seducer, seduced. And ultimately, she wouldn't have him.

His head was down. He was sloshing through water. He tried to tell himself this wasn't the real Vivienne. The real Vivienne was thousands of miles away in Mysore, back with her husband and lost to him.

But he hurried. Perhaps he hurried because he wanted to find Fiona before the tide rose. But maybe it was because his dream of Vivienne drew him on like a compass.

The water was around his ankles now. He splashed through it as he went deeper. The tunnels went deeper. Soon it would be too deep for him to progress. It would be too deep for him to get back. He broke into a run.

But he ran into the rising tide. It was round his thighs, then his waist. He held the lamp up high so the water wouldn't douse it. The heavy claymore was an unbearable weight. The wound in his shoulder burned like fire.

The water was below his breast as he forced himself forward. He had a plan that he would find a higher rock and stand there, wait the tide out. But he saw wet seaweed hanging from the ceiling of the cave.

They'd lured him to his death.

THORPE HEARD A VOICE. He had heard so many voices here but they had never belonged to a human. But this one was the voice of someone in need and pain.

"Fiona?" He yelled.

"William?"

He gritted his teeth, this could be another mirage, another test, but he shouted, "Fiona, I'm coming."

He came to a low archway in the rock. It was the entrance to a tunnel. The water was waist high here. In the gloom, he could trip and fall in an unseen hole and go under the water.

"William," Fiona's voice called again.

He had to go to her. He ducked and went through the rock archway. The walls here were veined in quartz and amethyst, glinting white and purple in the light of his dying lamp. He shook it to see how much oil was left; not so much. He had hoped that this low rock arch signalled an end to his journey, but it was not so. Ahead, the darkness stretched. He glanced up at the ceiling with its sparkling quartz. It was still damp from the last tide. Seaweed hung down. This was a place for drowning.

How could Fiona be down here? It was too far—too deep under the earth. This was the banshee again, and all the banshee wanted was his death.

His shirt and jacket were soaked and the brine stung his wound. He had lifted the lamp clear, but it was only inches above the tide now. If it got swamped, then he would have no hope, because it was as black as pitch down there. All the time the sea flooded higher into the cave system. The lamp flame flickered low.

If the tunnel was climbing, it didn't seem to make much difference to the water level, which still rose. His arms ached from holding up the claymore and the lamp. He was struggling to keep going. Each step was an ordeal. He held the lamp as high as he could, keeping it out of the water. He was going so slow, inch by inch. The tide was now at the level of his heart. But still, he laboured on, his breath coming in gasps. He thought of his own death. To come to this—to have faced the guns and anger of the enemy and live, to be saved only to drown like a rat in a hole.

He listened to the swishing water as in rushed in behind him. And then the lamp died. He held it, useless, for a minute and then he dropped into the sea water. The hot metal hissed as it disappeared. The darkness was now perfect. The blackness was so complete that it was as if nothing really existed. He hoped he would not lose his dignity in those last moments. He hoped he would die like a man.

And then, a soft white light bathed the cave. He saw his hands again—swimming out before him, one empty, the other grasping the sword. He felt his body buoyed up by the salt tide. The light was diffuse, and it was difficult to tell where it came from.

Ahead of him, on a bank of sand, Fiona lay. He waded out of the water, splashing his way towards her. He still held the claymore. The illumination came from somewhere past Fiona. He rushed up to her, knelt on the sand and she reached and took his hand.

"Alastair tried to rape me. He hit me and ripped off my dress."

He squeezed her hand. "I know."

"I ran. I didn't know where I was going. I was bleeding but he didn't catch me. I was so scared."

He saw her face was bruised. There were smears of blood beneath her nose and she had mottled thumb marks at her neck as if Alastair had tried to throttle her before she got to her knife.

"I'm so sorry, Fiona."

"And I got to the cave and he caught me, but I had my knife and I stabbed him. I meant to hurt him. I think I did."

"You did."

"Good. Then, in my panic I went down the hole. I thought he would come after me."

"No, he was too badly wounded."

She looked away, but muttered, "I said good, but I'm sorry I hurt him."

"He deserved it."

"I knew there was a way out of the caves the far end. I just hoped I'd find that. I didn't know how vast they were."

"There's light up there," Thorpe said.

All the time, Thorpe waited for her to change into another face of the banshee: another temptress, another dream. But she stayed human, her hair plastered, dark-blonde over her forehead. The light was brighter ahead. "Wait here a second," he muttered.

"I don't think I've got anywhere to go, really," Fiona said, forcing a smile.

Thorpe went forward to see where the light was coming from. He stepped a few yards past Fiona, then he looked up. There was a hole, surrounded by glittering amethyst. And through the hole, he saw Gráinne reaching down.

"Take my hand William," she said.

He looked at her, amazed.

"Don't drop the sword." She was wearing a white dress; the same one he'd seen her in the first time they met in the Castle.

"Fiona's back there."

"Go and get her, but then come back here."

He helped Fiona up. He shook his head, frowning deeply. "Your mother's there," he said.

Fiona said, "It may look like her, but it's not my mother."


Thorpe got to the hole and lifted and pushed Fiona until she could get out of the caves. When she'd disappeared from view, Gráinne said, "Take my hand."

"Do I still need the sword?" he said.

She said, "Yes, bring the sword. There is a use for it."

He held back. Fiona had gone up into the place above.

Gráinne smiled. "Don't let your courage fail you here, right at the end."

He reached up with his free hand. She grabbed him with both hands on his left wrist. She pulled. The water helped him up. His foot caught on a rock, and he used that as leverage. He pushed himself and grabbed the stone on the edge of the hole. He managed to pull and then reached and held with his left hand. He dragged himself up, and he was there with her in the cavern. It looked drier—as if the sea never or rarely reached this high.

He couldn't see Fiona.

"Lady Gráinne," he said, but couldn't continue, the words stopped, and he stared. "How are you down here? Where is Fiona?"

Gráinne stroked his cheek. "She's gone ahead. You have done well so far. Only the last test now."

He said, "I don't understand. What's going on?"

She nodded. "The price must now be paid—a price of submission or a price of wisdom."

"How do we get out of here?"

"Not down there," she pointed down the hole to the broiling sea which had by now almost filled the tunnel.

"Is there another way?"

She nodded. "Come with me."

He followed her then halted. "What about Vivienne?"

"Your wife?"

He rubbed his eyes. "I don't know. I don't think so. I think she's the spirit."

"Don't you know what she wants yet?"

"She wants power over me."

Gráinne said, "You think so? You still haven't learned?" She held out her hand, and he took it. They walked on. The tunnel looked man-made. The floor was beaten clay, packed down over the years as if by many feet.

"What is this place?"

"It's an old smugglers' tunnel."

"Where does it go?"

"To the crypts beneath the church. It's how the smugglers brought in their rum and tea once they'd landed it on the beach in the cove."

His heart filled with hope. He thought that they would get to the church crypt then come up into the daylight again. Then all would be well. Fiona must be already out.

He trudged his way up the steps behind Gráinne until they emerged into a stone-clad crypt. The boxes of the dead were all around. He smelled the dust and the dry decay of centuries, but they walked on. Gráinne led him up some steps until finally she lifted open a wooden hatch, more like a lid, and he smelled the musty book smell of church. They stepped up. Thorpe recognised the chapel in the Castle. There on the altar was the ancient carving of the Three Mothers.

THORPE WAS in the old chapel. He saw watery footmarks leading out and guessed that's where Fiona must have gone, back into the castle

Gráinne pushed the door closed. She turned the key, and locked them in with a click.

Thorpe looked around the room. There was the strange stone altarpiece. He looked to the east, and beyond the altar was a throne. He saw that clearly now. It was a throne made for three. Sitting in the centre seat of the throne, wearing a robe the colours of a peacock's feather was Vivienne. She was young and beautiful; dark-skinned with eyes like a snake. He saw her bare feet and her slender ankles, and he knew that under the robe she was naked. Round her neck was a necklace and at her throat as its centrepiece was a silver moon.

To Vivienne's left, red-haired Màiri sat. Màiri wore a necklace of iron shaped like a star. Golden-haired Gráinne took her place to the right. She wore a necklace of gold shaped like the sun.

"You've come," said Vivienne. Hers was the voice that whispered in his ears before he woke all the mornings of his life. Hers was the voice of the woman who lives in men. She was the divine dream of woman that flowers like a white rose in the hidden garden.

Vivienne stood, and the robe dropped from her. The tan of her skin, her breasts, her throat, her waist and soft belly and the flaring of her woman's hips all drew his eyes. Between her legs, was her sable hair. Lust rose in him and with it fear. He reached for something to hold onto, to keep him steady. "Vivienne," he said, voice trembling. "Is it really you?"

He held the claymore in his right hand.

Vivienne walked towards him. She put her left hand on his shoulder. As she spoke, he saw blood-red lips and teeth white as sharpened bone.

"Do you want me?" she said and her serpent's eyes glittered gold and black. He shook his head, trying to clear his mind of the heaviness that had come upon him.

"Hmm," she said, her eyes gone smoky between dark lashes. She reached down between his legs. "You want me," she said. "You always want me."

Gráinne stood and descended toward him. She too was naked now, her white robe dropped at her feet. Her skin was golden where Vivienne's was dark.

"The sword," Gráinne said.

He held it tight.

"You know what you must do," Vivienne said. "It is the price you pay for us."

Vivienne unbuttoned his shirt, beginning at his throat. She opened the shirt to his collar bone and leaned to kiss his neck. He smelled her hair—the perfume of jasmine and bitter nightshade. Her mouth brushed his throat, her teeth raked his carotid artery, her lips lingered like leeches. Her other hand held him harder between his legs.

"Give it up to us," Gráinne, standing in front of him. "It will be quick. The sword is sharp."

From his left side Màiri said, "Sacrifice or wisdom, which is it to be?"

He tried to pull away from Vivienne. He stretched back and took the sword in his right hand. Vivienne said, "You wanted to take me once against my will," she said. "Now I will allow you. For a price."

He looked around and saw Gráinne's eyes fierce and bright. "Give us the sacrifice," she hissed. "Be a man."

He stepped back, his lust for Vivienne, for all of them, almost overwhelming him.

To his left, Màiri had cast off her fairy-green gown. She stroked his arm and came to kiss his neck. Her small teeth brushed his skin.

Vivienne stood to his right, Màiri to his left and Gráinne in front of him. They undressed him. He ached for them.

Vivienne looked amused. She pushed her hands beneath her breasts and cupped them to him in offering, their dark tips red and hard. "Do you know what we want yet?" she said.

He still held the sword. He knew the price he would pay if he gave the wrong answer—the price Eachann had paid.

"So?" said Vivienne.

"What do you want most?" he said.

She nodded. The women watched, waiting for him to answer.

"I thought it was power over men," he said. He could feel their eyes on him. "But now I know it's not that."

"So what is it?" said Vivienne.

"You want to be free to choose."

Vivienne looked at him, and her eyes were tender. And then all three of them were gone.

Lady Gráinne found him collapsed in the old Chapel.

"Is Fiona all right?" He asked.

"Yes, it's been terrible, but are you unhurt? She collapsed but told me you'd be here."

He nodded. "Why did you send me into the sea caves?"

Gráinne looked concerned. "Do you know where you are?"

"Yes, at Dungarvan Castle, in the chapel. But you and Màiri sent me into the Sea Caves."

Gráinne shook her head. "I think you must have imagined that. Màiri and I have been looking for you."

"Where's Fiona now?"

"She's safe now. She's back in the castle with her father and Dr McKinnon. The police are on their way for Alastair. She stabbed him, it was in self-defence. Heaven knows what he'd have done to her if she hadn't had her knife."

"Thank God for her little *sgian dubh*."

"I carry one too."

Thorpe smiled. "I thought you might."

"Eachann thought it was you who'd attacked Fiona."

"I know."

"But after you'd gone, it became obvious. He wants to apologise. We went looking for you in the grounds. "

"Did you go to the Well?"

"Yes, but the tide was full and the well overflowing. We couldn't get down. I didn't even think you would go down there."

"It was some kind of test."

"Just like in the old stories. And it seems you have proved yourself a true and honest knight."

CHAPTER

# TWELVE

The great hills around Dungarvan were covered in snow, and the pine trees swayed darkly in the breeze from the sea. The waters of the burn were locked by ice, and the great boulder against which William's car struck, still bore the scar of their fateful meeting.

But Dungarvan Castle overflowed with light and joy. It was decked for Christmas and for a wedding.

William married Fiona McScaigh on Christmas Eve. Her father gave her away. Kit Thomason came from India to be Best Man. Alastair went to prison and then emigrated and was never seen in Scotland again.

After the wedding ceremony, William's father stood with Lord Eachann enjoying a malt whisky by the blazing log fire in the Library.

William's father said, "Lovely service."

"Yes, it was nice."

"Bride looked beautiful."

"And the groom very handsome."

William's father hesitated. "By the way, that was a strange altar piece."

Eachann sipped his whisky. "It's very old. It belongs in the family."

"Is it a lucky charm?'

Eachann smiled. "Not exactly, but it reminds us of our obligations."

Mr Thorpe said, "Oh, and what obligations are those?"

"To love, to loyalty and to the land we spring from."

"Ah, well, can't say fairer than that," Thorpe's father said. "I think my William has met his match."

Eachann studied his glass. "Your William is a better man than I ever was–braver, more honest."

Mr Thorpe said, "That's jolly nice of you to say, but he wasn't always that way. For a long time he was a bit of a beast."

Eachann said, "But now he's a man you can be proud of."

"Yes, indeed, Lord Eachann. I think you're right."

# ALSO BY TONY WALKER

Christmas Ghost Stories

More Cumbrian Ghost Stories

Further Ghost Stories

Haunted Castles

London Horror Stories

Horror Stories For Halloween

www.ingramcontent.com/pod-product-compliance
Lightning Source LLC
Chambersburg PA
CBHW072056190726
48294CB00005B/1558